KILLER AT THE COUNTY SHOW

KATE WELLS

Boldwood

First published in Great Britain in 2025 by Boldwood Books Ltd.

Copyright © Kate Wells, 2025

Cover Design by Head Design Ltd

Cover Photography: Alamy and iStock

A CIP catalogue record for this book is available from the British Library.

Paperback ISBN 978-1-78513-459-3

Large Print ISBN 978-1-78513-460-9

Hardback ISBN 978-1-78513-458-6

Ebook ISBN 978-1-78513-461-6

Kindle ISBN 978-1-78513-462-3

Audio CD ISBN 978-1-78513-453-1

MP3 CD ISBN 978-1-78513-454-8

Digital audio download ISBN 978-1-78513-457-9

This book is printed on certified sustainable paper. Boldwood Books is dedicated to putting sustainability at the heart of our business. For more information please visit https://www. boldwoodbooks.com/about-us/sustainability/

Boldwood Books Ltd, 23 Bowerdean Street, London, SW6 3TN

www.boldwoodbooks.com

For Jon and Nick, with many happy memories of a childhood spent adventuring on the farm and in the hills.

1

Jude Gray had been going to the Three Counties Show every June for as long as she could remember, although she'd never shown any livestock before. This was a challenge that Frank had set her soon after he'd moved into the pink shepherd's cottage at Malvern Farm the previous autumn.

Always up for trying something new, Jude had thrown herself into the task of choosing her first pedigree Kerry Hill lambs from a breeder in Shropshire and tending them in preparation for their first ever show. It was a far cry from the skills needed to rear her fair-sized flocks of Suffolks and Cheviots. She'd been doing that for years and had developed an instinct that meant she knew exactly what was needed – most of the time at least. When it came to pedigrees though, she was very glad to have the wisdom and experience of Frank behind her.

'Pull up over there, behind that trailer,' Frank said as Jude drove into the exhibitor's area behind the stock sheds. 'I'll go and see where our pen is and then we can unload and get the animals settled in.'

Once parked, Jude got out whilst Frank went into a cavernous metal-framed shed. It was one of several that would house the long list of sheep and cattle breeds waiting for their turn to shine. There was a real buzz about the place as people came and went carrying the tools of their trade and stopping for a chat with other farmers. Jude, who knew no one other than Frank, hung back and watched. She was excited by the scene but not without a certain amount of nerves. These people took the art of showing their top animals very seriously. Many had been doing it for years: for some of them, generations. And here she was, rocking up with her two shearlings, Henry and Helen, suddenly feeling as though she was a complete imposter. She looked through the slots in her trailer at the beautiful animals inside.

'Well, there's no going back now,' she whispered to them.

'Get that bloody vehicle moved on.' The angry shout over Jude's shoulder made her jump and she turned to see a red-faced man pointing his finger towards her.

'I'm so sorry,' said Jude, mortified that she'd already made her first mistake and the sheep hadn't even left the trailer. 'I was told this was where to park for unloading.'

'Not you.' Jude realised the man wasn't talking to her but rather someone beyond her at the next trailer along. 'Him. He's had his sheep out of there for an hour or more but his rusty old tin can is still clogging up the place.'

'And who made you the Lord Mayor of the Three Counties, ey, Jim Martin?' asked a scrawnier, taller man dressed in the same farmer's uniform of checked shirt rolled up to the elbows, moleskin trousers and a flat cap. He was leaning against his pickup with his hands tucked into the pockets of a fleece gilet, showing no sign of moving his vehicle.

'Don't need to be the mayor of anything to know when someone's flouting the rules,' said the first farmer, Jim.

'You and your rules.' The second farmer stood up and took a step towards him. 'Piss off, old man. Go and tend to those scrawny animals of yours and stop wasting my time.'

Some of the other exhibitors stopped what they were doing to see what the noise was all about.

'Nowt scrawny about my sheep. And I can hold my head up knowing that the judge will see nothing but honest rearing.' Jim pointed a finger at the other man. 'Not that you can always say the same, ey, Griff?'

The arrogant sneer on the taller man's face dropped as he flushed, matching his sparring partner. 'You're going to need to watch that tongue of yours if you don't want it to come unstuck.'

'Are you threatening me, Griff?' Jim waved his arm in an arc to indicate the people watching. 'In front of all these good people?'

'I'm telling you to leave me to my business and bother yourself with your own,' Griff replied. Jude could see his balled fists, knuckles white from tension.

'And I'm telling you to get that rust bucket out of the way and let others come in.'

The two men took another step towards each other and squared up, short and round facing tall and lean. Both red-faced and both showing no sign of backing down.

'Come on now, gents.' Jude held her hands up to

try and pacify them. 'I'm sure there's no need for this.'

Frank arrived back on the scene at this point. 'Jim. Griff.' He nodded courteously to them both. 'Everything alright here, is it?'

At Frank's gentle interference, the men turned away from each other to greet him, their squabble temporarily halted.

'Alright, Frank?' Jim held his hand out to be shaken. 'I didn't know you were showing again.'

'I'm here with Jude Gray,' said Frank. 'You'll have known her husband Adam, and his father, John.'

'Aye,' said Griff, also holding his hand out for Frank to shake. 'Good men, both.' He nodded at Jude but didn't address her directly – something Jude found sometimes still happened when meeting male farmers of the soon-to-retire generation.

'Well, I'll leave you both to get on with your animals,' said Frank. 'Griff, that your vehicle ahead?'

'Aye.'

'You about to move it, are you? Only we're at the end there and need to pull up to unload.'

Griff shot Jim a look of undisguised hatred as his rival smirked in his minor victory. Then he climbed up into the cab of his pickup and drove it away to the parking area with the trailer bumping along behind.

That was clearly all Jim had been waiting for and he disappeared off to his own sheep pens to start the process of preparing them for the following day's show.

'What's the deal with those two?' Jude asked.

'Old rivals,' said Frank. 'They have neighbouring farms out Leigh Sinton way, both grew up there so they've known each other since they were nothing but babes in arms.'

'A lot of shared baggage no doubt.'

'You could say that,' Frank chuckled. 'As long as I've known them, they've been at each other's throats. Seeing who could draw first blood.'

'Could be interesting,' said Jude as she climbed back into the Land Rover.

She drove to the far end of the shed and expertly turned the trailer so that it was backed up against the entrance. Then she got out and went to look inside. The enormous shed was split up into pens by sturdy, metal hurdles. Some of them were already occupied with sheep settled on beds of straw, others were still waiting for their tenants to arrive. Frank had located the pen that would house their two shearlings, one ram and one ewe – the sum total of their show stock – and had opened the front hurdle out ready for them.

'Okay, Jude?' he said as he joined her at the entrance of the shed. 'Let's get 'em out.'

Jude dropped the ramp from the back of the trailer and opened out the sides to stop her sheep escaping. Then she released the inner door and went in to fetch her animals. Helen backed tightly into the corner but Henry was a little braver and stood his ground. Jude took her time and, when she had him in prime position, she launched herself forward and caught him neatly by the thick fleece around his shoulders.

'It's okay, boy,' she whispered. 'You'll get a nice drink and something to eat as soon as we get you out.'

Henry skipped about and tried to burst free of Jude's grip but she held firm until she'd guided him out of the trailer and down the ramp. Helen wanted to stay with her mate so she followed nervously, stalling at the top of the ramp, not quite brave enough to follow Henry down into the shed.

As soon as Jude had the ram safely in the enclosed walkway between the pens, she let go of him. Henry took one look at Frank and turned to head back into the darkened safety of the trailer, but Jude was waiting and waved her arms, making noises to encourage him to go forwards. Frank shook a bucket of sheep nuts, a sound that the ram knew well, and it was enough to tempt him in. As he ran down towards the food, Helen close behind him, Frank threw some pellets into the pen and, when Henry and Helen were safely inside, he closed the hurdle quickly.

Jude went back to the Land Rover to collect her show box which she set down in the second pen they'd been assigned. This was where she would be able to keep everything she and Frank needed to get the shearlings ready for showing the following day.

'Here.' Frank handed over a hay net and an old sheep lick bucket. 'Why don't you get things sorted whilst I move the car?'

'Thanks,' said Jude, tossing him the keys. 'Meet you back here?'

'Aye, and then p'raps we can go and get ourselves a pint at the Stockman's Bar.'

Jude looked at her watch. It wasn't even half eleven yet, still Frank and his beer clock had a habit of keeping their own time. As Frank drove off, she turned her attention to her sheep, filling the bucket with water and stuffing hay into the net. The much larger pen opposite her had other Kerry Hills in them and Jude looked at the impressive set up. A lovely collection of five ewes looked right at home, all with the trademark panda black rings around their eyes to go with the black muzzles and erect ears. Behind them, cable-tied to metal poles, was a professional banner advertising the farm they had come from:

Dafad Bryniau Ceri. Batters Farm,
Abergavenny. Ffion and Carl Proctor.

There were contact details and a professional-sounding website address too.

It straddled the hurdle into the next pen where two exceptionally handsome rams were sharing a net of hay. A third pen contained lambs. With the kit pen at the end, the Batters Farm setup stretched all the way up to the top of the shed and made Jude feel a little out of her depth.

'Do you think we'll ever hit those heady heights?' Jude asked Helen. The sheep just looked at her quizzically as though she was still very much unsure of what any of this was about.

'I'd say they're set to win quite a few rosettes in the show tomorrow,' said a woman with long, dark hair tied back in a plait that hung across one shoulder. She was perched against the hurdle of the pen next to Jude's nursing a paper cup of coffee.

'I'm Tara Watson.' The woman held out her hand

and when Jude took it she was surprised by the strength of the grasp from someone so petite.

'Jude Gray. Lovely to meet you.' She indicated the sheep waiting expectantly behind Tara. 'Are those your Kerries?'

'Yes.' Tara turned to look at the animals. 'Well, mine and Mam's. We've run the farm together ever since Da died a few years back. He was Kerry mad, he was.'

'Judging by those beauties you've got there, he obviously passed his passion on to you,' said Jude.

'Thanks.' Tara smiled at her. 'I don't think we've met before, have we?'

'No. I'm new to the breed,' Jude confessed. 'In fact, I'm totally new to showing as well so I'm just hoping not to stand out as a complete idiot.'

'You'll be fine. We're a friendly bunch on the whole.' Tara pushed away from the hurdle. 'Once I'm done here, I was going to head for some lunch in the bar if you want to join? I can introduce you to the Proctors.' She pointed to the smart set up from Batters Farm. 'Ffion and I used to go to the Young Farmers things together and her family are friends of ours. You'll love her, everyone does. She's so easygoing and friendly, Carl too. That's her husband.

You'll be part of the Kerry Hill gang before you know it.'

'Thanks, that would be nice.'

This introduction already made Jude feel less unsure of herself and start thinking she might be in for a really good weekend.

At that moment, a spotless hybrid Range Rover with darkened windows and a personalised number plate purred up and stopped at the mouth of the shed. It was at odds with the pickups and old 4x4s that Jude was used to seeing on farms and she wondered whether it was a vehicle that had ever actually seen a day's hard labour.

'That's Zander Pettiford,' Tara said as a man stepped out of the expensive car. 'My best friend from agri college grew up with him and they work together now. This is the first year they're showing their sheep.'

Zander Pettiford was as equally polished as his car and stood out from the other exhibitors. In a sea of corduroy, fleece and yard boots, he wore tight jeans with a box-fresh designer shirt and trainers that were so white they had no place in a livestock shed.

As he closed the door, he took his sunglasses off and ran his fingers purposefully through his hair in a way that looked well-practised and no doubt had made many a teenaged girl swoon.

Jude wasn't into the life of celebrities, it not being a world she felt remotely attached to. Yet she still knew who Zander Pettiford was, everyone in the farming community did. Once the lead guitarist of the hugely successful band The Spods, he'd decided to use the fortune he'd made to buy a large farm near Ross-on-Wye which he'd renamed the rather saccharine Greener Days Farm. Unlike some of the other high-profile names who'd chosen a rural life to escape from their celebrity status, Zander had clearly decided to use his to promote his brand.

And that brand was an eco-warrior single-handedly responsible for turning around British farming and making it – in his words – *more sustainable and responsible for the future of the planet.* In reality, from what Jude could tell, all he'd done was rewild a huge area of previously well-managed arable land and stick up a load of solar panels on what was left. Neither groundbreaking initiatives nor viable in the long term or on a big scale. In fact, both potentially very damaging in their own ways to the future of British farming.

But the public loved him and he'd made a nice living as a social media phenomenon, posting regular videos on his YouTube channel which was followed by almost six million people. The sponsorship that he attracted must have been worth a small fortune each year, not to mention the royalties from the book deal that had come off the back of it. Jude wondered how much of that money he was putting back into the farming community he'd so publicly adopted. Probably not a bean.

'What's he doing here?' she asked.

'According to my friend Olivia – that's his farm manager – he's trying to prove that animals reared out on the wilds of his farm can beat any competition.' Tara rolled her eyes.

Jude stared at the man leaning against his car.

'I suppose we'll find out tomorrow if the judge agree with him,' she said.

There was a clatter from Jude's pen and she looked over to see that Henry had managed to kick the water bucket and the contents had sloshed out over the straw bedding.

'I'd better sort that out,' said Jude.

'See you in the bar later?' asked Tara with a smile that made Jude feel as though she was in for a fun weekend.

'See you there.'

* * *

With the sheep settled, Jude and Frank joined Tara and some of the other exhibitors at the Stockman's Bar. It was a relaxed and friendly area set aside purely for the use of those showing their animals and it was fairly busy as everyone piled in to grab a bite to eat and have a chat.

Whilst Frank went off to share a pint with some of his old farming friends, Tara took Jude under her wing and ushered her over to join the group of fellow Kerry Hill breeders sitting around a large table. Tara introduced Jude to her mother, Penny: a jolly woman with a strong stance that made her look as though she was no stranger to wrestling rams and lugging hay bales. Ffion and Carl Proctor – owners of the impressive setup in the pens next to Jude's – were there too, along with Zander Pettiford. There was no sign of Tara's friend Olivia, who Jude suspected was busy with the sheep.

'How are you enjoying the show so far, Jude?' Ffion asked. 'I think Tara said it's your first one?'

Before Jude had a chance to answer, Zander decided he needed to cut in.

'My first time as well,' he said as he thrust a hand in Jude's direction. 'Zander from Greener Days

Farm. Organic, wild, sustainable farmer and guitar player.'

As she shook his hand Jude wondered what made a guitar player wild or organic and then smiled inwardly at the images the thought conjured up.

'We're obviously the newbies then, but how about the rest of you?' Jude asked. 'How long have you all been breeding Kerries?'

'I'm the group's usurper.' Carl had an open, engaging face with creases under his eyes that made it look as though he was always just about to burst out laughing. He looped his arm around his wife's waist. 'I grew up in the middle of Cardiff and always thought I would become some hotshot power player in a designer suit. But then I met this farmer's daughter from Abergavenny and I swapped my life for one of sheep and tractors.'

Ffion poked him playfully in the ribs. 'What are you talking about? You love it.'

Carl kissed her shoulder. 'I do now,' he said.

'You two are so cute together.' Tara went to stand behind them and rested an arm on each of their shoulders. 'The Kate and Wills of the farming community.'

'Have you always farmed then, Ffion?' Jude asked.

'I'm one of those who can't tell you how many

generations back the family farm goes. Mum and Dad are still there with my sister, Caitlin, but I moved out and took over the tenancy on my first farm four years ago when Carl and I had just started dating.'

'It was your tractor I really fell in love with.' Carl grinned.

'Did you have Kerry Hills from the start?' Jude asked.

'Yep. They might be stubborn and bolshy but they're what I know and I wouldn't have anything else.'

Jude concurred with the accurate description of the breed. Beautiful to look at and full of character, they were flighty animals who tolerated humans only because they brought food. Jude had other breeds on the farm that were far friendlier and easier to handle, but there was something about the Kerry Hills that made them special.

'Ffion and Carl's sheep are the ones to beat,' said Tara. 'Mam and I had a look earlier and you've got some incredible animals there.'

'Thanks.' Ffion looked as proud as any mother would be if someone complimented her children. 'We've worked really hard on the flock since we moved in. I'm particularly proud of the aged ram we've brought to show this year.'

'He's a handsome boy, alright,' said Penny in clear admiration. 'You've done well there, Ffion. Good stocky bones, flat back and a strong physique. He says *look at me, I'm a little bit wild,* and the judge will like that.'

'I'd put my money on him not just winning his category but also overall breed,' said Tara.

'Bloody well hope so.' Carl crossed his eyes comically and pulled a face. 'The money we've ploughed into these sheep, it's about time they started to pay us back.'

Carl, like all the farmers there, knew that the top breeding rams were worth their weight in gold. The best rams led to the best lambs and good lineage was highly sought after.

There was a loud huff then as Jim came and sat down next to Jude. He banged a pint of beer down in front of him which sloshed, spilling amber liquid down the side and onto the table.

'What's the matter, Jim?' Penny, asked. 'Griff and you still not buried that hatchet yet?'

'There's no hatchet to bury,' said Jim. 'And if there was, I know exactly where I'd like to bury it. He's a born cheat, that one.'

Jude looked around to see if she could see the taller man but there was no sign of him.

'Ah now, here's my son.' Jim waved a hand towards the far side of the bar and a well-built man raised his hand back and started to head across to the table.

'Thought I might find you in here.' The man addressed his father first and then turned his attention to the rest of the folk gathered around the table.

'Tara Watson,' he said as his face split into a wide grin. 'It's been a while since our paths last crossed.'

Jude noticed Tara blush as she half-scowled at the newcomer. 'David, nice to see you,' she said unconvincingly.

'When was the last time? Some Young Farmers event no doubt, when we all still remembered how to have a good time.'

The glower Tara gave him made Jude suspect that she hadn't enjoyed their meetings quite as much as he had.

'Gosh, and Ffion Davies too.'

'I'm a Proctor now.' Ffion wasn't as cold in her greeting but Jude wouldn't have said that she was exactly pleased to see David either. 'This is my husband Carl.'

'The rest of the family here too?' David asked. 'I haven't seen Hugh in years. Top bloke, your brother.'

'He's actually coming to the show on Sunday.'

'Shame he didn't stick around to take your dad's farm on.'

This clearly made Ffion bristle. 'Farming's not for everyone, you know that. But my sister Caitlin's at home still and she'll be taking over the farm at some point.'

Zander stood up and held his hand out again, this time for David to shake, and Jude noticed he had his phone in his hand as though he was filming the interaction.

'Hi, I'm Zander from Greener Days Farm. Organic, wild, sustainable farmer and guitar player.' This was obviously a well-rehearsed introduction that would be rolled out goodness knew how many times before the show was over.

'I know who you are,' David said with a disapproving glare. 'You're the wanker trying to persuade the public that their little worlds will be so much safer if all us naughty farmers stop growing crops and turn our fields over to massive glass panels or wild deer.'

Zander took his sunglasses off and set them down on the table so he could calmly eyeball the man confronting him before looking directly into his phone.

'This is the challenge I face constantly,' he said, confirming Jude's theory that he was recording himself. 'And it's my responsibility to spread the word about what I do widely.'

'What are you doing with that thing?' David asked.

'I'm running an Instagram live. Shining a light on the inside workings of the show and reminding my followers that we can't keep draining our land without giving anything back.'

'You're streaming live, right now?' Ffion asked.

'It's part of my drive to educate and inform.' He fixed a concerned look on his face. 'As custodians of the countryside it's our responsibility to look after the wildlife and we owe it to the next generation to do all we can to protect their future. We've over-farmed for too long and now it's time to give the land back to nature.' Zander delivered his speech as though performing in some emotive play and it made Jude wonder if he had the capacity to ever go off script.

David gave him a slow, mocking round of applause. 'Well done. It's shite like that that's making you a very rich man, no doubt. Quick question though, to you and whoever else is watching your little farce. Where do you see the nation's food coming from? You know, if all the farmland is run your way?'

'I produce a good amount of food on my farm.

The farm shop is always well-stocked with venison and wild boar.' He looked into his phone screen again. 'Open six days a week, check out my bio for details.'

'Ah yes, the food of the masses. Affordable too, no doubt. Great job.'

Jude felt David's annoyance. It was a topic that was often discussed in farming circles and there was an increasing concern about the public appetite for repurposing arable fields and pasture in the name of sustainability.

Not that there wasn't a place for rewilding, but only where the land had been overworked and was no longer fit for crop production. As for solar panels, it seemed sinful to her and everyone she knew that these were being slapped on perfectly good food-producing land when there must be thousands of acres of car parks, shopping malls, factories, hospitals, schools and housing that could be used instead.

'And tell me, how do those sheep of yours fit into the whole wild farming model you want us all to adopt? I assume they've all been registered with the Flock Book Society and you're adhering to the strict breeding standards, despite the fact they're apparently roaming wild?'

'I have the best farm manager and she's teaching

me everything she knows.' Was Zander sidestepping the question? 'We bought all of our Kerry Hills in the Ludlow sale last year. You might have seen it on my YouTube channel.'

'Dad and me know Olivia well, she worked with us for a while and she's a bloody good farmer, but what the hell she's doing pissing about with the likes of you, I have no idea.' David snorted. 'And as for your YouTube videos, I wouldn't watch that trash if I was strapped to a chair with my eyelids glued open.'

There was a shout of *here-here* from someone in the bar. Jude glanced around her and saw that many of the exhibitors had stopped their own conversations to watch the spectacle.

'My videos are bringing the realities of farming to the public,' said Zander.

'You think that what you're doing showcases the realities of British farming?' Jim decided that now was the time for him to get involved in his son's argument. 'You're a disgrace and you've no place here. It breaks my heart thinking of Olivia wasting her time with the likes of you.'

'Things need to move forward and she can see that, even if you can't,' said Zander. 'You've done it your way for so long you can't see that. And you don't like the fact that at Greener Days I represent the new wave of conscientious farmers.'

'There's nothing conscientious about what you're doing.' David leant across the table so that his face was inches from Zander's. He grabbed the phone from Zander's hand and glowered into the screen. 'And to anyone out there listening to this charlatan, perhaps have a little think about what it would be like if the only food you can get hold of to feed your family is the scraps of some wild deer that you had to fight a thousand other muppets for.'

Zander tried to snatch the phone back from David but he was too fast and the table that stood between them hindered his attack. Jude noticed that nobody else was quick to move and let him through either.

'You might also like to consider how someone who lets his sheep roam wild can also exhibit them at an agricultural show.'

'Give that back.' Zander pushed his way roughly past Ffion and Carl who were in his way.

'I'd say your farming hero is full of shite. And he's earning more than the rest of us put together, so what exactly would he know about the realities of farm life?'

'Well said, son.' Jim clapped David on the back.

There were a few raucous cheers from other farmers before Zander managed to grab his phone and switch it off.

'I will have my lawyers on you for this,' he snarled at David.

'Oh, go ahead. Short of ruining your latest PR stunt, I don't know what you think you can pin on me.'

Zander opened his mouth to say something else but closed it again, choosing instead to extricate himself from the Stockman's Bar.

2

Most of the other exhibitors were camping at the ground but as it was only just over the hills from Malvern Farm, Jude and Frank left them to it and went back to the Land Rover.

'Some interesting people there today,' said Jude as they left the Three Counties. 'What do you make of our competition?'

'Mixed bag,' said Frank. 'Some really know what they're about. The Davies girl has some beauties for sure.'

'Davies?' Jude couldn't remember who that was.

'Her from Batters Farm. Proctor I think she said her name was now.'

'Of course. Ffion and Carl, yes. What about the celebrity in our midst?'

Frank snorted. 'Waste of space if you ask me. Load of nonsense he's spouting and did you notice him do any of the work because I certainly didn't.'

Jude rolled her eyes in agreement. 'All glitter and no substance if you ask me. He left everything to his farm manager.'

'Olivia Cook. Now she's a nice girl.'

'You know her?' Jude was often surprised by the smallness of the local farming community, especially amongst those who had been born into it.

'She used to work on Jim Martin's farm when she was first out of college. We all thought he was mad, hiring a girl, and a townie at that.'

'Seriously, Frank?' Jude looked across at him and raised her eyebrows.

'Sorry, Jude. I'm old and fusty, but not above being proven wrong. And in this instance we all were. That girl was an asset to Jim's farm from day one. Did more for him than that useless son of his ever did and Jim knew it.'

'He must have been upset when she left to go and work for Zander,' said Jude.

'Oh, yes,' said Frank. 'To start with I thought she was going for the money but Jim reckons she and

Zander Pettiford had some sort of past that made her want to go and work for that daft bugger.'

'Tara said they grew up together,' said Jude.

'That'll be it then. Jim won't hear a word said against Olivia. She's like a daughter to him.'

'Can't say the same about her boss though,' said Jude. 'Jim and David definitely didn't like Zander.'

'Yeah well, he was asking for it, wasn't he?'

'I suppose he was,' said Jude.

The talk moved away then to the plan of action for the next day: show day for Jude and her sheep. By the time she pulled up outside the pink cottage at the top of Malvern Farm's drive to drop Frank off, she didn't know if she was more nervous than ever or more excited.

'See you in the morning,' she called to Frank as he pulled his keys out to unlock his front door.

Jude carried on past the duck pond and into the yard where she parked the Land Rover and jumped out to head inside.

'How did it go?' Jude's sister, Lucy, asked when she walked into the kitchen.

'Sheep are settled and I've met some of the other Kerry Hill farmers.' Jude threw her car key down on the kitchen table. 'Interesting bunch of people.'

'Interesting good?' Lucy asked as she lifted the

heavy kettle and set it on the top of the Aga to boil. 'Or interesting bad?'

'Both. There was a really lovely couple from Abergavenny and a woman who'd come from the Brecon Beacons with her mum. But there were also a couple of old farmers Frank knew who bickered like they'd been in a disappointing marriage together for decades.'

Jude sat down at the kitchen table as she regaled her sister with stories from backstage at the county show. When she got to the part about Zander Petti-ford's disrupted Instagram video, Lucy snorted with laughter.

'Oh, I wish I'd seen that,' she said.

'Maybe you still can.' Jude took out her phone and opened Instagram.

Having searched for Zander's profile she looked for the recording of the incident but he'd obviously taken it down already.

'I'm not surprised,' said Lucy as she pulled her chair closer to see. 'From what you told me, it doesn't sound as though he came off very well.'

'Let's try this.' Jude clicked on the latest video that Zander had posted, clearly shot when he had gone back to his swanky caravan.

'Some of you may have seen the Instagram Live

post that went out earlier today. In it, I was attacked for my views on farming and my passion for pre-serving our countryside. I want to assure you all that I'm okay and won't be beaten by this sort of archaic, out of date rubbish. I know what's worth fighting for and I promise that I refuse to be broken by those who aren't willing to accept that change is needed.'

Jude wondered where the enormous caravan, and the big engine that would have been needed to pull it to the show, came into Zander's green vision of the future. She also wondered how showing sheep at a traditional livestock show, the largest in the country, fitted his rewilding ethos.

'That's it for now but I will be keeping you all up to date with how I'm getting on at the Three Counties and hope to prove to the world that wild-grazed sheep really are the best in the show. Right, I'm off to chat to some of the other farmers. See you all soon.'

He held two fingers up in a peace sign and then the video ended.

'What a prize plonker,' said Lucy. 'I bet the farmers love him.'

'Love who?' Noah came into the kitchen, four border collies at his heel, and dropped a kiss on Lucy's head.

When Jude's shepherd, friend and confidante had

proposed to Lucy, Jude couldn't have been happier for them. Noah was a gentle, kind man who had proven himself worthy of her precious sister on countless occasions. She loved them both and it had made sense for Noah to vacate the small pink cottage and to move into the big house. Lucy and her young son, Sebbie, were already living there and Noah had been a constant visitor so making it all official had not seemed like too big a change.

A little way down the track and things were still going well. There had been a few times when Jude had felt like a spare part and there had definitely been times when she'd longed for a little bit of peace but generally she loved having them around. At some point Lucy and Noah would no doubt want to find a place of their own but for now, Jude was happy to share her home with them.

'We were talking about Zander Pettiford,' said Lucy. 'Jude's been rubbing shoulders with him at the show today.'

'What's that numpty doing now?' Noah ran the tap in the kitchen sink and picked up a bar of soap.

'He was trying to persuade the farmers in the Stockman's Bar that rewilding their land or sticking up a load of solar panels is the way to go,' said Jude.

Noah rolled his eyes as he scrubbed at the layers

of dirt on his hands. 'I think he's going to find he's got the wrong audience at the Three Counties. It's like walking into a bar in Cardiff wearing an England rugby shirt and trying to persuade all the Welsh fans to swap red for white.'

Jude chuckled at the analogy.

'Talking of white clothes,' said Lucy, pulling out her iPad and shielding it from Noah as she handed it to Jude. 'I think I may have found my wedding dress today but I want you to have a look before I buy it.' She tapped at the screen and an image of a beautiful fifties-style dress appeared on the Oxfam website. Full-skirted and nipped in at the waist, it came to the model's mid-calf and was decorated with lace and pearls.

'It's stunning,' said Jude, already picturing her sister in it. 'Just what you've been looking for.'

Lucy beamed at her. 'That's what I thought. Look at the back of it too.' She clicked through the pictures to give Jude the full tour of the dress. 'I thought simple shoes with a medium heel, and something warm and furry to cover my shoulders seeing as it will almost certainly be freezing cold in December.'

'You don't have to go for a winter wedding,' said Jude. 'Ignore Noah and all his talk of fitting it in with the farming calendar.'

'I'm just being practical there, Jude.' Noah came over to try and sneak a look at the pictures but Lucy was quick to pull the iPad away.

'And it does mean he'll take time off to whisk me away for a honeymoon, even if it is only Swansea for a long weekend.'

Lucy looked expectantly at Noah who shook his head. 'Doesn't matter how much you push, I'm not going to tell you what I've got planned for us.'

'Gah!' Lucy exhaled. 'At least tell me if it's better or worse than a weekend in Swansea?'

'There are worse places than the south coast of Wales.' Noah kissed her again. 'Now, looking at the time, I'd better get down to school and pick Sebbie up.'

* * *

The next morning Jude awoke early with a nervous buzz of excitement already running through her. It was Friday, the first day of the Three Counties Show, and the Kerry Hills were due to be in the ring at around one that afternoon.

That gave her the morning to get her two shearlings ready for their debut. She had her white coat ironed and ready, new white halters for the sheep and her box of tricks to get them looking their best. Noah had offered to do all the farm rounds that morning so she could get up leisurely and have plenty of time to prepare. Of course, Jude's body clock wasn't exactly aligned with the gesture and she was still the first one out of bed.

By the time she was due to pick Frank up and go to the showground, she'd been dressed for hours. The car was packed and she'd tried to take her mind off things by visiting the growing menagerie of petting animals that she kept as an extra draw for her paying campsite guests.

'Everything okay with you, Jude?' Frank asked as he climbed into the passenger seat of the battered Land Rover.

'I don't think I've felt this nervous since my wedding day.'

As she drove down the driveway, Jude thought about her husband, Adam. If it hadn't been for him then she would almost certainly still be teaching. Instead, she was running a farm and about to exhibit her animals in her very first agricultural show. She wondered what Adam would have made of it and imagined for a moment that some part of him was still with her, encouraging her and giving her strength.

'He'd have been proud of you,' Frank said, somehow reading her expression perfectly. 'You can be sure of that.'

Frank had known Adam as a child in the days when Adam's family had farmed the land and Frank had been their shepherd. He'd watched him grow and had been there for Adam when his parents moved to Canada and ownership and responsibility had passed to him. By that time, Frank had taken his own tenancy, making room at Malvern Farm for his son Noah to become shepherd. The two families had been closely woven together and Jude was grateful that support had been passed on to her when Adam died and she took over the farm herself.

'Looks like another fine day today,' said Frank as they crossed the hills and began their descent down towards the showground.

There was already a queue for parking and Jude navigated towards the area set aside for exhibitors. She felt the butterflies in her stomach start to twitch into life as she took in the hordes of people making their way into the showground.

'Most of these buggers are here for the food,' said Frank drily. 'Bet you only a handful will even know what a Kerry Hill is, far less come to watch them being shown.'

Jude knew he was right. Whilst still being the largest agricultural show in the country, the vast majority of people who walked through the turnstiles were there for the motorbike displays, craft tents and maybe the farm machinery or sheep dog demos. Hardly any of them would take more than a cursory glance around the livestock sheds, and most wouldn't even get that far. But that didn't stop the nerves as she also knew that the ones who did turn up to view her sheep were the ones who would know what they were looking at.

'Come on then, Jude,' said Frank when they'd parked the Land Rover. 'Let's go and see those animals of yours and get them up to scratch for the judge.'

Although it was still several hours until show time, there was much to do. Jude led the way to the sheep shed where those who were showing in the earlier categories were already hard at work with their stock.

'Morning, Jude,' said Ffion who was busy clipping the fleece of an ewe whilst Carl was giving the rams a last wash. 'All set?'

'Not a bit of it,' said Jude. 'Mind you, I've only got two to prepare. You must have been here for a while already with yours.'

'It was an early start but we're used to it.' Ffion glanced towards the back of the shed and raised her eyebrows. 'Look who's here.'

Zander Pettiford was walking in with Olivia, the real farmer behind the sheep he'd brought with him to show. Whilst Olivia headed straight for Zander's pen, he pulled his phone out to start recording the day's social media posts.

'I wish he'd put that thing away.' Tara came over to join Jude and Ffion. 'I find it really embarrassing when I never know if I'm going to be caught out on the camera. Did you see the video he posted last night?'

'The one where he's in his fancy caravan talking about the argument he had with David?' Jude asked.

'No, he posted another one after that. Snippets of conversations he had with some people in the Stockman's Bar at the end of the day.' Tara looked furiously towards the celebrity as she spoke. 'Mostly taken completely out of context and basically trying to prove that all us farmers are responsible for ruining the environment and it's down to him to change the entire industry himself.'

'He's bloody bonkers if you ask me,' said Carl, who'd finished with the rams. 'I don't know how he has the balls to turn up here this morning after the things he had to say about all of us.'

Ffion ran her hand over the fleece of her ewe. 'Probably reckons us dark ages thinkers don't know how to use our mobile phones, let alone get on to Instagram to see what he's up to. He's not even a real farmer. Just some idiot with a lot of money who's got a bunch of people to do it for him. You know his farm manager, Tara. What does she think of him?'

'Olivia is lovely. We were at Hartpury ag college together and she was always top of the class even though she had zero experience of farming before she started. She and Zander grew up next door to each other in a block of flats somewhere in London,' Tara explained. 'She went off to work for Jim Martin when she graduated, which is where she fell for the Kerry Hills. Then Zander bought that farm of his and she went to work for him.'

'I always get the feeling that he doesn't really like the farming so much as the attention it gets him,' said Carl.

'I think you're right,' said Tara. 'When I first met Olivia at Hartpury, Zander had only just joined the band and they were still doing gigs at local pubs and weddings. She talked about him all the time, but he never came to see her. Then all of a sudden he's a mega star and has bought a farm.'

'At least David Martin stood up to him yesterday.' When Ffion mentioned David's name, Tara visibly stiffened and Jude wondered again what the history between them was.

'I noticed the video of their argument made it on to the BBC News app this morning,' Carl said. 'Although Zander took it off Instagram, it had already been shared and moved to other platforms so he can't get rid of it. That surely won't do his reputation any good.'

'Not that his daft followers will pay any attention,' said Ffion.

Frank, who'd gone off to try and find a spare trimming stand from one of his old farming acquaintances, came back to join Jude then.

'Bob Jeffries isn't showing his Jacobs until tomorrow so he said we can have his stand today. He's going to get someone to bring it over for us.'

'Thanks, Frank,' said Jude, distracted by Zander Pettiford who was heading straight for Jim Martin's sheep pens.

In the pen a little way from her, Jude could see Jim was busy with his ram whilst David watched with his hands in his pockets. Zander was still holding his phone in his hand and, as he got close to David, he held it up, pointing it directly at him. As though everyone in the shed knew that something was about to happen, the buzz quietened and all heads turned towards the men.

'I'm here with David Martin, who you might recognise from last night's Instagram Live where he became quite aggressive towards me and my opinions on building a greener Britain. After a little bit of digging, I can now see why and I've come to talk to him about his own plans for the farm he recently had passed to him from his father.'

As David turned around, Jim stood up to face their common enemy together.

'Get that thing out of my face.' David swiped at the phone but Zander moved it quickly out of the way.

'You are being recorded,' Zander warned him.

'What is it you want?' Jim demanded. 'Isn't it enough you're trying to ruin the industry we all work in when times are already tough enough for most of us?'

'You misunderstand me,' said Zander. 'I want to help farmers breathe new life into their farms. There's money to be made in sustainable farming, I'm living proof of this.'

'Not really a realistic comparison, is it?' Carl whispered. 'Olivia doesn't look very impressed.'

Jude looked over to where Carl was pointing and saw Olivia Cook standing by a pen that was now sporting a very smart *Greener Days Farm* banner with a picture of Zander in a flat cap on it. Olivia was staring at the scene with a look of horror on her face as the owners of both farms she'd worked at clashed antlers. Frank had told Jude how close Olivia had been to Jim, and yet she had grown up with Zander. She'd worked on both farms and so no doubt the unravelling row was not something she had hoped to see today.

'You're talking out of your arse, Pettiford,' said Jim. 'Like you always do.'

'What's going on here then?' Griff Gould approached to stick his nose in.

'I'm just here to find out what farming really looks like these days,' Zander said, 'and I wanted to talk to David about his plans for developing a large area of his farm to include twenty new houses over the next eight years.'

Jim let out a deep laugh from the pit of his belly but Griff and David didn't join him.

'Like I said, you're talking out of your arse. My son and I have no such plans for our farm so you can take your lies and your fake concerns and you can push off so we can get on with what we're best at. Our animals.'

'But it isn't a lie or a fake concern if it's the truth, is it?' Zander wasn't going anywhere, it seemed. 'You see, I thought there was something not right yesterday when David attacked me like that so I asked around and discovered a paper trail that very much leads to development plans for your farm. Oh, sorry – the farm that you recently signed ownership of over to your son.'

Jim's wide forehead creased as he looked to David, waiting for him to overturn Zander's accusation. Something that David didn't do.

'David?' Jim asked, less certain now.

'I was going to run it past you before I signed anything but it makes sense, Dad. We won't miss a few acres and we stand to make a lot of money from this.'

'You little git.' Griff launched forward and caught David by the neck of his shirt. 'And what about my farm, ey? What about neighbourly courtesy and respect?'

Jude remembered Frank telling her that the two farms bordered each other and she could see why Griff was so angry at the thought of land being turned over to developers. The noisy, disruptive work could last for years and end up with a scar across Griff's part of the countryside.

'You see the total lack of care that this man has for nature?' Zander had turned the camera back to himself again. 'No wonder he wasn't happy with my views yesterday when all along he's been planning on digging up fields in order to build new houses. It makes me so sad that this is allowed to happen.'

'You can't do this, David,' said Jim. 'I won't let you ruin the farm. It's been in our family for centuries. I passed it to you because I thought you'd continue to farm it, as my only child. Not so that you can turn it over to developers.'

'You can't stop me.' David looked forceful. 'The farm is in my name alone and at the moment it's barely even paying its way. You might be okay living like that but I'm not. We're sitting on an asset that I want to explore and make some proper money out of.'

At that moment, there was a mighty growl from Griff who launched himself at David, swinging his arm back to land a punch on the younger man's jaw.

Several people around them then sprang into life to break up the fight before it got out of control.

'You always were a lazy, spoilt arse,' Griff shouted as he wriggled to get free from the grasp of the two men who were holding him back. 'If you're arrogant enough to carry on with this plan of yours then don't expect me to make it easy for you. I will fight you all the way.'

'I expected nothing less.' David ran his fingers over his jawline and opened his mouth widely to test it out. 'Hit me again though, old man, and I'll have you up on charges of assault. You won't find it so easy to fight me when you're in prison.'

Three of the show's security guards rushed in and Griff shrugged himself out of the hands that had been restraining him. 'It's okay,' he said. 'I'm not going to touch him. I'll find a better way of bringing him down.'

Like everyone else in the shed, Jude watched for a moment longer as things calmed down and the men involved were separated. David disappeared, leaving Jim with the sheep and Zander looked smug as he tapped something into his mobile phone.

'David's such a dickhead,' said Tara.

'Do you remember when you had a mega crush on him?' Ffion teased. 'You went out with him for a bit too.'

Jude remembered Tara's reaction when David had joined them in the Stockman's Bar on the first afternoon. She'd definitely not been pleased to see

him again after so long which suggested any relationship they'd had did not end amicably.

'Yeah, well that was a long time ago.' Tara looked
beyond uncomfortable about the whole thing. 'He
used to be quite sweet when we started going to the
Young Farmers things.'

'Before he became a dickhead?' Ffion said.

Tara laughed. 'Exactly.'

'Well that was fun.' Ffion clapped her hands
against her thighs. 'But now we've got even less time
to get these beasties ready for their big moment.'

3

It was difficult to know when to stop clipping the sheep, or at least it was for Jude who had next to no experience. With her ewe firmly held in place on the trimming stand, she snipped away with old-fashioned metal clippers which were razor sharp and reminded Jude of some sort of medieval torture device.

The fleece needed to be short and neat to show off the strong physique and good lines of the sheep she and Frank had chosen back in the autumn when they were still lambs.

'I'd say she's ready.' Frank handed Jude the fixing spray and she finished the ewe's new hairdo with a good spritz.

There was still a little time to wait for their categories to take to the ring and Jude set about tidying up her pens whilst Frank returned the stand they'd borrowed. She was just closing the lid on her grooming box when she saw a familiar and welcome face appear amongst the small crowd of people moving around the shed.

'Marco!' Jude felt the flush of pleasure she always felt when she was with him. Although they had never been a proper couple, he was the closest she had come to a romantic relationship since Adam had died and he had a way of making her feel both happy and calm.

'I thought I'd come and see the product of your hard work after all those months of giving these two the special treatment.'

He walked over to the pen and leant over the hurdle to kiss Jude's cheek, leaving behind a heat that burnt its way through her nerves and took her mind away from the show.

'How are you feeling?' Marco asked.

'As ready as we'll ever be,' said Jude. 'I've learnt so much from Frank and the other breeders here but we'll just have to see what the judge say.'

Marco looked around the shed at the buzz of activity as the exhibitors all prepared their animals.

'It's a serious business, isn't it?'

'It really is,' Jude agreed.

Like the others, she had already put plenty of time into preparing her two Kerry Hills for this moment. They'd been sheared months ago when the weather was still cold, so the wool had the chance to grow back enough to be clipped into shape. Whilst the other sheep were all out to pasture, Henry and Helen had been kept in the lambing shed and fed well to bulk up nicely.

'It's a big task,' Jude told Marco. 'Expensive too. But for some farmers, success here means they can add another notch to their breeding credentials and that means more money coming in.'

Marco rested his hands on the top rung of the hurdle and Jude noticed how the muscles of his forearms flexed beneath the rolled-up sleeves of his shirt.

'So who's your biggest competition?'

Jude indicated to her right. 'The Proctors. Their ram should win the show.' She dropped her voice a little. 'And it sounds as though they need to do well this year. It might be the difference between keeping the farm afloat or not.'

'A win can really make that much difference?' Marco looked at Jude incredulously.

'It certainly helps. There can be big money in the best breeding animals. I think the most expensive ram ever sold in this country went for over £350,000 a little while back.'

Marco's eyes opened wide. 'Are you kidding me?'

'Look it up,' said Jude. 'It was a Texel, they're always the ones to go for the most money because of their meat and wool quality. But this was crazy. Mind you, he'll sire some pretty decent lambs himself and if they sell for even a quarter of the price the farmers paid for their dad, then it won't take long to start making a big, fat profit.'

Marco's eyebrows shot up to meet his hairline. 'I learn something new every time I see you, Jude,' he said.

* * *

It was finally time for the Kerry Hills to be shown and Jude was ready in her white coat with the ram haltered. Frank had introduced both sheep to the halter as soon as they'd come to live on the farm and, whilst they still hated having anything on their faces, they were at least used to it and didn't object as much as they might.

Once the aged rams had taken their turn and been judged, surprisingly without the Proctors coming out on top, it was the turn of the ram shearlings.

'Come on then,' Jude said as she led her boy out of the shed and into the sunlight.

The grass outside had been split into a grid of mini paddocks and Jude made her way to the right one. Jim, Tara and Griff were already there with their rams standing in the middle of the show ring and Jude inwardly thanked Henry for letting her lead him in to join them without too much of a bid to escape.

Zander Pettiford made his entrance next accompanied by a cheer from some spectators followed by a rumble of disapproval from plenty of others. Carl was the last to bring out his animal and Jude noticed the thunderous look on his face as he came to stand next to her. She assumed this was because of the disappointment of the previous category and hoped that he'd find success elsewhere in the competition.

The judge walked around the animals, looking at their stance and physique before coming in closer to check the fleece and teeth of each sheep in turn.

'Nice lad,' she said to Jude when she'd finished with her ram.

Jude looked over to the edge of the ring where Frank, Marco, Lucy and Noah were congregated. Jude gave them a smile and was rewarded with an enthusiastic display of thumbs up and fingers crossed.

The judge walked around the ring one more time before making her decision and picking up the rosettes to award. Before she could make her announcement though, David Martin rushed into the ring, waving a box of what looked like Just For Men hair dye and shouting for the proceedings to stop.

'What's going on?' the judge asked.

'He's a bloody cheat.' David pointed at Griff Gould.

'What are you talking about?' Griff said.

'I found this in your pen.' David turned to the judge. 'Check the ears and knees on his ram again. I bet he's used it to blacken them artificially.'

'I think I'd have spotted that,' said the judge, but she went over nonetheless to have another inspection of the sheep in question.

'I bet that's not all he used it for.' Carl turned on Griff. 'We had a ram in the previous class who had perfectly white fleece when I cleaned him up this morning. By the time Ffion took him into the ring, there were black marks on the back of his neck and above his tail. They cost us the win and you went on to take the rosette.' He jabbed an angry finger in Griff's direction.

'I did nothing of the sort,' said Griff. 'You'll find no dye on my sheep, doesn't matter how hard you look for it.'

The judge declared the rest of the Kerry Hill category to be postponed until an enquiry had been carried out and called for a steward to be brought to the ring.

'What are we supposed to do now?' Jim demanded. 'We all have to pay because of one cheat? Take him out of the ring and let's carry on with the job.'

'You know we can't do that,' said the judge. 'Please, Jim. Just take your sheep back to their pens for now and we'll wait for the results of the enquiry.'

'Well, I hope you're happy,' Jim shoved the end of the halter into David's hands and stomped over to challenge Griff who was looking equally stormy.

'I told you, I had nothing to do with that. Bit funny, don't you think, that your son was the one who just happened to find a box of hair dye in my things.' Griff pulled himself up to make the most of his height advantage. 'What I want to know is, what the hell was he doing going through my things in the first place?'

'I saw you earlier fiddling around with the Proctors' sheep and I had a hunch you were up to no good so I thought I'd have a look whilst you were out in the ring,' said David. 'Glad I did.'

'So it was you.' Carl's face was thunderous. 'You've cost us, and I don't just mean a rosette. Ffion and I were banking on our rams being top this year and we worked hard to get them here. And then you go and bugger it all up by messing around with hair dye.'

'I'm telling you, it wasn't me.'

'Calm down everyone,' said Zander. 'This negative energy isn't good for our animals.'

'Oh sod off, Pettiford,' Carl spat before being the first to march out of the ring back towards the shed.

Jude looked across to her friends and gave a wide-eyed shrug before leading her ram out with the other exhibitors. Only Jim, David and Griff remained in the ring, arguing between themselves. Jude imagined they'd stay there until some show official came to remove them.

* * *

Once a thorough investigation had been carried out it was decided that dye had been used to both blacken the knees and ears of Griff's sheep and damage the fleeces of not just Carl and Ffion's ram but also Jim's ewes. With no evidence that it had been

Griff who'd applied the dye other than David's word, the officials felt they couldn't just penalise one farmer and so the entire category was cancelled.

The mood was glum and there was a feeling that everyone just wanted to pack up and return to their farms, something that wasn't possible as the sheep couldn't be moved until the end of the three-day show.

Noah and Lucy went home, taking Frank with them, but Jude decided to stay and was delighted when Marco said that he would too.

'Why don't we make the most of it and have a look around?' Tara suggested. 'See what else is going on. Ffion, are you up for that?'

'I need to just go and sit in the caravan on my own for a bit.' Ffion looked so dejected but this wasn't really a big surprise. 'If we're still barbecuing later then I'll catch up with you all then.'

'Do you want me to stay with you?' Carl asked.

'No, you're okay. I'll be better on my own to be honest.'

Carl glanced at Tara and gave a conspiratorial wink. He clearly wasn't as put out by the results of the show as his wife was, but then Jude got the sense that the sheep were really Ffion's babies and he was just along for the ride.

Olivia was keen to have a look around too so the little group ventured away from the livestock sheds and out into the vast grounds of the wider show.

Marco pulled a timetable with map out of his back pocket and looked at it. 'There's a heavy horses show in the main arena in half an hour, or some guy is using a sheep dog to round up Runner ducks if you'd rather see that.'

Nobody had anything in particular they wanted to look at but it was nice to wander. It was also nice to get to know Olivia away from Zander Pettiford's shadow.

'You met Tara at Hartpury,' said Jude.

'God, that was a long time ago now,' said Olivia, 'but yes. Tara was one of the first people I met there and we hit it off straight away.'

'What made you want to go into farming?' Marco asked. 'Jude said you were brought up a city girl.'

'That's right, I was. I'm sure you already know that Zander and I were next-door neighbours.' Olivia picked up a woolly jumper from a country clothing stand they'd stopped to have a look at. 'When we were little we used to dream about moving to the country, so when I had the chance to go and study at agricultural college, I jumped at it.'

Olivia turned the price tag of the jumper over and

her eyebrows shot through her hairline before she hung it back on the rail. The act detached Olivia somehow from the showy, expensive lifestyle Zander had carved for himself and it made her seem more relatable somehow.

Tara linked her arm through Olivia's and pulled her close. 'And I'm so glad you did. Just imagine if you'd never gone to Hartpury and we hadn't met.'

The next stall along was full of pretty nick-nacks, all with a farming theme. Tables along the front were full of interesting things to tempt potential shoppers into the marquee behind.

'Ooh, look at these.' Tara let go of Olivia's arm and wandered into the tent where a table of hand-painted mugs were stacked.

Jude and Marco followed her in whilst Carl and Olivia chose to stay outside. Jude's eye was caught by some perfectly crafted little enamelled animal charms, one of which was of the instantly recognisable black and white panda face of a Kerry Hill.

'Just like Helen and Henry.' Marco picked one from the stand and held it up for a closer look.

'What have you found there?' Tara came to join them. 'Oh, that's gorgeous.' She also picked one up and rubbed the smooth enamel between her fingers. 'The perfect love token.' She wriggled her eyebrows comically and took out her purse. 'Only don't tell my mum. She's already a big enough nightmare every time I come back from a date. Sometimes I think she's just desperate to get me married off.'

Tara went off to pay and Jude turned around to find Marco but he'd already wandered back outside.

The little group left the show stalls then and went to have a look at the farm machinery although Tara was less interested in that.

'My dad used to make us spend hours looking at new tractors and stuff. It was like an addiction to him and now I'd rather just stay away and keep patching up our old kit.'

'We don't need to hang around the shiny tractors,' said Carl. 'In fact, we've been gone a while. I suppose I should head back and see how Ffion's doing.'

'Yeah, I should check Mam as well,' said Tara. 'Maybe we should start the barbecue early, try and cheer everyone up again after all that business with the hair dye and them cancelling our category.'

Carl frowned. 'I'm still fuming at the nerve of that man,' he said. 'If I see Griff Gould again before we leave...' However he intended that sentence to end, he obviously didn't think it appropriate to voice out loud.

'We don't actually know for sure it was him,' Tara

reasoned. 'Don't you think he had a point when he said how strange it was for the dye to be found by David?'

'I agree,' said Olivia. 'And we all know what sort of a man David Martin can be. I remember when I first got the job with Jim, you warned me about him then.' She looked at Tara.

'What do you mean?' Carl asked. 'He's a bit of a tit, that's for sure. But why should he come with a warning?'

'Tara knew him from the Young Farmers,' Olivia carried on, not noticing the discomfort that Jude saw tugging Tara's joviality away. 'I remember your words exactly before I started at the farm. You said that he was a chancer and a letch. Lazy and handsy and that I shouldn't trust him an inch. You were right about that.' There was an edge to Olivia's voice as she spoke.

'What?' Carl was almost accusatory as he turned back to Tara. 'Ffion never said anything like that.'

'Yeah, well, Ffion was always better than me at dealing with attention, in whatever form it was thrown at her.' Tara bit her bottom lip and Jude wondered again exactly what happened between Tara and David whilst they were both members of the Young Farmers. 'Anyway, that's all water under the bridge. But you're right, Liv. I wouldn't trust him as far as a bull could butt him.'

They'd been walking in the direction of the campsite and had come to the first rows of caravans and horse boxes that were being used by the ex-hibitors.

'I'm that way,' said Carl, pointing to the far corner.

'Over there.' Olivia waved a hand towards the opposite corner.

'You can spot us a mile off,' said Tara. 'Mam insisted on putting the flag up to make it easier to find our caravan. When you come and find us for the bar-becue, just look for the Welsh dragon.'

Jude looked over in the direction Tara was pointing and saw the red dragon on a green and white background flying proudly.

'What time shall we come over?' Olivia asked.

'Whenever you like. I'm heading back to crack a beer open and put my feet up. Mam will probably be doing the same so just come over whenever.'

'We'll be with you in a bit,' said Jude. 'I want to pop into the food hall first and find something to add to the barbecue.'

'Don't worry about that, there's usually more than enough to go around,' said Tara.

Jude was adamant though and she and Marco went off to buy some sausages, a block of cheese and some bread from the vendors in the delicious-smelling food hall. They took their time, people watching, chatting and laughing as they wove their way through the crowds.

'I got something for you,' Marco said as they started to make their way back to the campsite. He took a little paper bag from his pocket and handed it over to Jude.

'What's this?' she asked, tipping the bag to let a tiny velvet pouch fall into her hand.

'I thought you should have something to remember your first show by – for the good bits and not the bad,' said Marco. 'And also to bring you luck for all the shows you'll do in the future.'

Jude opened the pouch and took out an enamel Kerry Hill sheep. For a second her breath caught in her throat but she couldn't be sure whether it was the loveliness of having a friend like Marco or the words she'd heard Tara say before she bought one for the person she was secretly dating: *The perfect love token.*

'It's gorgeous,' she said. 'Thank you.'

'You're welcome. Now let's go and cook some sausages.'

* * *

When they found the Watsons' caravan the grills had already been lit, glasses filled and snacks shared. Camping chairs had been set out and Jim, David, Ffion, Carl, Olivia and Zander had joined Tara and Penny. Jude and Marco were welcomed with bottles of lager and they sat down on a couple of stools that someone had brought.

Only Griff was missing and Jude wondered how many of those sitting outside the Watsons' caravan had already tried and convicted him of tinkering with the hair dye.

'I still can't believe that's it for the show,' said Ffion despondently. 'All that work and preparation just down the drain. And we were counting on a win as well. I need to get top money for my rams this year to fill the hole in the farm's coffers.'

'There's always the Cheshire Show next and the Great Yorkshire and Royal Welsh coming up,' said Tara.

'You must all see a lot of each other, touring the county shows like that,' said Marco.

'We do get to know the regulars.' Penny held her hand over the portable gas barbecue to check if it was hot enough to put the meat on. 'Some folk come and go but then there are old buggers like us who stick around for ever, ey, Jim?'

Olivia, who was sitting next to Jim, patted him affectionately on the knee. 'What would we do without the old buggers?'

Jim raised his pint and smiled. Possibly the first smile Jude had seen from him since they'd met the day before. 'You still left me for that twit over there,' he said, nodding at Zander. 'It's not too late to come back to me, Olivia. None of this wild deer and foraging for mushrooms mumbo jumbo, just good old-fashioned farming – how it's meant to be.'

'That's the problem with you lot,' said Zander tersely. 'You're not even willing to listen.'

'It's been a long day, Zand,' Olivia cut in. 'Just leave it for now, hey? Jim was only messing with you.'

Zander and Jim said nothing more and a silent truce was drawn between them, neither wanting to upset Olivia.

'I have to say it's good to be here, despite the obvious shadow that a little Just For Men cast over today's proceedings,' said Tara. 'My dad would have loved to have seen such a good show of Kerry Hills doing us breeders proud, wouldn't he, Mam?'

Penny smiled and nodded at her daughter but Jude noticed that it seemed a little half-hearted. 'I'd say the barbecue's hot enough now if anyone wants to throw some meat on. Carl, how are yours doing? Almost ready?'

Carl was sitting near two large disposable grills which were glowing a satisfying orange now that the smoke had died away. 'All good here too, Penny.'

There was a flurry of activity as sausages, burgers, chicken drumsticks and some of Zander's venison steaks were loaded onto the barbecues. With the meat cooking, filling the air around the caravan with tempting smells, spirits lifted and everyone joined in with chatter about their farms. Even Zander kept a lid on it for a while and Jude found she was enjoying herself, perhaps even more so because Marco was sitting next to her.

There was a definite tension between Jim and David but otherwise there was a lovely feeling of ca-maraderie and togetherness amongst the farmers as they swapped their stories. Even Ffion lost the gloominess that she had brought with her and, with the help of a glass or two of cider, she was back to her jolly self again.

The afternoon slipped into evening and the show officially closed on its first day.

'Good to see Griff's keeping away after what he did,' said David. 'I told you he was a cheat, Dad.'

'Not the only one though, is he?' Jim's eyes blazed as he looked at his son, the resentment and hurt that he'd been trying to keep a lid on bubbling over.

'Oh, so you think I'm a cheat now as well as everything else?' David yelled. 'Come on, Dad, don't hold back. Tell us all how disappointed in me you are, how disappointed you've always been.'

'Stop being such a fool.' Jim turned away as though he couldn't stand to look at him any longer. 'You know that's not how it goes. I've never been disappointed in you, David. But I am today. Trying to build houses on the land your family's worked for generations, it makes me sick.'

Olivia rested her hand on Jim's forearm, a gentle action that only seemed to pour oil on the fire.

'Oh that's right, Liv. Golden girl to the rescue as always.' David stood up and sneered at Olivia. 'Turned up from heaven when the rascal son wasn't pulling his weight on the farm. Isn't that right, Dad? Bet you wished you could swap her for me on a permanent basis, don't you? I'm surprised you didn't hand the farm on to her instead of me.'

'Maybe I should have.' Jim's tone was low and measured. 'Don't suppose she'd go lying to me about what she wanted to do with the place.'

'I didn't lie,' said David slowly through gritted

teeth. 'I was going to tell you about the development when there was more substance of planning to give you.'

'When would that have been?' Zander asked. 'When the diggers came in to tear out the trees and desecrate the landscape?'

In one swift move, David turned round, raised the can of cider he'd been drinking and threw it at Zander. There was a stunned silence around the camp as everyone watched Zander blink in shock.

'You are going to regret doing that.' Zander fixed David with a steely stare.

Zander stood up and Olivia went to try and help but he pushed her away.

David grinned as the golden liquid soaked into Zander's designer clothes. 'Oh, trust me, nothing could possibly make me want to take this moment back. Now will you just keep your bloody nose out of my business.'

* * *

After Zander's dramatic departure, closely followed by David, the others remained around the camp for a little longer, although the atmosphere had been ruined.

'I fancy a bit of a walk before we head home,' Marco half whispered to Jude. 'Clear our heads and walk off the sausages before we get in the car. What do you say we sneak back into the showground for an amble whilst it's quiet?'

'Love to,' said Jude.

After the hustle and bustle of the busy day, it seemed almost eerily quiet around the empty show rings. All of the visitors had left and the ground had been turned over to a group of people carrying bin bags and litter pickers. As they walked, Jude felt Marco's hand brush hers and she thought how easy it would be to just reach out and take it.

'Home time?' he said once they'd walked the perimeter of the grounds.

'Sure. I just want to pop in and check on the sheep before we head off, if that's okay?'

Jude and Marco walked back to the sheep shed which was quiet now that almost everyone had packed up for the evening. There were only a few people in there, a man busy at the far end and a woman in the pen next to him. Down at the end by the Kerry Hills, Jude could only see David and Tara standing with their backs to her. As Jude and Marco neared them, she caught some of what they were saying.

'We had fun back then, didn't we?' David ran his finger down Tara's arm but she pushed him away.

'You had fun with anyone who was drunk enough to let you.'

'Maybe you could use another drink then, ey?' There was a slur to his voice that made Jude think he had already had several drinks himself.

'Just leave me alone, David.' Tara folded her arms defiantly but David clearly didn't want to hear the rejection and pushed his face closer to hers.

'Come on now,' he teased. 'Dad'll be in the bar all evening and I've got a bottle of white back in the caravan.'

Marco and Jude both sped up at the same moment to bridge the gap between them and Tara.

'Everything okay, Tara?' Jude asked.

'Jude!' David draped one arm across Tara's shoulders and looked lasciviously at Jude, making her feel as though she was standing half-naked in front of him. 'Don't be jealous. There's plenty of me to go round.'

Jude felt, rather than saw, Marco come to stand at her side. He stepped forward with a look of anger that seemed out of place on his usually gentle face. 'I'd think about your next step carefully, mate, if I were you,' he said.

David looked at him with a smirk. 'Oh calm down, *mate*. We're all just having a bit of fun.'

'I don't see anyone having fun, actually,' said Jude. 'I see a pathetic man who has to beg for attention from women who'd rather sleep on the shit-covered hay with their sheep than give him what he wants. Now, if you don't leave Tara alone and go and sober yourself up, the only place you'll be sleeping tonight is the police station.'

At that moment, Penny came into the shed through the door opposite and saw her daughter, whose face and body language screamed discomfort.

'What's going on here?' The stocky woman marched up with a fearsome look on her face, making David drop his arm quickly.

'Tara and I were just catching up.' David's bravado had gone, yet he still had a sense of untouchable pomposity about him. 'It's been so long since we last saw each other.'

'Well this time you're out of luck, I'm afraid,' said Penny. 'Tara's coming back to the bar with me. She clearly isn't keen on any form of catching up where you're concerned.'

'Actually, I think I want to go back to the caravan,' said Tara. 'It's been a long day.'

Tara turned quickly and ran out of the sheep shed, leaving her mother to confront David.

'You're finding all the ways to make yourself unpopular today, aren't you?' Penny said. 'If I were you, I'd make myself scarce.'

Penny didn't wait for David's reply before bustling out after her daughter. David turned to Jude and Marco with a drunken shrug as though they were suddenly his allies. 'Seems everyone is on a bit of a short fuse after today.'

'I think they have every reason to be,' said Marco. 'I'd take the advice you've been given if I were you and head off to bed to sober up.'

Jude was exhausted and just wanted to be back at home, collapsing into the saggy old sofa with her dogs at her feet and a cup of tea in her hands. Whilst David pretended to busy himself in Jim's sheep pens, hopefully taking Penny's advice and keeping low for a bit, Jude topped up her own sheep's water bucket and gave them a little more hay before gladly retreating back to her car with Marco.

It wasn't until she had already started the engine that she remembered she'd taken her phone from her pocket whilst she was dealing with her sheep and it was still sitting on the kit box in her pen.

'Bugger,' she said. 'I'll have to go back and get it.'

'Can we drive round?' Marco asked. A sensible question as the car park was a fair walk from the sheds.

'I don't think we'll be able to get through as they lock the gates,' said Jude. 'It'll be easier just to walk.'

By the time they got back to the shed, it was deserted and the lights had been switched off for the night. It was almost midsummer and the sky was still blue although the sun was heading rapidly over to the west side of the hills. Marco waited outside and Jude ran in to collect her phone.

Whilst she was in her pen, she heard a clatter at the top end of the shed in Zander Pettiford's pens and looked up. To begin with, she couldn't see anything and assumed it had just been one of Zander's sheep knocking into the metal hurdles. But then she saw something out of place in his kit pen. Something that she couldn't entirely make out through the bars with all the sheep partially blocking her view.

'Marco?' she called, suddenly wanting him close. 'Marco, could you come here a moment please?'

Before he'd reached her, Jude had walked to the end pen and seen the horror of what was inside. She clapped her hand over her mouth and stifled a gasp as she took in the image of a man slumped like a discarded scarecrow on the ground. His eyes were unblinking as they stared at nothing and his arms flopped loosely by his sides. Sticking out of the side of his neck, in line with his Adam's apple, was a pair of trimming shears. One of the pointed blades was deeply embedded whilst the other only scratched the surface. Jude wondered which had done the most damage as it was the second blade that had severed the carotid artery, judging by the amount of blood that had spilt from the wound.

'Holy shit,' said Marco as he arrived and saw what had happened.

Jude already had her phone in her hand and was dialling the emergency services.

'Police,' she said when prompted. 'I need to report a murder at the Three Counties Show. I'm there now, in the Avon Hall. The victim is a man called David Martin.'

4

Jude was relieved to see her good friend Detective Inspector Binnie Khatri arrive to lead to investigation and she resisted the urge to give her a hug when she walked into the sheep shed.

'Ouch!' exclaimed Binnie's partner, Sami Abadi. 'That looks nasty.'

'Thank you for your useful summary, DS Abadi,' said Binnie. 'Make sure to note it officially.'

Sami and Binnie had worked together on many large cases before and Jude knew there was no better team. When in work mode, Binnie was serious and professional whereas Sami was more jovial and had a tendency to make jokes on the edge of being acceptable. To a casual onlooker, perhaps it would seem like Sami exasperated Binnie and she didn't take him seriously. The reality was that there was a deep respect and understanding between the two and Jude knew they loved their working relationship.

Binnie turned to Jude and Marco. 'What can you tell me?'

Jude looked at the white-clad team that had already moved in to gather any evidence they could from the crime scene.

'Shall we do this over there?' Jude pointed to the other end of the shed where some old plastic chairs had been left out.

She began talking as the four of them made their way over to the chairs. 'His name is David Martin. He's here with his father, Jim, one of the other Kerry Hill exhibitors.'

'Did either of you see anyone else around here when you found him?' Binnie asked.

Marco shook his head. 'It was pretty quiet. I was standing outside the main door there whilst Jude went in to get her phone and I didn't see anyone.'

Jude pulled one of the chairs out and sat down. 'No, nobody. The place was empty.'

The others sat down too and Sami pulled out a notebook. 'What do you know of the victim?'

'He was a fairly dislikable man. Firmly invested

in his own gains and inclined to think of himself as not only irresistible to women but also entitled to help himself.'

Binnie raised an eyebrow. 'Do go on.'

'Earlier this evening Marco and I came in when he was giving one of the other female farmers far more attention than she was comfortable with.'

'Name?' Binnie was always direct when she was working a case.

'Tara Watson.'

'And then he turned his attentions to you,' said Marco, still bristling from the encounter.

'I bet he regretted that pretty quickly.' There was a glimmer of mischief in Sami's eyes and Jude knew it was because he understood her well enough to guess correctly exactly how that situation had played out.

'So we could be looking at someone using the shears as self-defence to ward off the unwanted attentions of a pest,' said Binnie. 'What else can you tell me?'

'I'm not sure if you keep up with these things but he had a bit of a run in with Zander Pettiford yesterday and that spilt over into today as well,' said Jude.

'Zander Pettiford from The Spods?' Sami asked.

'That's him. You know he's a farmer of sorts these days?'

'Can't miss him on social media,' said Binnie. 'So he had an argument with David Martin. Do you know what it was about?'

Jude outlined the row that had been streamed live to Zander's followers the evening before, along with the argument Zander had started when he'd revealed David's plans to build houses on a large chunk of the family farm.

'I think we'll need to bring Zander in and ask him a few questions,' said Binnie. 'Who else should we be speaking with, Jude?'

Jude picked a strand of hay absent-mindedly from the net that was tied up behind her. She thought of the other people she'd met and wondered if any of them had enough motive to kill David. Surprisingly, several faces sprang to mind.

'Looking at the choice of weapon, location of death and nature of injury, I'd say this was not a premeditated killing,' said Sami.

'I agree,' said Binnie. 'More of an impulsive act of passion or anger. Jude?'

'David certainly made an impact on the Kerry Hill contingent here.' Jude twisted the hay around her finger. 'His father was furious when Zander told him about David's development plans, as was another old farmer called Griff Gould. His land borders the Martin farm and so a project of the scale David was planning would impact him hugely.'

'Wasn't Griff also the one who David accused of cheating with the hair dye?' Marco asked.

'Hair dye?' Binnie raised an eyebrow.

'David said he found a box of Just for Men in Griff's kit box and the stewards agreed that it had been used to blacken the knees and ears of Griff's sheep whilst also spotting the fleeces of some of the other animals,' Jude explained. 'Markings are important when showing sheep. You want a pure white fleece with no blemishes and black knee pads, ears, noses and the panda rings around their eyes. All hell broke out when the others discovered there'd been foul play.'

'You're kidding me,' said Sami. 'A bit of hair dye could cause that much bother?'

'We've seen people killed for less,' said Binnie.

'It's not so much the dye itself but the fact that it could stop a particular sheep from winning. The very best animals are worth a lot of money when it comes to breeding from them.'

'If it wasn't David who used the dye, what might this have to do with who killed him?' Binnie asked.

'Because there's a fair chance that it was him,' said Jude. 'It just seems a bit convenient for him to be the one to have found it.'

Jude knew that Carl and Ffion had been banking on a win in order to be in a good position to sell their sheep. With their plans scuppered, at least temporarily, had either of them been so angry with David that they'd lashed out with the closest thing at hand?

Jude talked through her theories. Zander, Jim, Griff, Carl and Ffion all had potential motives, and then there was Tara. She clearly had a murky past with David. Jude and Marco had witnessed first-hand the episode between them just half an hour or so before they'd discovered David's body. Tara could have come back in to find him when the shed was empty. Or perhaps it was her protective mother, Penny, who had gone back to warn him off her daughter. And what about Olivia? She'd worked on Jim and David's farm and there had been an edge to her voice when she'd talked about the warning Tara had given her. It was possible something happened there that had been unresolved until they'd met again at the show.

Jude let each scene play out in her head and realised she couldn't strike any off her list of suspects.

'Well, thanks to you we have a pretty accurate

time of death,' said Binnie. 'He was here, alive and well, when you both left the shed at around twenty past six.'

'That's right,' said Marco.

'And you came back for Jude's phone and found his body at around ten to seven.'

Jude nodded and Binnie turned to Sami. 'The first thing to do is talk to everybody on Jude's list and find out where they all were between these times. See who we can eliminate from our enquiries.'

Sami stood up to leave. 'On it, boss.'

'It's going to be a long night for you,' Jude said to Binnie. 'Can I help out with anything?'

'I think I've got everything for now but I'll be in touch soon.'

Jude found that she was reluctant to leave. Partly because she wanted to be on hand if there was anything she could help with, and partly because she was keen to hear what the other Kerry Hill farmers had to say. Over the years Jude had played a vital role in the investigations of several murders and she found it difficult to step away when a new mystery had just begun. This was not her territory though. Here, she was a member of the public and that meant she couldn't stay. She'd just have to be patient and wait to hear from Binnie when there was news.

'What about the rest of the show?' she asked. 'Will it be able to go ahead?'

'I don't know,' said Binnie. 'Obviously this shed is now a crime scene so as few people should be moving around here as possible. The rest of the show though? Legally, I suppose there's no reason why it would have to be cancelled so I guess that's a decision for the organisers to make.'

Jude thought about the tens of thousands of people with tickets planning on showing up over the coming weekend. The exhibitors, those who had stalls set up and those who would be taking to the rings to showcase their animals, skills or machinery. There was a lot at stake and she was very glad she wasn't the person in charge of making the decision.

'I assume we'll be able to get in to look after the sheep though?'

'Of course, but they can't be moved until we've been given the all clear from the forensics team.'

'Understood,' said Jude. If the sheep were staying put then their owners also would. As far as the investigation went, that would definitely make things easier.

Jude and Marco left Binnie and her team to their enquiries and went back to find the car. It was a sombre journey back to Malvern End and Jude didn't want to part ways outside Marco's cottage in the village but she didn't quite know how to broach the subject. She'd rejected his advances several times before and they'd fallen into a happy rhythm of friendship. Jude knew he wanted more and she often thought that perhaps she did as well. The ball was firmly in her court but that didn't mean it was easy for her to run with it. The last thing she wanted to do was mess with Marco's feelings and risk the wonderful friendship that they shared. And so, when she stopped outside his cottage and he leant over to kiss her goodbye, Jude offered her cheek and watched him get out of the car. He paused before he put his key in the front door and turned to wave at her, and she bit her lip to stop herself from shouting out for him to wait so she could join him.

As she drove in silence the short way to Malvern Farm the car felt empty. Perhaps one day she would know for certain what was the right decision to make where Marco was concerned. But that day was not when they'd both been thrown head first into a brutal murder investigation.

* * *

There was a carefully worded email from the show organisers waiting for Jude when she woke up the next morning.

The decision had been made that, whilst there would be certain restrictions around the livestock area, the Three Counties Show would go ahead as planned for the remainder of the weekend. The police had asked for minimal movement around Avon Hall, meaning it would be impossible to allow any showing of the breeds currently housed there. It was, of course, understood that there would be a need for all owners to have access to their animals but that they should keep this to the essentials only.

As she read the message, Jude wondered how the others would be taking the news. Binnie and Sami would almost certainly have talked to each one already and Jude was desperate to know if they had uncovered anything important.

After the chaos of the past two days, Jude needed to give herself some much-needed breathing space. Fuelled with coffee and toast, she called the dogs to her and walked across the yard to the paddock where she kept a motley assortment of rescued and petted animals. These were always a firm favourite with the visitors who came to stay in the shepherd's huts and bell tents in her campsite.

'Morning, ladies,' she said to the two curly fleeced Valais Blacknose sheep. They were waiting by the top gate as always for their breakfast with their ridiculously cute ewe lambs at their sides. Maud and Marley were two of the friendliest members of the paddock contingent and also two of the hungriest. They'd had pregnancy as an excuse for a while, and then milk production for their growing offspring, but Jude knew they'd always find some reason. They were so big that when Rodney Trotter, the Shetland pony, came over to see what was going on, Jude could see virtually no difference in size between the animals.

There was a certain kind of magic steeped into the pasture and stable block of the paddock. It had always had the power to calm Jude's mind, and she wasn't the only one. Her once toxic next-door neighbour, retired headteacher Mike Trout, had discovered the therapeutic effects of the animals. Jude often found him pottering around or just sitting in the paddock with a flask of coffee and the daily newspapers.

It wasn't Mike though who was already down by the stables. It was Kerry Shepperton, a young woman who had stumbled onto the farm and into Jude's life the previous year and who now had her own tent in the campsite. It was a bolthole from a sometimes difficult home life and in return for the use of the tent, Kerry helped Jude out when it came to cleaning the huts and tents.

'You're up early,' said Jude. 'I thought you'd be having a lie-in now that your exams are all over.'

'I can't stop thinking about them papers and all the things I did wrong in them.' Kerry's hair was tied back in a loose topknot which bounced as she spoke. 'What if I don't get my grades and they don't let me on the course?'

Kerry had impressed Jude greatly by studying for the GCSEs that she'd failed whilst still in compulsory education. Despite the fact that she had been as good as written off by her mother and stepfather, she'd secretly studied so that she could apply for a course in childcare.

'You worked so hard, Kerry. I'm sure you'll be fine.'

Kerry didn't look convinced and Jude knew that it was going to be a killer of a summer for her whilst she waited for the results that were still two months away.

'Come on, let's get those ducks out.' Jude went over to the second stable that the little flock of Indian Runner ducks were rounded into at night to keep them safe from the foxes. The gentle quacking started as soon Jude moved the bolt, and as soon as the door was open, the funny little ducks waddled out. Their quirky upright gait never failed to make Jude smile and she watched them step into the early sunlight with tails shaking and necks stretched long.

There was no need to feed any of the animals as the summer had gifted the paddock with a smorgasbord of choice. Slugs for the ducks, fresh grass for the sheep and a good array of goat-friendly wild plants for Gertie, the golden Guernsey. Only Rodney Trotter was fed his usual bowl of horse nuts every morning.

'How'd you get on at the show yesterday?' Kerry asked. 'I was gutted my last exam was the same time as the Kerry Hills or I'd have been there to cheer you on.'

Jude supposed it wouldn't be too long before the news of David Martin's murder filtered its way through to the public. Journalists and gossips had a habit of making that happen but until it did, Jude thought it better to be minimal with what she said.

'There was a bit of skulduggery where the Kerries were concerned so we were cancelled.' Jude pulled the end of a yellow hosepipe off the stable wall and walked with it over to the old four-seater canoe that had been repurposed as a duck pond.

'That's a bummer,' said Kerry. 'What happened?'

'Two old farmers had a bit of a bust-up over a box of Just for Men,' said Jude. 'Turns out someone had been using it to change the markings on some of the sheep.'

'Shocking, that,' said Kerry looking genuinely disgusted. 'Did they get to the bottom of it all?'

'Not really.' Whilst Jude held the hose in position, Kerry turned the tap on. 'The farmers are old rivals, well-known in the field apparently. Griff Gould and Jim Martin. Anyway it was Jim's son, David, who found the dye in Griff's things but Griff swears it had nothing to do with him.'

Kerry looked at Jude thoughtfully. 'David Martin, did you say? Not from Leigh Sinton way, is he?'

'That's him,' said Jude. 'Do you know him?'

'I met him once or twice. He used to go drinking with my brother in Worcester, used to get... stuff for him now and again. I didn't like him much.' Kerry pulled a face to show just what she thought of David. 'Too handsy for my liking.'

'What do you mean he got your brother stuff?' Jamie Shepperton was near the end of serving a prison sentence for theft. Kerry adored her brother and swore that he was a good person who'd got messed up in bad things with bad people. Was there a chance that David Martin had been one of these bad people?

Kerry looked at her a little sheepishly. 'I don't know I want to let on. Jamie ent a bad person and I don't want to get him in trouble or nothing.'

Jude decided that now was probably a good time for a little more honesty about what had happened at the show.

'Kerry,' she said gently. 'David was killed yesterday. So if you know about anything dodgy that he was tangled up in, then I think it would be for the best that you let me know.'

'What?' Kerry looked at her in shock. 'He's dead?'

'I'm afraid so.'

'Was it murder?'

Jude thought back to the trimming shears that had been rammed into David's neck.

'The police aren't sure at the moment,' she lied. 'But if someone did kill him and you know that he was mixed up in something...' Jude tailed off to give Kerry time to pick up on the insinuation. Kerry sighed and turned the tap off, the water having reached the top of the canoe.

'Jamie only got a bit of weed from him,' she said. 'It wasn't a lot and he only used it himself, never sold it on or nothing.'

Jude raised her eyebrows at this new piece of information. If David Martin had been involved in dealing drugs then this would open up a very interesting new line of enquiry.

'Don't look at me like that.' Kerry's demeanour had instantly changed to become more challenging and defensive, something that Jude was used to seeing when the girl felt as though she was being backed into a corner.

'I'm not judging Jamie,' said Jude quickly. 'I just think that this could be a very useful piece of information for the police.'

'Keep Jamie out of it,' Kerry said. 'Promise me, Jude. He's coming up for parole soon and I don't want to piss on him and stop him from getting out early.'

'This isn't on Jamie,' said Jude. 'I promise it won't have any effect on his parole.'

'How do you know that?' Kerry looked like a trapped wild boar. Frightened and yet ready to attack if she was pushed too far. 'Jamie don't need anything going wrong for him now.'

Jude knew how much Kerry loved her older brother. She visited him in prison regularly and had always made it very clear that she didn't think he belonged behind bars. She idolised him, which made Jude a little anxious about his release as there was always the chance he wouldn't measure up to the pedestal Kerry had put him on in his absence.

'Nothing will go wrong, I promise. I'll talk to Binnie and she can do the probing without causing any ripples.' Jude put her hand on Kerry's shoulder. 'You did the right thing, telling me about the weed. If David was dealing then he would have come up against some unscrupulous people and it's those sorts of people the police will be interested in, not Jamie who just had the odd joint now and again.'

Kerry relaxed a little. 'S'pose you're right, Jude.'

'I am right. Now what are you doing today to celebrate being a lady of leisure after finishing your exams?'

'Mike and Val asked me round for lunch later and I said I'd help Mrs James in the shop this morning.'

Jude smiled. When she'd first found Kerry squatting in one of her tents having just stolen from the village shop, Jude had assumed she was trouble. But circumstances had meant that she'd got to know Kerry; found out about her home problems and her drive to forge a better pathway for herself. Less than a year later and here she was, a regular presence on the farm, friends with the neighbours and casual employee of the shop she'd once stolen from.

'What about you?' Kerry asked. 'Are you going back to the Three Counties today?'

'I've got to go in and feed the sheep.' Jude pulled a face to show that she'd far rather be staying in the paddock with Kerry and the animals. 'I'd better get going. Say hi to Val and Mike for me.'

Jude was not looking forward to revisiting the scene of the crime, but she was hoping she might see the other exhibitors. If one of them had been the person holding the trimming shears then perhaps they'd give themselves away somehow.

5

There was a security guard standing outside the back entrance to the sheep shed when Jude arrived. She had to show her exhibitor's paperwork before she was allowed to go inside and the pen where the body had been was now cordoned off with plenty of police tape. Although the body had been removed, there was still a large amount of blood staining the hay and the sight of it made Jude shiver.

Frank had offered to come in and sort the sheep out for Jude but she'd wanted to do it herself. She wanted to see the rest of the Kerry Hill gang and find out how they were all doing.

Penny and Olivia were the only people Jude

recognised in the shed and when Jude stopped to talk to Penny, the guard called over to her.

'Quick as you can in there, love. You'll have to take the chat outside, I'm afraid.'

'They're all in the Stockman's Bar,' said Penny. 'I'm heading that way when I've finished here, come and join us.'

Jude nodded and went into her own sheep pen to check her sheep and top up water and food supplies. She saw her own trimming shears on the top of her kit box and it made her think about David and the brutal way in which he'd died.

What had he been doing in the shed in the first place? David had shown little interest in his father's sheep, hardly lifting a finger to help, so why wasn't it Jim who'd been there to settle them for the night?

Except, David hadn't been with his father's sheep. When Marco and Jude saw him with Tara he had been by the Watsons' sheep and his body had been discovered in the Greener Days pen.

Whilst she filled the water tub, swept out the muck and topped up the hay net, Jude went through everything she had seen the night before. The shears had been stuck in the left side of David's neck which indicated the person wielding them was right-handed.

There had been a lot of blood, suggesting that the murderer would have got at least some on them, although the shears being left in the wound could have stemmed the initial flow. David might have died instantly – there had certainly been no sign of a struggle or any indication that he had tried to move, unless the deeper of the two blades had served to incapacitate him.

'I'm heading out now, Jude,' said Penny, breaking into her thoughts. 'See you in the bar when you've finished here?'

'I'll come and find you.'

As Penny left the shed, Jude heard a familiar voice greet the security guard. She looked over to see Binnie walking in with a reusable coffee cup in her hand. Even though the nature of the investigation created a need for sensible footwear, Binnie hadn't let her professional standards slip and was immaculately dressed in a dark trouser suit with her hair coiled up in a neat chignon.

She waved when she saw Jude and walked straight past the crime scene to get to her.

'Did you get any sleep last night?' Jude asked.

'I could ask the same thing about you.'

'Difference is, you look like you've just come back after a week off being pampered, whereas I know I look as though I've been dragged across my fields tied to the back of a tractor.'

Binnie held her coffee cup aloft. 'Strong doses of caffeine, that's the secret.'

'Nice.'

'Seriously though, how are you?'

'Been better,' Jude admitted. 'But not as bad as David Martin, I suppose.' She looked around the shed to make sure nobody else was in the vicinity. 'Any news there?'

'Not much at this stage. We obviously have the murder weapon, which is currently being tested for prints, et cetera, and we're waiting for pathology to see if his body will uncover any hidden secrets. Other than that, just going through the list of suspects to find out what we can about their histories with the deceased, and their whereabouts at his time of death.'

'Any alibis confirmed?' Jude asked.

'Not strong ones. Penny and Griff were both in the bar, and there are plenty of people who saw them although nobody can say for sure if they left at any point. Olivia had gone to have a drink with Jim in his caravan. Said she'd gone to check on him, to see how he was after David's betrayal with the development plans.'

'And the timings match?' Jude asked.

'They were both clear on time but that doesn't necessarily mean their alibis are watertight. It's still possible that one of them manipulated the other's perception of time. Easy to do as long as the other person doesn't check for themselves.' Binnie looked at her hands and tapped the names off on her fingers.

'Zander Pettiford was in his own caravan messing about with social media content. A post on his Instagram did go out during the time but I have it on good authority that it could have been a pre-timed post.'

'So you're taking it with a pinch of salt.' Jude leant against the metal hurdle.

'Jude, until we know for sure who did it, I will be taking everything with a hefty dose of salt.'

'Very sensible,' said Jude. 'So who does that leave us with? Tara and the Proctors.'

'Who say they were all together.' Binnie folded her hands together. 'Carl found Tara coming out of the shed at around six-twenty.'

'Which matches the time Marco and I saw her leave.'

'Exactly. He saw she was looking distressed so he took her back to her caravan. Then Carl left her to get showered and changed whilst he went back to fetch Ffion. They were all together until the end of the evening.'

'Was there enough time for Tara to sneak back to the shed and kill David first?' Jude asked. 'Or for Carl or Ffion to do it on her behalf?'

'It would be a stretch but I suppose not impossible,' said Binnie.

'So nobody is off the table?'

'Absolutely not.'

'There's something else you should know,' said Jude. 'Something that Kerry told me about David. He has a history of supplying drugs.'

Binnie opened her eyes wide; her interest had been piqued. 'Really? There's nothing on record about him.'

'Perhaps he just never got caught. I'm not sure on what kind of scale he was involved but Kerry's brother used to get weed from him.'

'Interesting.' Binnie tapped her coffee cup against her bottom lip.

'Please tread carefully with Jamie Shepperton if you need to involve him,' said Jude. 'Kerry's worried that by telling me about the drugs, she might have got her brother into more trouble. He's coming up for parole soon and she's anxious she might have scuppered things for him.'

Binnie waved her hand dismissively. 'The parole hearing won't be interested in a bit of dope Jamie bought before he was sent down. As long as he hasn't been accessing drugs inside then there's no reason it even needs to be mentioned.'

This was as Jude had expected but it was a relief that she'd be able to set Kerry's mind to rest.

'I take it you didn't find anything like that in his pen or the Greener Days Farm one where David was killed?'

'Nothing,' said Binnie. 'Although there must have been some reason for him to be there in the first place. We did find traces of something dark staining the tips of his fingers. Not immediately obvious as the marks were so small and he'd clearly tried to wash them off, but definitely there. After what you told me about the hair dye, I think we have a good idea what it is.'

Jude had thought the real culprit behind the sheep tampering was more likely to be David Martin than Griff Gould and now it seemed there was proof of this.

Another exhibitor came into the shed, moving to the Jacob sheep a couple of rows away. This put a stop to Jude and Binnie's conversation and Jude packed her things away whilst Binnie moved off to

have another look at the Greener Days Farm pen to
see if there was anything she'd missed.

The Stockman's Bar was full when Jude went in
to find the others, although there was an understand-
able air of gloom lying heavy across the assembled
farmers.

'Jude, over here,' called Tara from a table at the
edge.

Jude made her way to where Tara was sitting with
her mum, the Proctors, Zander Pettiford and Olivia.
Griff was nursing a large whisky, despite the fact that
it wasn't yet ten in the morning. There was no sign of
Jim which was unsurprising and Jude wondered if he
was still in his caravan. To have outlived his son
would be a horrendous thing to come to terms with,
but the nature of David's death coupled with the
bitter argument they'd had on the day he'd been
killed would surely elevate Jim's grief exponentially.

'Morning,' Jude greeted them all as she took a
seat next to Zander. 'How is everybody?'

'It's all a bit surreal, isn't it?' said Carl who was
sitting opposite, holding hands with his wife.

'You could say that,' said Penny. 'I've never known
anything like it in all the years I've been showing animals. Terrible business, just terrible.'

'I was surprised to hear that the rest of the show

was going to be allowed to carry on, if I'm honest.' Zander had his phone in his hand and Jude glanced at the screen to make sure he wasn't doing some more surreptitious videoing for his social media. Not even Zander would stoop that low though it seemed: the screen was black.

'Not easy to stop everything, just like that.' Griff was half slumped with his elbows on the table. He looked awful, as though he hadn't slept a wink since the news had broken. 'Too many people wrapped up in the show to just pull the plug.'

'Maybe so, but it seems heartless to me after what happened to our good friend and fellow farmer last night.' Zander did a very good job of portraying de- mure sadness with his downcast eyes and slight shake of the head. It was almost as though he was playing a role and it made Jude check his phone again to make sure it really wasn't recording.

'Bollocks to that.' Griff snorted into his whisky glass but didn't look up.

'What did you say?' Zander demanded.

'I'm just thinking about yer interesting choice of words there.' Griff spoke lazily and Jude wondered just how much whisky he'd already had. 'Good friend and fellow farmer, you say? Not sure you're either of those, are you, Mr Pettiford?'

'What about you?' Zander said. 'Sitting there slurring into your whisky as though you're in mourning for the man, when it was only yesterday you were begging me to help you bring him down. What's to say you didn't find your own way to stop the development?'

Griff looked up then and glowered at Zander. 'I don't like the way you said that. I only asked you to use your Instant-grammar whatsit to tell everyone what he was up to.'

'That's enough.' Carl spoke with authority. 'We've all had a difficult night and tensions are high but you two aren't the only ones here and the rest of us could do without the sniping and accusations.'

Griff wasn't ready to let things lie though. 'It sounded like that plonker over there was insinuating I might have had something to do with what happened, and I don't like being accused. Anyhow, I was here in the bar last night. Where were you?'

All eyes turned to Zander who clasped his hand to his chest. 'Not that it's anything to do with you, but I was on my computer. I did a post for my followers, you can check the time of that if you don't believe me. And then I was doing a bit of research into my plan to introduce some old native species back to the farm. Things that were hunted to extinction in this country.'

'Lord above.' Griff rolled his eyes. 'Please tell me you aren't bringing wolves and bears back to the British countryside.'

'Of course not,' said Zander. 'Beavers, lynx and eventually bison.'

'Give me strength.' Griff downed the remainder of what was in his glass and then sucked at his teeth. 'Or at least some better whisky than this paint stripper.'

Jude tried to picture a herd of bison trudging around Zander's land. If he wanted to make a splash in the rewilding world then that was the way to do it. It was certainly an interesting discussion but for Griff and Zander it was clearly very black and white. Two polar opposite opinions coming from two people who were both custodians of large areas of farmland. It was no wonder they clashed.

'Has anyone seen Jim this morning?' Jude mindfully moved the conversation along to avoid any further arguments.

'I popped over earlier to take him some breakfast and see if he wanted a hand with his sheep.' Olivia puffed her cheeks out and exhaled slowly. 'He was like a hollowed-out shell, hardly said a word and I'm sure he had no intention of eating the bacon butty I gave him.'

Ffion shook her head and Jude noticed that she was crying as Carl put his arm around her.

'Hey, it's all right,' he said, drawing her into him.

Ffion pushed back a little. 'It's not all right though, is it?'

'Actually, no it isn't,' said Olivia. 'I know David could be a bit of a dick but Jim was still his dad and he's broken. But here we all are, supposed to carry on like nothing happened. And do you know what the worst bit is? There is a killer sitting round this table, one of us, hoping that they will get away with what they've done.'

Olivia's tirade was met with a wall of shocked faces as the rest of the group took in what she'd said.

'Surely not,' said Penny. 'It could have been any-one. David did have a way of rubbing people up the wrong way. He always did, ever since I remember Jim bringing him to the shows when he was a little boy. I don't like to speak ill of the dead but he was a difficult man and there were plenty outside of this group who had reason to be aggrieved by him.'

'Penny's right,' said Carl as he gently rubbed his wife's shoulders. 'Come on now, it's been a very long night and I think we could do with a bit of a rest. Let's get back to the caravan and I'll make you a proper cup of tea whilst you put your feet up for a bit.'

Ffion nodded in silent submission and allowed Carl to guide her up out of her chair.

'We'll see you around,' Carl said.

The already subdued group became even more pensive with the departure of the Proctors and Jude reflected on what had happened. Penny's mention of David as a young boy was a reminder to her that, although she had only just met the Kerry Hill breeders, Zander aside, they had all known each other for a very long time. A death of one of their number, even one who wasn't particularly well thought of, was going to make a huge impact on them.

Just as she was wondering how to extricate herself from the bar, Jude had a call from Binnie.

'I'm so sorry.' Jude took her chance and stood up. 'I need to get this. I'll catch up with you all later.'

She left them to it and waited until she was out of earshot before accepting the call.

'How's everything going?' Jude asked.

'You were right about the hash,' said Binnie. 'A quick search of David's truck gave us not only the ready to go, dried stuff, we also found a couple of fresh leaves.'

Jude headed towards the car park, trying to be

careful with what she said in case her side of the conversation was overheard. 'Meaning?' she said.

'Meaning there's a chance he was not only dealing in the stuff but also involved in growing it.'

'Interesting. So what next?'

'Next, Sami and I will take a team to search the Martins' farm to see if there's any sign of something more than wheat and barley being harvested there.'

6

Jude left the Three Counties Showground with a feeling of great sadness. So far, David's death had been kept out of the news and the throng of excited visitors who'd come to see the exhibits and attractions had no idea of the turmoil that was going on behind the locked doors of the restricted Avon Hall.

She was deep in thought as she drove through Little Malvern and up to British Camp where she joined Jubilee Drive to take her round the West side of the hills. Penny had a point when she'd said that David had been difficult and there were plenty who hadn't liked him. There was already a lot of evidence to show that almost everyone in the Kerry Hill circle had reason to dislike him. But which one of them had been pushed to pick up a pair of shears and ram them into his neck with enough force to embed them so deeply?

Penny had been quick to move the focus away from the group and Ffion seemed more affected by David's death than most. Was that because Ffion was the one who'd killed him, or was Penny trying to divert attention away because either she or Tara had? Both had reason to be angry with him, but then so did everyone else there.

As she got to the bottom of the hill, Jude decided that she didn't want to go straight back to the farm. She found herself drawn into the village and before she had really known she'd made the decision, she was parked outside Marco's cottage.

The row of old stone workers' cottages marked the edge of Malvern End and their gardens backed out on to Jude's fields. It was a pretty place to live and Jude had been more than delighted when Marco had chosen to settle there after a short stint away from the area.

Jude climbed out of the car and pushed open the little gate that led up to the cottage. Marco had trained white jasmine plants to grow up each side of the door and they were in full bloom, filling the air with an intoxicating scent of summer. In a few years, the plants would meet in the middle, creating a gorgeous entrance. This pleased Jude as she felt it showed that Marco was planning on staying in the village for at least the foreseeable future.

The unmistakable tones of Billie Holiday drifted through the half open window of the front room and Jude could see Marco inside, sitting at the stripped-back oak table that he used for sketching. She rapped on the window and he turned to greet her with a welcoming smile.

'Door's unlocked,' he called. 'Come on in.'

Jude lifted the latch of the heavy wooden door and pushed it open. Since he'd moved in, Marco had redecorated every inch of the cottage and it was both beautiful and quirky inside. A gentle colour palette of calming pastel shades, accented with bright splashes from a painting, antique vase or piece of reclaimed furniture. All perfectly chosen and all absolutely Marco.

'This is a nice surprise,' he said, coming out of the sitting room to meet her in the hallway. 'I thought you'd be tied up today. How are you doing?'

Jude kicked her filthy old shoes off and followed Marco into the kitchen where he put the kettle on.

'I've come from the showground,' she said. 'It was

horrid there so I thought I'd pop round for a bit of cheering up.'

'You've come to the right place.' Marco took two handcrafted clay mugs from the cupboard and put them next to the kettle. 'I can put in these whatever you want. Tea, coffee, cider, vodka – what's your poison?'

Jude smiled, already feeling better for being in Marco's house and company. 'Tea's fine,' she said. 'But if you have a biscuit lurking in one of your cupboards, I might go for one of those too.'

'I can do better than that.' Marco pulled out a battered Cadbury's Roses tin that looked like it came from the seventies. He popped the lid off and handed it over to Jude.

'Flapjacks,' she said. 'Did you make them?'

'Actually, you're not my first visitor of the day. These came from Janet Timms.'

Jude furrowed her brow at the sound of the village busybody's name. 'I assume she wasn't just here to bring you flapjacks?'

'She did invite herself in to decant them into my tin because she needed her Tupperware back. And whilst she was here she thought she'd ask after you, having heard from someone who knows someone who knows Penny Watson that you were the one who found David Martin's body.'

'She's incorrigible.' Jude bit into one of the flapjacks. 'But she does know how to bake!'

'Back to my initial question,' said Marco. 'How are you? Really, I mean, not just the usual Jude Gray reply of "I'm fine."'

'Do you know what? I actually am fine. The whole thing is horrendous obviously, and I feel desperate for Jim, but selfishly I am okay. I didn't really know David and what I saw of him I have to say I didn't hugely like. I'm glad to have stepped away from the whole thing.'

Marco brought the two mugs, now full of perfectly brewed tea, over to the table and sat down next to Jude.

'Are you telling me that you're not going to do any investigating?' he said, his eyebrows raised.

'That's Binnie's job.'

'So you haven't started to put together your own list of suspects and tie them in with motives, opportunities and evidence?'

Jude picked up her mug of tea and blew into it, avoiding the question.

'I thought so,' said Marco. 'Any obvious front-runners?'

'A couple,' Jude admitted. 'He definitely had the knack of pissing people off.'

'I'd say whoever did that to him was a bit more than pissed off. I reckon they'd either have been beyond furious or frightened.'

Jude knew he was right. She imagined someone confronting David and being met with either a frustrating level of arrogance and disinterest or fury perhaps to match their own. Both might lead to a possible overspilling of anger that could have made them grab the nearest thing to hand without thought and lash out. The other option was that David had backed his murderer into a corner, made them feel threatened either mentally or physically, perhaps in the way he had threatened Tara.

'You're thinking about who could have done it right now, aren't you?' said Marco.

'Sorry.' Jude realised that she'd been staring at a patch on Marco's wall as she digested her thoughts. 'Let's forget about it all. Talk to me about you instead. What are you up to today? I saw you sketching through the window.'

'Doodling, really. I sent some of my work to a greetings card company and luckily they liked them enough to commission a series.'

'That's great news.' Jude was a little surprised as

she'd only ever known Marco paint in oils, beautiful works of art which sold in two local galleries as well as through a contact he had in Cornwall.

'Not my first choice but it does pay the bills and lets me keep working on the things that I love too.'

'Seems very sensible.'

'Clara gave me the idea.' Marco leant backwards to reach a sideboard and slid the drawer open. 'She's been great, helping me research and picking a style to go with.'

Jude wasn't one who often felt the unhelpful stab of jealousy and when it came it annoyed her greatly. Clara was Marco's next-door neighbour and there had been an instant and immediate camaraderie between the two when Jude introduced them. They shared a love of art, something that had never really been on Jude's radar. It stood to reason that when he needed artistic advice, Marco would turn to Clara and yet for some reason the thought of the two of them sitting at the same table she was currently resting her elbows on, heads together discussing his work, caused the green-eyed bug of jealousy to needle her.

Marco pulled a bundle of paper from the drawer and spread it out on the table for Jude to see.

'These three here are the ones they've already

taken.' He pushed some watercolour illustrations towards her, each one depicting a characterful animal set against a background of flowers and trees. Instead of the usual highland cattle and hares that were already widely seen on cards, Marco had chosen animals very familiar to Jude.

'That's Marlie,' she said, picking up the picture of her beautiful Valais Blacknose sheep. 'You've caught her cheekiness perfectly. And this is Gertie. I can almost read her thoughts from the expression you've given her.'

'They also liked Rodney Trotter but sadly they didn't go for this one.' He passed her a picture that was clearly little Pancake, who Jude had rescued as a squashed and battered newborn lamb. Of all the animals she kept in the paddock, if pushed, Jude would name Pancake as her favourite and it saddened her to think that she hadn't made the grade for the greetings card industry.

'Well I love her and I think you've done a fantastic job.'

'That's what Clara said as well, but what do we know?'

Jude pushed the bubble of jealousy firmly away. 'How is Clara? I haven't seen her for a while.'

Marco tidied the pictures into a pile in front of

him. 'She's fine. Have you been to the cottages since she redecorated the sitting room?'

Jude shook her head. 'I bet she's done a good job.'

'It's nice. You should pop in one day and take a look.'

Jude knew she should. Clara was great company, and Jude enjoyed the walks they had shared together with the dogs over the winter months. Once lambing hit in the spring, life had become impossibly busy and time had marched on without a thought for those it trampled underfoot.

'I'll give her a ring and see if she and Rex want to come for a walk.'

'We could all go today,' said Marco. 'See if Lucy and Noah want to join us too. Maybe even finish at The Lamb for a pint and a bowl of chips.'

That was actually exactly what Jude fancied doing to take her mind off what had happened at the show, so she got out her phone and called Lucy.

* * *

It was always lovely to get out for a walk in the Malvern countryside, and Jude found that good company and fresh air did her the world of good. Lucy and Noah brought Sebbie and the dogs to join them at Marco's cottage. When they were all ready, they called in to fetch Clara and her rescued German shepherd, Rex.

'He's pleased to see you,' said Clara as Rex ran rings around the four collies. Pip, Alfie, Floss and Ned gave him varying amounts of attention, Alfie being the keenest by far to have another boisterous dog to play with. Floss, who had retired from farm work that year, was not at all interested and gave a low warning growl when Rex came too close.

'Let's get them away from the road and into the woods so they can be off lead,' said Jude, leading the way to the track that led up behind the cottages, skirting the fields of Malvern Farm and ending in a wood that clung to the bottom of the hills like a full Victorian skirt.

Jude fell into step with Clara and Lucy whilst Marco and Noah strode on ahead deep in conversation and Sebbie searched the ground for interesting things to take into school for the nature table.

'I was so sorry to hear the dreadful news about that sheep farmer,' said Clara.

Jude looked instantly at the back of Marco, wondering just how much he'd told her.

'I didn't know it was common knowledge,' she said, a little snippily.

'It popped up on my news feed when I turned my phone on earlier,' said Clara. 'Zander Pettiford was at the Three Counties Show and posted a video about it on Instagram.'

Jude felt guilty for blaming Marco and furious at Zander for turning David's death into a promo opportunity.

'Did you watch the video?' Jude asked.

'No,' said Clara. 'I don't really do social media all that much and this all seemed a bit, you know, tasteless.'

'I saw it this morning just before I came out, actually,' said Lucy. 'And you're right, it was a tasteless thing to do. He even managed to squeeze out a few tears for the camera, right before he plugged his YouTube channel.'

Tasteless as it was, Jude found she wasn't in the least surprised. The world loved a grizzly tale of true crime and David's death had definitely been that. There would no doubt be plenty of people wanting the inside gossip from not only someone who was there and knew the victim, but a personality as well-known as Zander Pettiford.

'He's such an arse,' Jude said. 'Making out like he's best friends with all the farmers when I didn't see him lift a finger once to help his farm manager out with the sheep.'

'Did you meet him?' Clara asked. 'What's he like in real life?'

'He's shallow and fake and one of those bloody nuisances who think they are somehow above everyone around them.'

'He comes across like that, actually,' said Clara.

'I used to think he was brilliant in The Spods.' Lucy took the skeleton leaf that Sebbie was holding out for her.

'What are spods, Mummy?' Sebbie asked.

'They were a band before you were even born. I had one of their CDs, I think.'

'That's so old, Mummy.'

'I suppose it is. Now why don't you see if you can find any more leaves like this. I think Miss Elgar would really love to see them.'

Sebbie bustled off to look in the detritus on the forest floor and the three women went back to their discussion about Zander Pettiford.

'I had a huge crush on the lead singer, Coby Tyler,' said Clara. 'I was heartbroken when he died.'

'He overdosed, didn't he?' Lucy said.

'Yes,' Clara replied. 'Such a waste. He was amazing but I guess the fame messed with his head.'

'It sounds like they went from nobodies to the biggest band in the country so quickly,' said Jude. 'It must have been a very weird time for them all.'

'Just look at how Zander turned out.' Lucy said. 'Money and fame didn't bring him much sense, did it?'

Jude wanted to have a look at the video he'd posted but there was no point in opening her phone as there was never any connection in the woods.

After a decent leg stretch, and when Sebbie had a poop scoop bag bulging with natural treasures, the group decided it was time to turn around and head back to the village for the promised reward of hot chips at the pub.

It was always busy at The Lamb, especially at the weekends and doubly so in the summer months when the hills were visited by droves of walkers, mountain bikers and fresh-air appreciators. Ted and Barbara, the landlords, always found space for Jude and her friends when they came in though, and a couple of smaller tables were grouped so everyone could sit together.

'What'll it be?' Barbara asked. 'We've had a fresh delivery of Appletiser and I know one young man who loves his fizzy apple.' She ruffled Sebbie's hair and was awarded with a winning smile.

'Yes please.' Sebbie looked at Lucy. 'And am I allowed crisps as well?'

'We were going to get some of Ted's chips as a treat,' Lucy said.

'Ah, yeah!' Sebbie punched the air and they all took this as a sign he was more than pleased with the arrangement.

'Come on, my grubby little tyke. You need to go to the loo to wash all that muck off your hands before you can have anything.' Lucy turned to Barbara. 'Two portions of chips for us, I'm not sharing with anyone! And I'll have half a pint of bitter. Don't mind what, surprise me.'

'Right you are,' said Barbara.

Lucy took Sebbie's hand and led him away to find soap and water whilst Barbara finished taking their order and headed to the bar to get the drinks.

'Here you go.' Clara passed her phone over to Jude who saw that it was open on the video clip of Zander Pettiford, posted earlier that morning.

'What's that tosser been up to now?' Noah asked.

'Shhh, we'll find out.' Jude held Clara's phone between them all and hit the play button.

'It is with such devastation that I'm coming to you from the Royal Three Counties Show in Malvern, the largest livestock show in the country, where I came earlier this week to show some of my pedigree sheep. As you may know if you're a subscriber to my You-Tube channel, I keep a breed of sheep called Kerry Hills, amongst my other animals on the farm.'

Jude glanced up. 'No mention of Olivia, the one who really does the hard work.'

'What perhaps isn't well known outside of the farming world is that when you meet other breeders and get to know them, they become almost like family to you. I was so very lucky to have been welcomed warmly into the close network of Kerry Hill experts and am eternally grateful to be able to call them dear friends.'

An expulsion of incredulity erupted from Jude with such force that several people on neighbouring tables stopped talking to look her way.

'Not the take you'd have had on the situation?' Noah asked.

'Could not be further from the truth.'

'With close friendship naturally comes the opportunity, and I did see it as an opportunity, to debate serious issues as David Martin and I often did. But at the core of things, David and I both had the same goals. To look after our animals and land as best as we could. I might not have always agreed with his methods but that didn't stop us from quickly becoming mates. I respected him deeply and therefore it is with a very heavy heart I must report on the mindless killing of my good friend last night as he was in the sheep shed tending his animals.'

Jude grimaced and shook her head in utter disgust.

'He was doing what meant the most to him when an as yet unidentified person, or persons, attacked him with his own fleece scissors.'

'So much wrong with that sentence,' said Jude, furious with the man for turning the tragedy into a drama for his own audience.

'I would like to ask for your understanding and peace at this terrible time whilst I mourn the loss of my dear friend and support the rest of the grieving Kerry Hill family.'

Jude skidded the phone across the table back to Clara. 'I can't watch any more of that nonsense,' she said. 'Did he even have permission to put that out?' Jude wondered if Binnie had seen it. It was almost inevitable that she had, but Jude would tell her about it anyway, just in case.

'Bet that little stunt doesn't go down too well with the other farmers still at the show,' said Noah. 'If I were him I'd be keeping a low profile right now.'

'Yeah, well we'll see about that I suppose.'

As Ted brought six bowls of piping-hot, triple-cooked chips to the table, Jude couldn't help thinking about Noah's words. He was right. Zander perhaps should be keeping a low profile when emotions in the group were so high and someone had already snapped once from their anger.

Internally Jude told herself to stop getting carried away. Just because there had been one brutal killing amongst the group already didn't mean the potential was there for a second. And yet experience had taught Jude that when there was a murderer at large, nobody was truly safe.

7

Later that afternoon, when Jude was sitting at the computer going through the ridiculous number of emails that always seemed to accrue, Binnie dropped round for a chat.

'I assume you've seen Zander Pettiford's Instagram video?' Jude asked as Binnie sat at the kitchen table and bent down to stroke Pip, the first of the dogs to go over and say hello.

'I did. Can't say I was very impressed that he took it upon himself to put that out there before we'd made an official statement.'

'What did you make of it?' Jude held out a jar of coffee and a box of tea bags.

'Coffee, please,' said Binnie. 'I thought he came across as a bloody egotist with his own agenda.'

'Precisely my thoughts when Clara showed it to me.'

'Using someone else's tragedy as a way of gaining a few more clicks online. What a complete arse.'

'Sadly though, it looks as though it worked. Lucy tells me he's gone viral. She reckons there will be a true crime special on his YouTube channel before the year is out.'

'That'd be about right.' Binnie took a piece of paper out of her bag. 'This is what I actually wanted to come and talk to you about.'

Jude sat down at the table and passed Binnie her coffee before taking the piece of paper from her. It was a photograph rather than photocopy of a note that had clearly been folded into three, suggesting it had been held in an envelope at some point in its life.

It was missing a recipient's name at the top but when Jude's eye flicked to the bottom she saw that it had been written by David.

'Do you know who it was meant for?' she asked.

'No. Tara and Ffion found it on the floor of the shed. Tara handed it in to us when she was questioned. Have a read.'

Jude looked back at the page of untidy handwriting.

I thought it better to write a letter to you rather than email as I don't know if you have a secretary screening your computer and I don't think it would be in either of our best interests to allow what I have to say to fall on the wrong ears.

I know about the issues you had with the farm coffers. And I know the little sideline you put in place to make some extra cash to help things keep ticking over.

'Do we think he's talking about the cannabis?' Jude asked.

'It's possible,' said Binnie. 'Keep going.'

Jude read on.

Whilst I applaud your initiative and would never normally concern myself with the ways in which other people supplement their income, I find that the time has come for me to ask you for a favour in return for my silence.

I'm in the process of putting together a planning application for 20 new houses on one of the fields of my own farm and I need to make sure there are no stumbling blocks and that this is all signed off with minimum fuss. I've been assured that you can make this happen and if you do, I can make sure that nobody ever finds out about the cash injection at the homestead. You can keep doing your thing to make some extra money and I will be able to do mine.

Doing this in the middle of the showground is not ideal so I think it would be a good idea to find time once the show has finished to talk about it. I will await your call.

David Martin

There was a phone number included, making it clear that whoever this letter had been intended for, it hadn't been someone who knew David well enough to already have him in their contacts list.

'Meant for someone who can push through a massive planning application, just like that,' said Jude. 'That can't be a very large number of people.'

'It depends on how blinkered David was,' said Binnie. 'Just because he thought this person could help him with his application, doesn't mean that they could.'

'There'll be obvious names to start with though, won't there?' Jude had been through the rural planning process when she had set up a campsite with permanent tents and shepherd's huts so she knew a little bit about how it worked, although she imagined it was infinitely harder when erecting brand-new houses. 'Anyone working for Worcestershire Planning Committee. Does Malvern Hills District Council go as far as Leigh Sinton?'

'I've got Sami looking into it at the moment,' said Binnie. 'I've asked him to cross-check with anyone who owns a farm. It's not much to go on but it's a start.'

Jude tried to put herself in David Martin's shoes. If she wanted to bribe or blackmail someone into pushing through plans for rural development, where would she go other than the obvious? Perhaps a local MP?

'Was the letter in an envelope when you found it?' she asked.

'Yes, although it had been opened so we assume the letter had been read. Annoyingly there was no name on the front either.'

'And I suppose we can't know for sure that the person who read it was who it was intended for.'

'We can't be certain,' Binnie agreed.

'Were there any fingerprints?'

'Yes, they're being run through the system but we already know it was touched by Tara and Ffion, and they showed it to Penny and Carl, who also held it. Annoyingly it's a similar story with the murder weapon. They were Olivia's shears which Zander would obviously have valid reason to have used. Ffion and Carl asked to borrow them as they only had one pair and wanted to clip at the same time and Tara offered to take them back to Olivia afterwards, so that gives all five of them a reason to have left prints on them.'

'Blast it,' said Jude. 'It's going to be one of those investigations where nothing quite goes our way, I can already see it.'

'*Our* way?' Binnie smiled. 'So you're in? Unofficial consultant?'

Jude sighed. 'I suppose I am.'

* * *

Sundays at Malvern Farm had always been traditionally the day when every member of the team would make time to have lunch together and go up on the hills for a walk. Adam's parents had been al-most religious in keeping this habit going as it was the only time in the week they were able to regularly get together.

Jude and Lucy had tried their hardest to carry on in the same vein but it didn't always work out how they would have liked. The final day of the Three Counties Show was one such Sunday.

Thanks to Zander Pettiford and his viral video that had been seen hundreds of thousands of times and led to outrage that the show was still proceeding, the organisers bowed to the pressure and cancelled the last day.

The police had given permission for the sheds to be cleared, so all exhibitors were required to go and collect their animals.

Jude had been expecting a bit of a crush as she and Frank drove into the showground but nothing like the queue of vehicles waiting to get to the back entrances of the three livestock sheds. She pulled up behind a large lorry, put the Land Rover into neutral and switched off the engine.

'We've only got the two sheep,' she said. 'I reckon I could bring them out on halters if you wait with the car.'

'I reckon you could,' Frank agreed. 'Why don't you go ahead and see about the state of things. I can move us on if needed.'

Jude left the driver's door open when she'd got out so Frank could take her place. After the eerie quiet of the day before, it was strange to see the inside of the shed so busy again, almost as though nothing had happened.

The bleating of sheep mingled with the low chatter of folk clearing up their pens.

Jude breathed deeply, inhaling the familiar smell that split people firmly into two camps. Whereas the warm animal shed scent offended some noses, Jude loved the mix of hay, the lanolin in the fleeces and even the soft earthiness of the ruminant droppings. It grounded her in the simplicity of being around animals.

The Proctors were already there, gathering up the contents of their pens and Jude went over to see them.

'Are you heading back to Wales this morning?' she asked.

'Can't wait to be back on the farm.' Jude noticed that Ffion's skin had a blotchy appearance to it, from crying or tiredness she couldn't tell. Perhaps a bit of both.

'I bet,' said Jude. 'How long does it take from here to Abergavenny?'

'Only about an hour once we get away from the

show traffic. My sister's been staying on the farm to look after things so there'll be a warm welcome for us when we get home.'

'Good luck with the next show, hopefully things will go a lot smoother there and your animals get the chance to really prove their worth.'

Carl glanced at Ffion and Jude thought she noticed a silent message being passed between the couple for a second. He looked forceful and she looked resigned but other than that, Jude couldn't decipher it. The disastrous show that they had pinned such hopes on was clearly weighing on them both.

'Maybe,' said Ffion.

'Have you seen Tara and Penny this morning?' Jude asked. 'I'd love to see them before they head off home too.' She could see that their sheep were still in the pens so she knew she hadn't missed them.

'They were in their caravan when we came over this morning,' said Carl. 'Perhaps they're waiting for things to clear a bit in here first.'

'I suspect that's what poor old Jim's doing as well,' said Ffion.

Jude looked at the pen that still housed Jim's Kerry Hills. She hadn't even thought to keep an eye on them whilst she'd been tending her own sheep.

But it looked as though they had plenty of water in their buckets and there was still hay in the nets, so someone had been looking after them. Perhaps Jim had found solace in doing the jobs that he had always done. There was never a day off for farmers where livestock was concerned, after all. No matter what happened, the animals still needed to be fed and watered and Jim would have lived by this principle every day of his life.

Griff was in with his sheep and Jude noticed that he was stooped low, focused on the task without taking in anything that may be happening around him.

'I'd better get on,' she said to the Proctors. 'Frank is waiting in the car. I'm hoping to get my pair out on halters so we don't have to queue.'

'Very sensible,' said Ffion. 'We managed to get a space right outside which is lucky as we've got a fair few to shift.' She followed her husband back to their pen to gather the first of the sheep for transfer.

Jude went to her pen and opened the box she'd brought all of her kit in. At the top were Frank's trimming shears. Goodness knew how many generations had used them on sheep over the decades but they'd always been kept rust free and perfectly sharp. It was a stark reminder of David's murder and Jude took the halters out quickly so she didn't have to look at them for too long.

A loud shout made her look up and she saw a red-faced Jim thundering down the shed towards the Kerry Hill section. It was no great surprise to see him stop by Griff's sheep pen and his entrance made everyone stop what they were doing.

'I want a word with you.' He reached the hurdle that marked off the pen where Griff had stood up.

Griff held his hands aloft to show that he didn't want to get involved in any trouble, but Jim paid no heed. He jabbed him sharply in the chest with the four fingers of one hand.

'Let's not do this here, Jim.' Griff stepped backwards, away from the hurdle. 'I know you're grieving an' all but this isn't the time for picking a fight.'

Jim fiddled with the baling twine holding the hurdle in place, trying unsuccessfully to unhook it so he could join Griff in the pen.

'I beg to differ,' he said. 'This is exactly the right time. I want to know if you did it? An' I don't want no bullshit. As his father, I have the right to know that happened to him.'

Griff looked at him in horror. 'Jim. How can you ask me that? Okay, so we've had our arguments over the years but we've known each other since we were nippers.'

'You're right, we have.' Jim managed to break through the baling twine and pushed the hurdle so roughly that it parted ways with the one it was clipped into and fell away. 'And it's because I've known you and your ways for that many years I ask you. Did you kill my boy? Did you kill my David because he was threatening to build on our land and mess with your peace and quiet?'

Griff pulled himself up to his full height, Jude guessed a good half a foot taller than his antagonist, and glowered at him. 'I feel bad for you, Jim. I wouldn't have wished this on anyone but I'm not going to let you talk to me like this.' He moved to where the rounder farmer was standing blocking the entrance to the pen.

Jim didn't move and Carl was amongst the men who stepped forward to intervene in what was a dangerously volatile situation between old sparring partners.

'Come on now, boys,' said a man of even more years than Jim and Griff. 'Let's not do things in haste that will come back to bite you both. Jim, it's a terrible thing that happened but you leave it to the police to work out the who and why of it. Griff, maybe it's as wise to let me help you get those animals of yours into your trailer there and then you can be on your way.'

Griff nodded, his face still knotted in consternation, but he held out a hand of peace which Jim batted away. It looked for a moment as though he was going to punch the other man but he decided against it and all the fight suddenly seemed to leave him. His head hung low and he scrunched his fists deep into the sockets of his eyes.

'There we are, Jim.' The farmer who stepped in as peacemaker now took on the role of comforter as he put his arm around the broken man's shoulders and led him away. 'Let's you and I get ourselves a cup of something medicinal and let things settle in here before I help you tidy those sheep of yours into your vehicle.'

Jude was warmed to see empathy like that on display from one man to another and she was glad to know that Jim would be guided through the rest of what would be another difficult day.

'Do you reckon he did it?' Carl asked when he rejoined them.

'I don't know,' said Ffion. 'It's hard to imagine.'

'It's hard to imagine anyone doing it,' Carl pointed out. 'But someone did.'

'Stop it, Carl.' Ffion scowled at her husband. 'Let's just get the sheep packed up. I'm ready to go home.'

The Proctors went back to their animals and Jude finished tidying out the kit pen, her mind full of what the Proctors had said. Murder was always difficult to imagine, unless it was carried out by a psychopath and Jude wasn't sure that any of the farmers she'd met at the show met that criteria.

As she closed the lid on her kit box and picked it up, along with her white show coat, she thought of the run-in she herself had had with David when she and Marco had caught him pestering Tara. He was a predator, that much had been very evident. He had still been in the sheep shed when Jude and Marco left, so it was possible that another woman had gone in there and found herself in his unwanted company. Perhaps striking back to protect herself if he had become too forceful.

Jude thought about Ffion. She had clearly not taken David's death well judging by her appearance and reactions. Was that because she had been the one to stick the shears in his neck? And if it was her, or Tara or any woman who'd acted in self-defence, what would that mean for them?

Jude started to walk back to the car with the box and passed Ffion and Carl who were taking down their signs. She nodded at them and couldn't help wondering if Carl had walked in on David and Ffion in the same way she and Marco had done when David was with Tara. If so, there was a very real chance he would have seen red and done something about it.

The same could be said about Penny if Tara had had cause to go back into the shed and found David still there. Or Zander for that matter if David had been forcing himself on Olivia.

Back at the Land Rover, Jude dropped the box in the boot of the car and then went back for the first of the two sheep. On the way, she bumped into Olivia and Zander who were walking together in the direction of the shed.

'Are you going to pack up?' Jude asked.

Olivia nodded. 'We were hoping to head off early but I couldn't sleep last night and then somehow managed to nod off at about five and was out for the count until Zander woke me ten minutes ago.'

'Well you must have needed it then,' said Jude, who was well used to the sleeplessness that came in times of busyness or high stress.

'I bet you'll be glad to put your first show behind you,' said Zander. 'I know I will.'

'It's not been the best weekend.' After watching

Zander's ridiculous Instagram video, Jude was not keen to fall into a conversation with him about what had happened. 'I was hoping to say goodbye to everyone before I go. The Proctors are in the shed already but I haven't seen Tara and Penny yet. I don't suppose you've seen them about?'

'I guess you're wanting to ask her more about her relationship with David Martin,' said Zander.

'Zander!' Olivia gave her head the tiniest of shakes as a warning. But it was one Zander chose to ignore.

'It's no secret. Ffion was teasing her about it yesterday, if you remember.' Zander flapped his hand at Olivia. 'I remember you telling me all about the arsehole your new college friend had got herself mixed up with at the time. I just didn't know that arsehole was the man you then went and got a job with.'

Zander was practically sparking with indignation and Jude got the sense that a conversation had been had between and Olivia already that morning.

'I knew you'd try and stop me working with Jim at Leigh Farm if you knew whose dad he was.'

'Too bloody right I would. It's making me feel sick just the thought of you putting yourself in the path of such a vile man.'

Jude fought the urge to mention the video that

Zander had made, telling the world what a good friend David had been to him.

'Just drop it, Zand. I don't want to talk about this any more.'

Zander ignored her again and turned back to Jude. 'She doesn't like to speak ill of the dead but he was awful. Back then I was away a lot with the band and Olivia used to go and stay with Tara during college holidays. Liv wrote me long emails about this arse who Tara had a thing for. She told me how worried she was about their relationship and that the guy was no good and had a reputation for sleeping around.'

'Zander, stop it,' Olivia warned again. 'Jude doesn't want to hear this.'

Jude was not one for gossip as a rule, and this sounded suspiciously as though it might fall into exactly this territory. But when murder had been committed she was definitely one for keeping her ears open for anything that could lead to something interesting.

'I told you I think everyone should hear this,' said Zander, putting his own anger above the comfort of his best friend. 'Including the police.'

'And I told you it's not relevant.' Olivia put her

hand on Zander's cheek and turned his head to make him look at her.

'I disagree.' Zander stared into her face. 'I was there, remember? When Tara came to stay with you at Greener Days just weeks after I'd bought the place. I saw how crushed she was after the abortion and I remember how angry you were with the man who'd treated her so abysmally. What you failed to tell me even then was that this was the same man you'd been working with for the past two years.'

'He got her pregnant?' Jude exclaimed, unable to stop the surprise in her voice.

'Zander!' Olivia was clearly furious with him for spilling such a private piece of information about her friend. 'Jude, that wasn't his secret to tell, please keep it to yourself.'

But that was a promise Jude wouldn't make as it had just given both Tara and Penny another motive for a killing born of fury.

8

Jude's two pedigree Kerry Hills were very pleased to be released back onto fresh grass when Jude and Frank returned to the farm.

Like her animals, Jude was happy to be back in the paddock, although a large part of her mind was most definitely still back at the Three Counties Show.

A noise at the far end of the field made her look across to the hedge that split her farm from her neighbours' garden. Mike Trout waved at her as he walked through the gate he'd installed and closed it behind him. She shaded her eyes from the midday sun and watched him cross the grass towards her.

'Penny for your thoughts?' he asked, coming to stand next to her as she leant against the stable door.

'Hi, Mike,' said Jude. 'I was just enjoying a bit of peace with the animals. It's been a busy weekend.'

'Sorry.' Mike pointed his thumb over his shoulder towards his house. 'I can leave you to it if you like.'

Jude smiled. 'Not at all. I know you feel the reviving nature of this place as much as I do, and I'm happy of the company. Just don't ask me about the show, okay?'

Mike smiled and came to stand next to her, resting his back against the wall and gently stroking Rodney Trotter's nose as the pony pushed against his pocket looking for treats.

'How are the wedding plans coming along?' he asked.

'They both want a low-key event.' Jude raised an eyebrow. 'And yet Lucy is planning every single low-key element with a very high-key level of precision. I've lost count of the number of canapés we've sampled.'

Mike grinned at her. 'Val was the same when we got married. Said she wanted to keep things simple but we ended up with all the trappings. I even remember having different styles of linen napkins thrust at me to choose from. Thing was, I couldn't really tell the difference between them!'

Jude thought back to her own wedding. She and Adam had been married under the apple trees in the orchard and then dined with their guests at tables set out in the farm's garden. It had been a beautiful day, although the lambing shed had been power-washed out with a temporary floor installed in case the weather turned. That was where they'd moved to as the meal was cleared away and the band started to play. The shed had been transformed into a ballroom with strings of fairy lights and a glitter ball hanging from the rafters. It had been perfect and Jude wanted Lucy's day to be just as special.

'They've decided on holding it in the lambing shed.'

'Won't that be a bit chilly?'

'Lucy has thought of everything. She's hiring special heaters and she's bought a job lot of extra chunky yarn too. The folk at the old people's home where she works are currently busy knitting it into blankets for anyone feeling the chill.'

'What a marvellous idea,' said Mike.

'Oh, my sister is full of those.'

Jude looked at the old open canoe that had been turned into a splash pool for the Runner ducks to enjoy. Three of them were bobbing about happily whilst Maggie and Mo, the two fluffy Valais lambs, skipped and gambolled in front of it. She took in a deep breath of the farm-scented air and allowed it to wash over her.

On the whole things were good. The farm was doing well, the campsite was pretty much fully booked for the summer and there was a wedding to plan.

Her weekend at the show had been draining and incredibly sad but, for Jude at least, it was over. She had given her witness statement and answered all the questions that Binnie had for her, but perhaps this time she should step away now and concentrate on what was happening around her in her own life.

Jude turned her face upwards to the June sun and closed her eyes.

'Better than any other sort of therapy,' Mike said. And Jude agreed.

In the tack room attached to the stables there were two camping chairs which had been stored there by Mike for just such occasions. He and Jude took them out and set them up on the grass. Jude gratefully sank into the canvas caress of one of them and Mike did the same in the other. No conversation was necessary as they both relished the gentle buzz of bees on the clover, snuffles from the animals and chatter from the ducks. It was Jude's version of heaven and she could feel her eyes fighting the urge to close when her phone buzzed in her pocket.

It was a text from Binnie.

> Black marks on David's hands were definitely hair dye.

> Jim has been arrested for smashing lights of Griff's pickup.

> Zander is milking the publicity opportunity and Tara is furious he told us about her abortion.

> Thoughts? Bx

And just like that, Jude was back in the investigation.

* * *

When there was something on Jude's mind, it rarely gave her a moment's peace until whatever it was had reached its conclusion. It therefore stood to reason that, having discovered the murdered body of a fellow farmer, Jude did not find it easy to channel her thoughts elsewhere.

Zander had clearly already told Binnie about Tara and the baby that she'd apparently conceived with David and subsequently aborted. Him discussing it with Binnie felt like an invasion of Tara's rights to privacy and kindness. Yet if David had treated her badly in the past and then appeared in her life again, she may have had a reason to lash out. Anger and fear were both equally possible emotions in this situation and both could have ended with Tara picking up the shears.

Jude swapped her work trousers and stained T-shirt for something cleaner and prepared for a trip into Great Malvern on the other side of the hills.

One of her dearest friends, Margot Lloyd, had moved out of her cottage in Malvern End and into the care home where Lucy worked, several years ago. A visit to Perrins House to see her was often one of the highlights of Jude's week and she always had the feeling it was very much mutual.

'Afternoon, Gerwain.' Jude greeted the care home manager as she walked through the front door and went over to sign her name in the visitors' book.

'Brought the sunshine with you as always, Jude.' Gerwain was wearing a white plastic apron and surgical gloves and was carrying a suspicious-looking bowl of something covered in blue tissue. Jude decided it was best not to go in for a closer greeting until whatever it was had been dealt with. 'Margot's in the day room. I think I saw her in a vicious game of Scrabble with Hector, who I'm sure will be very grateful to you for the distraction.'

'Thanks,' said Jude. 'I wasn't aware Scrabble could get vicious.'

'You've clearly never played it with Margot before.' Gerwain started walking off down the hallway to deal with the contents of his bowl. 'Good luck!' he called over his shoulder.

Jude went into the large, sunny day room where many of the residents of Perrins House were ensconced in various board games or reading quietly in their wingback chairs. Margot and Hector were sitting at a table near the window with a Scrabble board between them. It was a luxury one that had a little plastic turntable stuck to the underside and Granny Margot swivelled it triumphantly round to face her opponent.

'Bastard!' she exclaimed. 'The D of which is on a double letter score and the S turns your tinker into stinker so I get points for that too. And it's on a double word score for both so I think I make that forty-six points. Add on the fifty I get for using up all my letters and you can put me down for ninety-six all in.'

Jude smiled to herself. Granny Margot was cagey about her exact age but Jude knew she must be over the ninety mark and yet her brain was as sharp as most twenty-year-olds.

Hector caught sight of Jude and he broke into a broad smile, losing the hunted rabbit look the game of Scrabble had given him.

'Ah, Jude. How marvellous to see you.' He stood up and waved her over. 'I suppose you'll be wanting us to stop playing now so that you can have a natter with Margot here.'

'Oh no.' Margot jiggled her hand in the bag containing the remainder of the tiles and started to refill her stand. 'We've got a game to finish. It can stay set up whilst Jude and I have a natter and then we can finish it later on.'

Hector sighed. 'Right you are. Well, I'll get out of your way for now then and let Jude have my chair.'

As he stood up, Hector appeared to have a bit of wobble and put his hand out to use the table as support. Unfortunately, his arm caught the edge of the Scrabble board which tipped sideways on the turntable, scattering tiles across the table.

'Oh dear.' Hector did an admirable job of looking genuinely aghast at the fate of their game. 'What a pickle I seem to have made.'

He started to tidy the spilt tiles into a pile but Granny Margot pushed his hand away.

'Oh just leave it, Hector. Jude and I will sort it out.'

Hector took his opportunity and left Margot to the job of rehousing the tiles in their bag. As he walked past Jude he gave her a conspiratorial wink which made her smile.

'Jude, my darling. Come and bring some sanity to my day.' Granny Margot looked up at her through the thick, blue-tinged fringe of her bob. She was wearing a bright fuchsia-pink T-shirt that clashed wonderfully with her aubergine trousers.

Jude bent and kissed her on the cheeks before settling into the chair recently vacated by Hector.

'That blasted man,' Granny Margot said. 'He does hate losing but I ask you, why play if you don't want to take that risk?'

'This is very true,' said Jude. 'Although I do wonder exactly how much choice he had in the matter.'

'I don't know what you mean.' Granny Margot's eyes crinkled at the corners as she spoke.

Once all the tiles were safely back in their bag and that in turn had been returned to the box, Granny Margot rested her arms on the table.

'Now then, Jude,' she said. 'What's all this I hear about a body at the Three Counties Show?'

Jude rested her head on the high back of the chair. 'What do you already know? I suspect there has already been a lot of chatter about this over the morning porridge.'

'Well of course there has. Everyone loves a good murder to solve.' Granny Margot caught Jude's eye. 'Although naturally it is desperately sad for the poor man's family.'

Jude propped her elbows on the arms of the chair. She knew how much Granny Margot liked to be involved in the solving of any mystery. She was actually rather good at it, asking questions and putting a twist on things that Jude hadn't already thought of.

'It would appear that this was not a murder carefully thought about in advance,' Jude began. 'The victim, David Martin, who I'm sure you already know was the son of a farmer from Leigh Sinton...'

'I did, although they weren't a family I knew.'

'Not a very nice man from what I saw. Anyway, he was in one of the livestock sheds at the end of the day and someone had some sort of altercation with him that resulted in David being stabbed in the neck with a pair of sheep clippers.'

Granny Margot winced. 'Ouch,' she said. 'What a way to go.'

'It looks as though it wasn't a planned attack,' said Jude.

'Why?' Granny Margot asked. 'You think that whoever did it just grabbed whatever was handy rather than going in already armed?'

'It makes sense.' Jude could tell from Granny Margot's expression that she was about to lay a cloud of doubt over this working theory.

'It would make sense, yes. But it isn't the only ex-planation.' Granny Margot drummed her fingers rhythmically on the table. 'It's also possible that someone went in with the intention to kill and used the clippers to make it look as though it was an act of passion.'

Jude nodded. 'Of course you're right,' she said. 'And I should know better than to just make assump-tions because something looks cut-and-dry on the surface.'

'So we've got the gist of how this man was killed, but what can you tell me about the who did it and why?'

'David was the sort of person who seemed to walk through life making more enemies than friends as he went,' Jude said. 'There were plenty of people at the show that may have been driven to stab him, and then we discovered a link to the world of marijuana that might also have had something to do with it.'

Jude ran through the list of people she'd met, highlighting the motive each may have had for murder. Although some of them had alibis, Jude hadn't removed them from her suspect list just yet. As Granny Margot pointed out, it was far better when investigating a crime not to take anything at face value.

'Gosh,' Granny Margot said. 'So this man was trying to force a large housing development on good farmland, had tampered with several sheep and a box of hair dye, liked to force his unwelcome advances on women and was involved in supplying marijuana. Not to mention all that furore he started with some minor celebrity who thinks he's the saviour of farming. Have I missed anything?'

'That's about the size of things,' Jude said. 'David's father, Jim, is convinced that he was killed by Griff.'

'Neighbour and staunch rival?' Granny Margot checked.

'That's right. Yesterday when I went to fetch the sheep back from the showground, the pair of them had another very public, very unpleasant argument which ended up with threats from both sides.'

'I imagine both men were at boiling point from what you've told me.'

'Very much so. Binnie had to go round first thing this morning to arrest Jim for attacking Griff's car with a metal pole when he was coming out of his farm's drive.'

'Oh dear.'

'Binnie said he was furious when she arrived but he quickly crumpled.'

'Often the way.' Granny Margot bridged her fingers together. 'Did they charge him?'

'Griff didn't want to press charges against Jim, surprisingly, claiming that he felt sorry for his neighbour who'd already been through enough for one weekend.'

'Indeed,' said Granny Margot sagely.

Jude and Granny Margot were prevented from discussing things further by the appearance of Rani, another resident of the care home, barely visible behind the most enormous pile of thick yarn she was carrying.

'Are you coming into the conservatory, Margot?'

she asked. 'Bitch and stitch is about to begin and Lucy kindly brought us a new delivery of yarn to crack on with those blankets.'

Jude wondered at the power her sister had over these pensioners, not only getting them to make the chunky knit blankets for her wedding, but also thinking it was a kindness on her part.

'Not right now, Rani. I have a visitor.' Granny Margot eye-balled the heap of yarn. 'Throw one of those balls my way though. I've got my knitting bag under the table.'

Jude stood up to help Rani with the yarn.

'I'll help Rani take these to the conservatory.' She took two of the bags from her. 'Be back in a minute.'

'Make sure you bring a ball back for me, Jude. I know what those pensioners are like when there's new craft supplies. Yarn vultures the lot of them.'

'Don't you worry,' said Jude. 'My sneaky sister has obviously made sure there's plenty for all her minions.'

There was a steady flow of ready blanket knitters heading to the conservatory where the French windows had been flung open to let the air flow. Some keener members of the bitch and stitch group were already sitting on the rattan furniture with needles the thickness of Jude's thumb, clacking away.

By choosing such chunky yarn, Lucy had made sure that the blankets grew quickly under the expert fingers of the care home's knitting team.

'You've nearly finished that one,' Jude said to Ralph, a dapper gentleman who was always pristinely turned out.

She put the bags of yarn down on the table and went over to feel the soft thickness of the dusky pink blanket Ralph was working on.

'Just a few more rows and then I can start the next one,' said Ralph.

'It's really kind of you all to be doing this for Lucy.' Jude saw that the bags of yarn were, as Granny Margot had predicted, being pulled apart by eager hands. She grabbed a ball quickly before the lot went.

Ralph looked up at her with dewy eyes. 'It's for our Lucy and we're all just so proud to be a part of her wedding.'

Jude took the scene in and realised that every stitcher in the room was not just there because they enjoyed knitting. They were there to give back something to the woman who worked for a disgracefully small wage to offer them the best care she could in their twilight years. They loved her and this was their way of showing it.

Granny Margot had already got her knitting out by the time Jude returned with the new ball of yarn. Lucy was also in the day room helping Phylis, the oldest resident, into a chair. Jude knew that Phylis needed an extra caring pair of hands having recently mourned the tragic loss of her daughter. As Jude watched her sister at work she felt a bubble of pride swell inside. She was incredible at her job. Patient, empathetic, gentle but also strong.

Jude sat back down opposite Granny Margot and put the yarn on the table.

'It's quite the workforce in there,' she said.

'Your sister has made a mark around here.' Granny Margot leant over her knitting and lowered her voice. 'Gerwain and Jacinta are planning a special party for her here, the week before she gets married, seeing as not many will be able to go to the actual wedding. Keep it under your hat though.'

Jude tapped the side of her nose. 'She'll be so touched by that.'

'Touched by what?' Lucy had finished with Phylis and sneaked up without Jude noticing.

'Oh, I was just saying I'd look for some old photos of my cottage for you to show Clara.' Jude marvelled at Granny Margot's seamless capability to spin a white lie. 'She can see how much it's changed over the years.'

'That is sweet,' said Lucy. 'She seems really happy there.'

'She's the perfect tenant as far as I'm concerned. Always pays her rent on time and I hear she's getting on well with the neighbours too.' Granny Margot looked pointedly at Jude. 'Don't lose your chance there.'

Jude felt herself blush a little. 'I don't know what you're talking about.'

'Margot's right,' said Lucy. 'Marco and you are made for each other, we can all see it. But he won't wait for you forever.'

This was not a conversation Jude was keen to continue with. She ignored them both and pulled out her phone.

'Anyway, before all of this we were talking about the other exhibitors at the show who knew David Martin.' She found Zander Pettiford's Instagram page and passed the phone to Granny Margot. 'This is the guitarist I was telling you about.'

'I know who he is,' said Granny Margot. 'Sarah used to love listening to The Spods on full volume. Janet Timms was regularly banging on the door asking her to turn the music down.' She smiled at the memory of life with her granddaughter. 'And you say over two million people tune in to see what he's up to?'

Jude pointed at the number on his profile. 'It's actually gone up since he posted that video about David. People can't seem to get enough of him.'

'He looks like he's never seen a day of hard work in his life.' Granny Margot zoomed in on one of the selfies Zander had recently posted, back at his farm looking deliberately troubled as he carried on fake-mourning his fake-friend.

'It's enough to make my skin bristle,' said Lucy, taking the phone from Granny Margot and staring at the photo.

'He's taking this as a brilliant publicity opportunity,' said Jude.

'Enough of a reason to have killed David in the first place?' Granny Margot picked up her needles and looped the yarn over, her fingers finding their autopilot as they took up the rhythm of the knitting. 'You said there was no love lost between the two of them anyway.'

'I'm not sure,' said Jude. 'Look at some of these videos and tell me what you think of it all.'

Jude began with the video filmed in response to the Instagram Live recording where David had stolen

Zander's phone to put his own views across to all those tuning in.

'And then he goes from that to this.' The next video Jude chose was the one where Zander Pettiford had broken the news of David's murder to the world before the police. 'Zander has gone from hating everything David stood for to suddenly being one of his closest friends.'

'He certainly likes the sound of his own voice, doesn't he?' said Granny Margot.

'Full of shite if you ask me.' Lucy was leaning over the back of Granny Margot's chair to get a better look at the videos. 'And he posts an awful lot of them too.'

'Have you been through all of the ones he took at the Three Counties?' Granny Margot asked.

'Not yet,' said Jude. 'Although I think Binnie had someone doing that at the police station.'

'The police don't always see everything.' Granny Margot put the phone down and got on with her knitting. 'My eyes aren't good enough to stare at that tiny screen of yours for too long but why not have a look on your computer when you get home. Make sure you properly examine what's going on in the background as well as the obvious. You're not just watching this Zander character. If he was filming around the showground then who knows what else he caught?'

'I have to say that the idea of wading through streams of nonsense from Zander Pettiford doesn't exactly fill me with joy,' said Jude.

'It's called suffering for the cause.' Granny Margot pursed her lips.

Jude sighed. 'You're right.'

Lucy patted Granny Margot on the shoulder. 'Have you ever known this woman to be anything other than right?'

'If you could tell Gerwain that, I'd be very grateful.' Granny Margot winked.

'Well, I suppose I'd better get going then.' Jude was comfortable where she was and would have far rather stayed put for a while, soothed by the *clack clack* of the knitting needles and the odd detachment from the world outside. But she had work to get on with and an investigation to probe. 'It seems I have the Instagram account of a narcissist to go through with a fine-tooth comb.'

9

Jude settled herself in front of the computer in her office space at the farm and loaded Instagram. It wasn't something she did very often and when she did dip into the world of social media it was always small-scale on her phone.

Zander's face filled the screen and she had to promptly turn the volume down as his voice was so irritating; or at least the things he said were. In the four days since she'd first met him, he had posted fifteen videos and several reels consisting of carefully staged photos with links to his online shop.

Jude put some Edward Elgar on in the background to help dilute the awfulness of the man on her screen and then set about watching each video. The first one that featured the Three Counties started with him in an expensive-looking farmhouse kitchen, full of mod cons that were most unusual in Jude's world.

'I'm very excited today,' he said into the camera. 'I'm taking some of my wild sheep to their first ever agricultural show where I hope to prove that wilding and farming top animals can and should go hand in hand.'

Jude rolled her eyes, hoping that there was footage of how the hell he'd managed to catch the wild Kerry Hills. They were a skittish breed naturally wary of people anyway, hard to catch in an open paddock when they were well used to seeing humans in their territory. Wild sheep, out in the woods would be a different kettle of fish altogether and then there would have been the challenge of getting them used to being on a halter.

Jude imagined that Olivia had done all the hard work but she didn't get the chance to see how as the next part of the video showed the inside of the brand-new trailer with Zander's sheep ready for the journey.

'That was tricky but we've managed to get these beauties loaded and ready for the off.'

'How much were you involved other than waving the camera around?' Jude muttered.

Olivia had obviously taken over the videoing at this point as Zander was driving the state-of-the-art 4x4 down the motorway, eyes on the road but still more than capable of talking about himself.

Jude left the video running but she didn't start to properly take notice until they arrived at the show-ground. The screen showed the top end of Avon Hall which had been turned into the sheep shed for the duration of the show. And there were the other ex-hibitors, all busy preparing their sheep. Jude held a pen in her hand, ready to note down anything of im-portance.

The video panned the sheep shed and she saw, to her dismay, that it stopped on her where she was bent over the hurdle of her own pen to reposition the water bucket that Henry had hoofed over, with her rear end in the air.

'You're kidding me,' said Jude as her bottom waved at the camera. At least the waistband of her jeans hadn't slipped, she supposed. And from that angle she'd be difficult to identify anyway.

There was nothing of great use in the first video so Jude skipped to the next which was a compilation of snippets taken from interviews he'd obviously done with some of the other livestock exhibitors. There were a mix of sheep, cattle, goat and pig farmers and Zander had clearly spent a lot of time cutting just the right bits and piecing them together to form what she could only describe as a propaganda video. He had put a spin on everything that either showed farmers agreeing with him and his views and choices, or directly opposing him which gave him a noble cause to fight.

Jude guessed that almost everyone in the video would have been interested to see how their words were being used. David was neither included nor mentioned in this particular video although he was the main point of reference for the next one which Jude had already seen, filmed after the disastrous live streaming of David's rant against Zander.

Jude looked at the piece of paper she had in front of her, edged with swirly cartoons of cloud-like sheep which she'd doodled in lieu of having anything meaningful to write down. She still had several more videos to look through and the photos Zander had posted on top of that.

The next video was of the inside of the sheep shed on the morning of David's death and featured snippets of the big revelation as Zander had confronted him about his plans for developing part of his farmland. After footage of the ensuing argument between David, Jim and Griff, there was a short monologue from Zander about the sort of person he thought David was.

'Not only does he want to destroy the land his family have been custodians of for generations but he has shown no thought for his poor father who you can see from the previous clip was beyond distressed. As you know, I believe in looking after the older members in our families which is why I have made sure that my own mother is being cared for in the very best nursing home that money can buy. If only David Martin had the same thought when it comes to his dad.'

This video wasn't exactly in keeping with the ones that Jude knew followed when Zander took to social media to express his grief. But then she supposed he'd done such a good job of spinning things to suit his narrative that people had been taken in by him.

There was only one other video before David's death and it was again filmed in the sheep shed. It was buzzing with activity and Jude could see the Proctors getting their sheep ready to show. Tara was also in with hers, and Jude and Frank were busy with Helen and Henry. Whilst Zander spouted some inane drivel, Jude kept her eyes scanning what was going on in the background until she saw David Martin come into the sheep shed. He glanced around before walking a little way down where he stopped to talk to someone annoyingly just off-screen. Jude tried to work out who it could be and decided it must be Olivia who was probably putting in all the hard graft as usual as David had stopped close to the large run of pens where Zander's sheep were kept. And of course, David was known to enjoy the company of attractive women.

But as she watched, Jude noticed David's face cloud over and she could tell he was not enjoying the conversation at all. He was bent forward, perhaps so that he could speak without being heard by those in the other pens and he didn't look happy. Jude was frustrated that she couldn't tell for sure who was on the other end of the conversation but she could discount the Proctors, Zander and Tara because they were all elsewhere in the shed.

Jude tried to think back to that moment but she had been so focused on getting her sheep ready that she hadn't taken much notice of what was going on around her. There was a small chance that Jim, Griff or Penny had wandered over to that part of the shed but Jude knew that it was more likely to be Olivia.

Once she'd tuned into David's body language, Jude could see that he was getting angrier about something, perhaps forcing himself not to make a scene. She wished she could listen in to the conversation and wondered if Binnie's team of experts would be able to pick something out by lip-reading David's mouth. Even if it was only one side of the conversation, it might still throw up something interesting.

There was a single warning woof from Pip in the kitchen as the front door opened. The sound of skittering claws on the flagstones told Jude that whoever had come in was a friend and the low lilt of the voice that followed confirmed that it was Frank.

'In here,' she called out. 'If you're sticking the kettle on, I'll have a cuppa with you.'

'Right you are, Jude.'

Whilst she waited for her tea to be brought through to her, Jude carried on looking at the Instagram regurgitation of Zander Pettiford's time at the Three Counties. She watched the plaintive video he'd made shortly after he'd been questioned about David's death and she tried to decipher whether anything in his behaviour signposted him as the killer. He would have to be particularly cold-souled to produce a video like this only hours after murdering the man he was talking about. Was he capable of such callousness?

Zander liked to portray himself as the community-minded good egg with the best intentions but at the same time he was out to grow both his money pot and social brand. David had tried to put the kibosh on that with his abject and vocal opposition but his death had served to boost Zander's profile. Although it seemed that when Griff had asked him for his help in bringing David down, Zander had refused.

'Here we are now, Jude.' Frank set a welcome mug of tea on the desk next to her.

'Thanks, Frank.'

'Not still looking at that foolish bugger, are you?' He nodded at the photo of Zander that was on the computer screen.

'I'm just trying to help Binnie figure out what happened to David.'

Frank perched on the piano stool. 'Noah tells me they found some of that hair dye on his fingers.'

Jude nodded as she picked up her mug. 'It wasn't Griff after all.'

'Maybe not but he's still done alright by it.' Frank itched his chin. 'I heard he bought that ram of the Proctors for a snip. Odd that, don't you think?'

Jude thought of the pedigree ram that had been

everyone's favourite to take home the prize for best in breed before the hair dye scandal, possibly even the top prize of best in show. Despite the fact he hadn't won a first-place rosette, everyone could see that he was something special.

'That *is* very odd,' said Jude. 'There are still other agricultural shows for the ram to have shone in, and Ffion and Carl could have named their price if they'd really wanted to sell, but I'd have thought they'd have kept him for at least one breeding season first, wouldn't you?'

'I would indeed,' Frank agreed. 'Breeding stock like that don't come around very often. If it were me I'd have got one lot of lambs from him before I even thought of selling him on.'

The Proctors were strapped for cash, Jude knew that. Perhaps they couldn't afford to wait for another year before making money out of their prize ram. But neither could they afford to let him go for less than he was worth. Something strange was at play and Jude wanted to know what it was. Her mind was taken back to the look that had passed between Ffion and Carl as they were packing up at the end of the show. When Ffion mentioned showing again, Carl had looked at her as though trying to persuade her of something. Had Griff already mentioned his desire to buy the ram from them? If so, was Carl the one persuading Ffion to sell, or was he trying to stop her from making a mistake?

Something else rubbed at Jude's train of thought. Perhaps Griff had found some sort of leverage that gave them no choice but to hand the ram over for such a bargain price. Maybe the same thing that David had alluded to in the blackmail letter he had written.

Or was it possible that Griff had seen one or both of them kill David and was offering them his silence? Ffion and Carl had told Binnie they'd been with Tara when David had been killed but there had been some vagueness in the exact timing of when Carl had gone back to find Ffion and how long it had been before they returned to the Watsons' caravan.

On the piece of paper surrounded by sheep doodles, Jude wrote out a list of questions that she wanted answering.

Why did the Proctors sell their prize ram to Griff Gould?

Who had David been talking to in the Instagram video, and what had it been about?

Why had David been in the Greener Days sheep pen when he'd been killed?

Who had David's letter been intended for?

Did David know that Tara had aborted his baby? If so, had he been angry?

And of course the big one.

Who killed David Martin and why?

*   *   *

With the drama of the weekend, Jude had completely forgotten that she'd made plans with Binnie that evening so it was a surprise when her friend turned up on the doorstep.

'I'm all for the natural look—' Binnie's eyes were drawn to the short pyjamas that Jude was wearing under one of Adam's old hoodies '—but that's a bold choice for the cinema. Even for you.'

'Jude!' Lucy exclaimed from where she was chopping up freshly cooked sausages to add to the pasta sauce she was cooking. 'You didn't forget, did you?'

'Bugger!' Jude glanced at the calendar on the

kitchen wall and saw the note she'd made there to remind herself of the cinema trip they'd booked weeks ago. 'What time does it start?'

'You've got half an hour,' said Binnie. 'When you didn't answer my reminder text, I thought you might have forgotten so I figured it wouldn't harm to get here early.'

Jude blew Binnie a kiss before running upstairs to get herself ready. It didn't take her long to throw on some clothes, brush her hair and generally make herself a little more presentable. She was back in the kitchen ten minutes later where Binnie had made herself comfy chatting to Lucy whilst Sebbie ate his way through a plate of pasta.

'Ready when you are.' Jude picked up her phone and dropped it into her handbag along with her keys. 'If we leave now we'll have time to grab a drink before we go in.'

'Will you get pick and mix?' Sebbie asked.

'I was thinking perhaps a glass of wine instead,' said Jude.

'Poor you.' Deeply disappointed on his aunt's behalf, Sebbie went back to his pasta.

'We could get pick and mix if you wanted,' said Binnie as they crossed the yard to get into her car.

* * *

The road to Hereford was one of Jude's favourites as it cut through a variety of farmland, from fruit orchards to hop yards, cereal crops and livestock. It sometimes felt as though the landscape had changed so little in the past couple of centuries that her literary heroine, Bathsheba Everdene from Thomas Hardy's *Far From the Madding Crowd*, would not feel out of place if she came to visit. That was as long as she didn't come across any farm vehicles in the fields.

'We had the fingerprints back from the murder weapon,' said Binnie. 'Everyone we already expected to find plus Griff Gould, who says Olivia dropped them when he was walking past and he stopped to pick them up for her: a fact that she has confirmed.'

'So pretty much everyone then?'

'It definitely didn't give us any further clues.'

'What about the letter?' Jude asked. 'Any interesting prints found on that?'

'It's harder to lift prints from paper as the fibres tend to soak away the oils from the skin.' Binnie shifted down a gear, giving her little car more power to get up the steep incline of Fromes Hill. 'The letter had got damp from the floor of the shed too which makes it even harder. They're still working on it.'

'I've been thinking about what he wrote and something's puzzling me,' said Jude. 'We know that David was prone to a little dope dealing and so we assume that this is what he's talking about in his letter.'

'That is our best theory, yes.'

'If he was writing to the grower then the wording of the letter suggests this was the first time he'd spoken to them directly about it. He tells them that he knows what they're up to on their farm which doesn't fit if this is where he's been getting his supply of drugs from for the past few years.'

'True,' said Binnie. 'Which means that either there's a middle person dealing between the farm and the smaller suppliers like David, or the letter wasn't about marijuana production at all.'

'Unless there's more than one producer. Have you been able to go and look at the farms of all the suspects?'

Binnie shook her head. 'I'd never get clearance to do that with no evidence. Besides, if the person growing drugs for David was at the Three Counties, what's to say it was one of the Kerry Hill farmers? It could have been absolutely anyone. Farmer, visitor, even organiser.'

Jude sighed. Binnie was right. Tying David's

murder up neatly by looping the letter, the hash and the group of Kerry Hill farmers together was just that. Neat. But that didn't make it the truth. It seemed as though they were a long way from finding any firm answers and this was cause of much frustration for Jude. She had no strong starting point to go from, just a collection of scraps that still pointed a thousand different ways.

Had David died as a direct result of the blackmail letter? Or had his murky, underhand view of life caught up with him in another way?

Jude thought back to the list of questions she'd jotted down earlier that day and made the decision to take a trip over the Welsh border and pay a visit to the Proctors and the Watsons.

10

The Courtyard cinema in Hereford was a super find but Jude could not fully relax into her evening out. As the film rolled, she sat in her seat playing her own set of mini movies in her head. In each one she cast David as the victim but the part of the murderer was swapped around as she tried to find the best fit from the cast of supporting characters.

'What do we know about Olivia Cook?' Jude said as they sat in the cafe afterwards having ordered fish and chips.

'Zander Pettiford's farm manager? Not an awful lot other than that she seems to run the place whilst he fannies around with social media. Why?'

'There's a moment on one of Zander's Instagram

videos where David can be seen in the background talking to someone off screen and he doesn't look happy.'

'Can you tell what he's saying?'

'No, but it looks like it's a pretty intense conversation.'

Binnie pattered her fingertips against her bottom lip. 'And you think he was talking to Olivia Cook?'

'Possibly. He was standing next to her sheep pens and she's nowhere else in the shed, unlike Ffion, Carl, Tara and Zander who are all in shot.' Jude took the cutlery being offered by their waiter and put it down in front of her. 'Thanks.'

'It would be good to know what they were talking about,' said Binnie. 'How close were they to Zander? Is there an outside chance that his mic could have picked enough up for the tech team to try and hone in on?'

'I doubt it. They were quite a way back and the shed was full and noisy. I did wonder if you might be able to send it to a lip-reader to have a look at?'

'If there's a clear view of David's mouth then I can definitely ask someone to see what they can pull off. Of course there's also the old-fashioned method of actually showing the video to Olivia and asking her if it was her on the other side of the conversation and if so, what they were talking about.'

'Of course,' said Jude. 'Obviously bearing in mind that people lie.'

'They do indeed,' Binnie agreed.

The food arrived then and Jude felt her stomach rumble at the sight of the puffy batter and chunky chips.

'Speaking of going to talk to people who were at the show and who knew David, I was thinking of a trip to Wales to see some of my new Kerry Hill friends.' Jude looked up at Binnie innocently through her eyelashes, although she knew she wouldn't be able to fool her for a second. Binnie would know there was nothing innocent about any visit she made to the Proctors or Watsons. It would purely be a fact-finding, evidence-gathering mission.

'It's not against the law,' said Binnie as she squirted ketchup onto the edge of her plate. 'You are dealing with a murder investigation though so you don't need me to tell you to tread carefully.'

Jude held her hands up in submission. 'When have you ever known me not to be careful?'

Binnie picked up her knife and fork. 'I am not going to waste my breath answering that.'

* * *

Once Jude had made the decision to take a day trip to Abergavenny and the Brecon Beacons, it seemed pointless to wait. She called Ffion and Tara and made arrangements to pop over on the pretence that she was in the area anyway picking up more yarn for the wedding blankets.

Lucy was working the early shift and Jude had offered to take Sebbie to school which was something she loved to do. Not only did she get to spend time with her only nephew but she also enjoyed the connection to the school she'd once worked in as a teacher before Adam's illness had meant she was needed on the farm full-time.

'Aunty Judy, why do boys have teats?' Sebbie asked as Jude bundled him into the back seat of the Land Rover.

'Pardon?' Jude had heard his question perfectly well but she needed a moment to try and come up with a suitable answer.

Being five, Sebbie was at that inquisitive age that came without filtration and Jude, along with the other adults in his life, was often caught out by him. She was still recovering from the conversation they'd had during the tupping last year. Sebbie had been convinced that the raddle packs they strapped to the rams to mark which ewes had been serviced, contained hundreds of tiny lambs which the rams injected straight into the ewes to grow.

'Girls and ewes have teats to give their babies milk but I asked Noah and he says boys and rams can't make milk so why do Noah and me have teats.'

The thing about allowing Sebbie to be hands on with the lambing was that biology was thrust at him in a very visible way. This was great for lots of reasons; awkward questions about nipples on the school run was not necessarily one of them.

'I think it's got something to do with the way babies are built whilst they're still inside their mothers,' Jude hazarded a guess and vowed to Google it later. It was a pretty valid question, after all. Although, knowing Sebbie, he'd probably have forgotten all about mammalian milk production by the time he got back from school and would be on to something else.

'Have you got your costume for the summer concert?' Jude asked. She knew full well that it was already safely in his school bag but it made for a cunning distraction.

When Sebbie was safely deposited with his

teacher, Miss Elgar, in the school playground, Jude set off for the Welsh border.

She stopped off at a wool shop in Monmouth which handily supplied the mega yarn balls Lucy was using for the blankets. They usually delivered it and Lucy didn't actually need more but Jude found it much easier to lie if the lie was hidden under a cloak of truth.

The Welsh countryside was stunning, the Brecon Beacons standing twice as high and spread more widely than the crest of the Malvern Hills. The outline of the Brecons could clearly be seen from the top of the Malverns and Jude had been to Pen Y Fan, the highest peak, several times with Adam.

The National Park had been one of his favourite spots, mainly because of the rugged yet tranquil landscape with its waterfalls and lakes, but also because they had a way of taking him back in time to his childhood. Driving through them made Jude wonder why she hadn't come back since his death and decided to rectify that with her family; Sebbie especially would love it.

The Watsons' farm was on the north-east side of the nature reserve, only a short drive from where the Proctors lived in Abergavenny. A driveway even more potholed than that of Malvern Farm took

Jude up to the Welsh stone farmhouse with the usual assortment of machinery and vehicles in the yard. Two border collies came bounding out to meet the car and Jude had to slow right down for fear of running them over as they nipped at the tyres.

There were several outbuildings, barns and sheds that surrounded the courtyard and Jude found herself wondering if any of them could be housing a secret crop of cannabis plants. This was a thought that she pushed away quickly as Penny came out of the house dressed in overalls, with a red-spotted handkerchief tied round her head to keep the hair out of her face.

'Jude, how lovely to see you,' she said as Jude got out of the car and bent to let the dogs sniff her hands.

'I was in Monmouth anyway so thought I'd come on over to see how you and Tara are after the show.'

Penny's cheeks were covered in red thread veins that, along with her large smile and sparkling eyes, gave her a rosy, welcoming appearance. She seemed far more at home in the Welsh hills than she had cooped up in the sheep shed at the Three Counties and Jude could imagine her getting on very well with Granny Margot.

'Ignore Bryn and Ness,' she said. 'They're farm

dogs through and through, great with the sheep but think they have to protect us from everything.'

The two dogs sniffed Jude thoroughly, trying to work out what this strange creature was that looked human but probably smelt of dog and sheep.

'You're both very lovely,' said Jude as the dogs clearly concluded she was safe and let her tickle them behind the ears.

'Tara's in the kitchen getting some bara brith ready with a brew. She'll be so pleased to see you, come on in.'

Penny led the way inside and Jude found Tara buttering slices of the rich fruit loaf.

'You've been baking,' said Jude. It was almost unbearably hot in the kitchen with the heat of summer joining forces with the Aga.

'God, no!' Tara made it sound as though Jude had suggested she'd tried lambing in her bikini. 'I can't bake for toffee, take after Mam in that sense, I'm afraid. I buy it from the farm shop, it's my guilty pleasure.'

'If that's all you're guilty of then you're doing better than me.' The words were out of her mouth before Jude could stop them. Tara didn't bat an eyelid though so Jude swiftly moved on. 'I like the T-shirt.'

Tara looked down at the oversized shirt bearing a

picture of a sheep relaxing in a deck chair and smoking the most enormous spliff. 'Mam hates it,' she said. 'Although I'm not sure if it's the crudeness of the picture or the fact I borrowed it from the person I'm sleeping with and she's imagining me shacked up with a pothead. Look at her frown, it's like looking down the barrel of a gun.'

Penny shook her head and sighed in submission. 'She likes to try and shock me, Jude. Whereas really I couldn't give a stuff about this feller of hers.'

She went over to steal a piece of bara brith and was rewarded with a slap on the knuckles from her daughter.

'Manners, Mam. We have a guest.'

Penny was a good few inches shorter than Tara who played on the height difference by resting her chin on her mum's head.

Jude smiled at the banter between the two. 'Glad to see you got back safely after the show,' she said.

Tara put the plate of bara brith on the kitchen table and busied herself making a pot of tea.

'It's not really all that far, is it? It was my father's favourite show, he loved taking his Kerries there, or the *dafad bryniau ceri* as he'd call them. Always used the Welsh name.'

Jude remembered seeing the name on the Proctors' sign at the show as well.

'I saw some of your flock when I came down the drive,' said Jude. 'How many have you got here?'

'What is it now, Mam?' Tara looked at Penny. 'Around six hundred with this year's lambs.'

'That's it.' Penny sat down heavily at the table. 'All Kerry Hills now, although in the past we've had all sorts. The year my Clive trialled a few Kerries though, he never looked back.'

It wasn't a huge flock but it seemed to be enough to keep the farm afloat with the two women at the helm.

Jude took a bite of the fruity bara brith and wondered how she could swing the conversation round to the Three Counties. She needed to be subtle if she was going to get some of the answers she'd gone there to find.

'Are you stopping in at Ffion and Carl's whilst you're this way?' Tara put three mugs of tea on the table and sat down.

'Yes. Abergavenny is just down the road from you, isn't it?'

'It's less than half an hour.' Penny took a swig of tea and Jude thought her throat must be lined with asbestos as it had only cooled to a couple of degrees below boiling.

'I was so glad when Ffion and Carl took the tenancy there.' Tara rested her elbows on the table with a mug clasped between her hands. 'We always got on so well when we were growing up, although we only saw each other at shows and then Young Farmers events when we were a little bit older.'

Adam had been to many Young Farmers events and had loved the camaraderie and understanding of other people who knew exactly what it was like to grow up in the world of farming. They organised social gatherings, sports matches, career fairs and parties and it was at one of these that Jude knew Tara had got together with David.

'You met David there too, didn't you?'

'Ghastly man,' said Penny vehemently.

Tara didn't take her eyes off the surface of her tea. 'I gather you know about our past then. Zander did a good job there.'

'Sorry,' said Jude. 'I shouldn't have brought him up.'

'No, it's okay,' said Tara. 'That was all ages ago.'

'I wish you'd told me about it at the time.' Penny turned to Jude. 'I only found out she'd been pregnant a year or so after it all happened when I overheard Tara and Olivia talking.'

'You had your own problems with Da and the contracts not coming in to pay for his new combine. That's all water under the bridge now though, Mam.'

'Maybe, but I can't say I'm sad he's passed on.'

'Mam!' Tara sounded horrified.

'Well I won't lie.' Penny pushed her glasses further up her nose. 'He treated you so badly. In fact, he treated everyone badly. His poor dad, that lovely Olivia, Griff.' Penny's eyebrows were drawn together in a fierce V and Jude wondered at the intensity of her anger. 'Whatever we might think of that Zander Pettigrew, he's a damn sight better for her than David Martin was.'

'He didn't do anything to Olivia.' Tara spoke with exasperation. 'I keep telling you that. Olivia barely saw him whilst she was on the farm with Jim. Besides, he really wasn't all bad.'

'Pah.' Penny brushed her daughter's comment to one side.

'Olivia and Zander are really close, aren't they?' Jude tactfully moved the conversation away from David. 'I had wondered if they were attached romantically.'

Tara snorted with laughter. 'Heavens no! They're more like brother and sister. They've known each other pretty much their whole lives. It might look as though Zander has always been loaded but he actually grew up in a block of flats in Sheffield. Olivia lived next door and neither of them had particularly supportive families so they sort of looked out for each other.'

Jude saw a new side to Zander then and she found it gave her a little more empathy.

'That must have been tough.'

'I think it was. She said they both dreamt of doing big things that would take them away from their families and the tower block. She always wanted to live on a farm and he wanted to be a famous musician.'

'And they did it.'

'They helped each other. Olivia stole money from her dad, a bit at a time, until she had enough to buy Zander a second-hand guitar and he practised every evening whilst his mum was out at work. It's a gorgeous story actually, because he got really good and managed to start earning money playing gigs. He earnt enough to help Olivia get through ag college. By that time she'd graduated, Zander had joined The Spods, then they had that runaway success a couple of years later which meant he suddenly had enough money to buy Liv's dream farm.'

'That's incredible!' Jude really was impressed with the rags to riches tale. 'Why doesn't he talk about it more? Surely this is exactly the sort of story the public would love, mutualism between two child-hood friends who turned each other's fortunes around.'

'Zander has talked about his past before,' said Tara. 'In his book mainly. But Liv really hates the limelight and to give Zander his dues, he respects that so he keeps her out of things mostly now.'

'She's such a good friend of yours, isn't she?' Jude was thinking about the fact it had been Olivia Tara had turned to after the abortion.

'Olivia?' Tara smiled. 'She's the best. We were in-separable at college, saw each other through some tricky times. We drifted apart a bit after graduation and went our own ways. It's not so easy to catch up with old friends when you're both farming.'

'That's definitely true,' said Jude.

'It's easier now she's in Ross-on-Wye as it's so much closer than Leigh Sinton. We try and see each other every few weeks. And of course we can catch up at the shows now too.' Tara blinked and shook a thought away. 'Not the best circumstances this time though.'

'No,' said Jude. 'It was all very sad.'

'Liv went to see poor Jim yesterday and he doesn't know what to do with himself.'

'It's so lovely that she's still close to him,' said Jude. 'But she never really got to know David at the farm?'

Penny, who had finished her tea despite it still being too hot for Jude to manage, stood up abruptly. 'Anyone for a top up?' she asked.

It was a clear message that she thought quite enough had been said about David Martin.

'It was so nice of you to come out and see us,' said Tara. 'You said you were fetching something for your sister's wedding?'

Jude knew that the subject of David Martin was over and she obediently moved on to talk about Lucy and the blankets that she had the residents of Perrins House knitting for her wedding.

Although the rest of her visit was fruitless as far as the investigation went, Jude enjoyed the Watsons' company as they finished their tea and bara brith. They talked about the rest of the county show calendar for the year and reminisced about previous shows they'd been to when Tara's father was still alive.

Conversation eventually turned to Zander Pettiford when Penny brought up the topic of Greener Days Farm, something that she had strong and unshakable views on. 'It just seems such a shame. Olivia was a damn good farmer and she's wasting it on that fool and his rewilding nonsense.'

'She's happy, Mam,' said Tara. 'Okay, it might not be exactly what she planned but she's doing what she loves. You should be happy for her.'

'Maybe,' said Penny unconvincingly.

Jude felt herself starting to melt in the heat of the Aga-fuelled kitchen as they chatted.

'I'd better head off and leave you in peace,' she said when it became too much for her.

'You said you're stopping off to see Ffion and Carl on your way back home.' Tara dug through the pile of stuff on the kitchen table until she found an exercise book. 'Only it's a bit tricky to find and most satnavs don't get you there from the postcode.'

She opened the book and tore out a page, decorated with a border of ivy leaves. After making a few notes and marks on the paper, Tara passed it across to Jude. 'Here. This is where you come off the main road but then you need to turn left straight away by the cattery. That's The Great Catsby, I've marked it here. You'll pass what looks like the main farm house on your right, it's a massive black and white thing, but that's been turned into a B&B. Go on past it and then turn left here by a big old Dutch barn.' She pointed at another mark on her map. 'Down the drive for about a quarter of a mile and you'll end up in Ffion's yard.'

Jude took the note and picked her car keys from the table.

'Brilliant,' she said. 'Thanks so much, and good luck with the other county shows.'

'Are you sure you won't join us again?' Penny asked as Jude stood up.

'Not this year,' said Jude. 'One show was enough for me. But perhaps next year, if my Kerries produce any show-worthy lambs in the spring.'

'And you've got the wedding to prepare for too.' Tara stood up and showed Jude to the door where she was met by a welcome breeze. 'I hope that all goes well. Do pop in again if you're ever back in the Brecons.'

'I will. And if you find yourself in Malvern, you know where I am.'

Jude got in the Land Rover and headed away from the Watsons' farm feeling frustrated. There was something going on that involved Olivia, Tara and David and she wanted to know what it was. Penny obviously knew, well part of it at least, and there was a chance that Zander also knew, and that made her itchy.

She headed away from the Brecon Beacons, back towards the border and Batters Farm where the Proctors were expecting her.

11

The Proctors' farm was very different from the one Jude had just left behind in the Brecon Beacons. Whereas the natural Welsh stone walls of Tara and Penny's farmhouse felt as though they belonged to the land and had been around for centuries, Ffion and Carl's boxy house was covered in grey pebbledash that had a green wash of algae growing across many places.

Even in the brightest sun of near midsummer, it looked cold and uninviting, an appearance that wasn't helped by the presence of three overbearing evergreens that stood over twice the height of the house.

The welcome she received when Ffion opened the front door, however, was warm and sincere.

'You're here!' Ffion beamed in delight. 'It's so lovely of you to make the effort to come over.'

'It's not all that far and I had to go to Monmouth anyway.' Jude's half fib was now well practised.

'Well, we're glad you drove that extra bit to Aber-gavenny.'

To Jude's surprise, Ffion closed the door without inviting her inside. 'It's such a nice day, and after sitting in the car I thought you'd prefer to have a tour of the farm.'

'Great idea,' said Jude. 'I take it the Kerries all settled back into the field after their adventure?'

'They were definitely glad to be back on good pasture rather than cooped up with only hay to eat. Come on, let's go and find them.'

Ffion led the way out across the broken concrete yard and Jude followed. 'Carl's out here somewhere. He's been gradually replacing all the old wooden gates that have rotted through with new aluminium ones before they fall apart completely. Carl managed to get a bulk load of surplus gates which were a bargain, but of course they don't fit any of the existing gateways so each one is causing its own challenges.'

'That sounds like a big job.' Jude went through the smart, new gate that Ffion held open for her.

'Everything around here is a big job. Seriously, it's like nobody touched the place for years before we took over. We've had to replace goodness knows how many hundreds of metres of fencing since we've been here. All the posts were rotten through, same as the gates. The problem is, we're doing it all on a budget and we don't have much in the way of machinery to help us.'

The field they had walked into had some Kerry Hill ewes and lambs in who all ran off as soon as they caught sight of the two interlopers. A thick hedge ran up one side of the field and, through some small gaps, Jude could see a herd of black and brown cattle on the other side. She didn't know much about cows but she assumed they were for beef rather than dairy as she hadn't seen any sign of a milking shed.

'I didn't know you kept cows as well,' she said.

'Ah no, those belong to our neighbour. I don't think I could ever keep cattle after seeing my parents' farm absolutely devastated by TB.' Ffion shook her head at the memory. 'It wiped out so many animals we wondered for a while if we might have to sell the farm. I've never seen my father in bits like that before, or since for that matter. It was awful.'

'I'm so sorry to hear that.' Jude knew just how damaging the bovine disease was. It spread easily and any cow who tested positive was given an instant death sentence which was both tragic and costly for the farmer who had reared them.

'I'm happy enough to stick with my sheep,' said Ffion.

They'd been walking up the length of the field and found Carl at the other end with a pile of rotten wood next to him and a gate that was clearly too narrow for the gap he had to fit it into. A chestnut and white border collie was lying patiently on the grass nearby and his ears pricked up at the sound of people approaching.

'Hi there, Jude.' Carl stopped breaking up the old gate and took off the heavy-duty gloves he'd been wearing. 'Come to lend me a hand?'

'It's a bit hot to be doing that, isn't it?' said Jude.

'Hot and dry. The ground is like concrete and I have to make two holes big enough to drop the new gate posts into.'

Ffion turned to Jude. 'I told him he should wait until the autumn when the ground will have softened up but when he gets a bee in his bonnet about something, he just can't stop.'

'Imagine if I didn't sort it and one of the gates collapsed altogether. The sheep could get out,' Carl said.

Ffion theatrically hid her mouth behind her hand to stage whisper to Jude. 'He's probably right but don't tell him I said that.'

'Anyway, I've got my foreman here who won't let me slacken off.' He crouched down and rubbed the dog affectionately on both sides of the head whilst pushing his own forehead into the soft patch of fur between the ears. 'Isn't that right, Tom, my lad?'

Jude had always thought that you could tell a lot about a person by the animals they chose and the way they interacted with them. Anyone who loved their dogs as much as Carl clearly did was okay by her.

'He's a beaut,' she said. 'Do you work him?'

'In theory that was the reason for buying him,' said Ffion drily. 'Tom's a good worker too, but Carl spoils him. I sometimes think that if it came down to a choice between him or me, I'd come off second place every time.'

'You don't appreciate the long walks that Tom and I love.' Carl stood up and put his arm around his wife. 'And you don't appreciate it when I try and give you tummy tickles.'

He laughed as Ffion dug him in the ribs and

shrugged him away, but there was a loving look exchanged which made Jude smile.

'I heard you sold your star ram to Griff Gould,' said Jude, feigning innocent conversation. 'Didn't fancy breeding off him yourselves first?'

Carl turned back to the rotten gate and carried on breaking it into pieces which he started to lob into the waiting trailer.

'He offered a fair price and we needed the money.' Ffion sounded a little defensive. Her version of the facts was somewhat at odds with what Frank had told Jude but she knew better than to push.

'I'll be keeping an eye on Griff's lambs come the spring,' Jude said.

'Been caught by the Kerry Hill bug, have you?' Ffion smiled. 'It's easily done. First you find a couple of good pedigrees to breed from and before you know it you're several years into a breeding programme and filling any land you can afford to rent with more and more of them.'

'You've certainly built yourself a good reputation,' said Jude.

'My dad helped us out initially, buying us some good breeding stock as a wedding present to get going and we've taken it from there, really.'

'You've got some beauties here,' said Jude.

'I'm keeping my eyes on the ram lambs in particular.' Ffion looked across at her animals. 'When they go to the Ludlow sale in September, I'll definitely be keeping a few of the best ones back to breed from.'

'It'll be good to get some decent money coming in.' Carl had finished loading the trailer with the old gate and was taking his gloves off again. 'Until I met Ffion, I had no idea how hard it is for farmers to make any money.'

'It's easy to see why people go looking for other ways to make money from their land,' Jude said.

'Like David Martin and that development plan of his, you mean?' Carl said. 'I suppose Griff will be happy that's not going ahead now that sneaky little sod's out of the way.'

'That's a bit much, Carl.' Ffion turned to Jude. 'Sorry.'

'Not at all,' said Jude. 'There's no rule that says we always have to be sad when someone dies, especially when that someone was found to have ruined your chances at the show with the underhand use of hair dye.'

As the words came out of her mouth, Jude remembered how upset Ffion had been after David's death and she felt awful for being so glib.

'Maybe not,' said Ffion. 'But whatever he did, it

was still a horrid way to go and we should at least respect the dead. Struggling to keep a farm going can mean the best of us make dubious decisions now and again.' She looked at her husband meaningfully until he turned away.

'I mean, just look at my sister.' Ffion turned back to Jude. 'Caitlin thought it would be a good idea to run a pop-up nightclub in one of the barns when our parents were away one weekend. Oh my God, it was a total disaster. The neighbours called the police, one man was arrested for being drunk and disorderly and my sister was slapped with a fine for taking money for tickets without the right licences.'

Carl chuckled. 'Thank God she'd been sensible enough not to try selling alcohol, at least. Although bring your own booze wasn't her smartest idea.'

Jude laughed along with them but couldn't help wondering if this was the example Ffion had truly been reminding her husband of when she'd shot him with a look of warning. Was there something else going on at the farm involving the Proctors that sat outside the law in order to try and bring a cash injection in? Was it something that David had known about, perhaps linked to the drugs he'd been dealing?

There were no obvious signs of cannabis growing

on the Proctors' farm but then she hadn't been invited into the house yet.

'You're right about the need to diversify,' said Jude. 'I set up a campsite on my farm and it's bringing in enough money to take the pressure off a bit. And I can see where your sister was coming from but don't you think that what David did stepped outside the realms of what's okay?'

The laughter stopped and Ffion raised her eyebrows. 'Well, we didn't appreciate the hair dye, that's for sure.'

'I didn't know the man,' said Carl. 'Not really. But I agree with you, Jude. He came across as underhand and sneaky. It's one thing pushing the boundaries a little to try and bring some extra cash in for the farm but it's something else altogether when what you do affects other people. If I'm being completely honest, I can see why someone out there snapped and did what they did.'

Jude searched his face for signs that he might be talking about himself or perhaps veiling a message to his wife to tell her that she shouldn't feel guilty.

'It was odd that he was found in the Greener Days pen, don't you think?' said Jude.

'Do you know, I was wondering about that too.' Ffion bent down to pick up some small shards of rotten wood that Carl had missed. 'After the hair dye trick though, who knows what he was up to in there?'

Ffion threw the bits of gate into the trailer. 'We'd better let you get on with the new posts if you're going to make this field sheep-proof today.'

Carl saluted. 'Right you are.'

'He's a nightmare with things like this,' Ffion said to Jude. 'Hard ground and no mechanical help, just Carl and his auger. The cursing will be foul so let's leave him to it.'

'Good luck,' said Jude. 'It was nice to see you, Carl.'

'You too, Jude. Now that you're in the Kerry Hill fold, no doubt we'll be seeing plenty more of you soon.'

Back in the farm yard, Ffion stopped short of the front door into the farmhouse again.

'It's such a mess in there,' she said. 'Let's go and sit in the garden, it's nicer outside whilst the sun is shining.'

There was no boundary between the front and back of the house and they walked around the side where weeds sprouted through the many cracks in the concrete. Someone had made an effort to smarten up the back garden with some geranium-filled planters but it still gave Jude the same unloved, slightly depressing feel as the ugly grey house. The grass had been cut but, other than the geraniums, there were very few plants or flowers growing. In one corner there was a pile of rubble and opposite that was an empty greenhouse with several broken panes of glass.

'I'm sorry about the state of the place,' said Ffion. 'We had so many plans for clearing this all out and turning it into a haven, but we can't really make a start until we've sorted the farm itself out. Any spare time we have at the moment is spent decorating the inside of the house. It was last done up in the seventies and they chose the most hideous brown textured wallpaper for pretty much every room downstairs.'

'You've got super views.' Jude chose to hone in on the one thing that the garden did have going for it.

'We are lucky there.' Ffion looked out across the farmland towards the Brecon Beacons. 'We didn't take this place on for the house itself. We're here for the land and because it's cheap. One day, we'll get the house and garden looking nice but we've got masses of time for all that.'

Jude supposed the Proctors were still just in their twenties, early thirties at most. They were right at the start of their journey.

'Could I borrow your loo?' The tea Jude had

drunk at the Watsons had worked its way through and Jude was bursting for a wee.

'Of course.' Ffion pointed to a shack, tacked on to the outside of the house. 'There's one in there. You carry on and I'll go and find us something to drink.'

Jude opened the cobwebbed door and found a light pull dangling from the ceiling. The old workers' privy had been plumbed in at least, and there was a sink with soap, but Jude thought how odd it was that she'd been fobbed off with this instead of being invited in to use the house loo.

As she sat down with her shorts around her knees, a spider scuttled out from a crack in the wall and ran under the sink. Jude peed quickly and gave her hands a speedy wash so she could vacate the poky room. Back out in the sunshine, she shook her hands to dry them off and went over to sit down on a wooden bench, positioned so that it looked out over the fields.

Footsteps behind made her turn round. She expected to see Ffion returning with the drinks. Instead though she found herself staring at a man she didn't recognise who'd just come out of the farmhouse.

'Oh, hello there. Sorry, I was looking for Ffion.' The man approached with his hand outstretched. 'Hugh Davies. I'm Ffion's brother.'

'Jude Gray. It's nice to meet you.' Jude stood up and shook his hand. She could see the family resemblance in the sandy-red hair and green eyes. 'Ffion's gone in to get some drinks.'

'I must have just missed her.' Hugh pushed his hands into the pockets of his jeans. 'How do you know Ffion and Carl?'

'We met through the sheep, actually. We were both at the Three Counties over the weekend.'

Hugh's brow crinkled at the mention of the show. 'Nasty business, that.'

'Ah, Hugh.' Ffion came back then, carrying two glasses of something that had ice cubes bobbing about in it. 'I see you've met Jude.'

'Yes, she was telling me that she's also a Kerry Hill breeder.'

'Not yet,' said Jude quickly. 'I'm only at the beginning of the journey, really. I mainly have Cheviots and Suffolks. Are you still involved in your parents' farm?'

'Not these days, no,' said Hugh.

'He doesn't like getting his hands dirty.' Ffion laughed. 'Actually, he's here to help me with my financial planning and all the boring paperwork. Would you give us a second whilst I take him inside and get the computer running for him? I know he can't spare me much time today.'

'Of course.'

Hugh looked a little surprised as his sister bustled him away and Jude wondered if he knew that was the reason he was at Ffion's house.

'It was nice to almost meet you, Jude,' he said over his shoulder.

'You too.'

As Jude watched Ffion and Hugh disappear back into the house, she thought how strange the whole meeting had been. It was almost as though Ffion hadn't wanted Hugh and Jude to have the opportunity to talk. It was the same feeling she'd had when she'd been denied access inside to use the loo.

Ffion and Carl seemed to be desperate to hide something and Jude wished there was a way of finding out exactly what that was.

* * *

Jude arrived back in Malvern End a little too early to collect Sebbie from school so she decided to stop off at the village shop to get a few things first. Mrs James, who'd run the shop and post office for as long as anyone could remember, had taken to perching on a stool behind the counter in recent months to take the weight off her corns.

'Hello there, Jude,' she said when the little shop bell over the door alerted her to a customer's arrival. 'Are you on school duty today?'

'Just about to head over there and thought I'd see if you had any baps left.'

One of the bakers from Malvern Link supplied the shop with daily deliveries of fresh bread and they were always fast to disappear off the shelves.

'I don't have any plain ones I'm afraid, but I do have a few filled if you haven't had your lunch yet.'

'It was lunch I was hoping for,' said Jude. 'I know it's late but I've been out all day and forgot to pick up something to eat.'

Mrs James laced her hands over her pinny-clad waist. 'You'll fade away, Jude. Go and have a look in the fridge next to the cheeses and you'll find whatever we have left. I think there might be a couple of smoked ham and salad, a coronation chicken or an egg and cress.'

The shop door tinkled again and Jude turned to see village busybody, Janet Timms, enter.

'Afternoon,' said Janet. 'Nice to see you, Jude.'

'Afternoon, Janet.'

Whilst Janet Timms went straight to the

counter for a natter, Jude went over to the fridge and found that Mrs James had been spot on with her mental stocktaking. She chose the coronation chicken bap and took it over to the counter where she added the *Malvern Gazette* she'd missed from the Friday before and a packet of Maltesers that she would share with Sebbie in the car on the way home.

'Little did they know, ey?' Mrs James tapped a fingernail on the front page of the newspaper where the headline was one of excitement at the prospect of a sunny weekend at the Three Counties Show. 'I suppose it will be a different tone on Friday when the next one comes out.'

'I suppose it will,' said Jude.

'You were there, weren't you, Jude?' Janet Timms was practically vibrating in anticipation of a good piece of gossip to pass on.

'I was.' Jude was always a little cagey around some members of the Malvern End community.

'Did you know the poor man who was killed?'

'Our paths crossed briefly at the show, but I didn't know him.'

'Kerry told me he was a rough sort anyway, dealing drugs and the like,' said Mrs James.

Jude was aware of two pairs of eyes boring into

her as she waited for Mrs James to ring through the rest of her shopping.

'I'm not really sure,' said Jude.

'Do you think that had something to do with why he was killed?' Mrs James asked.

'It could have been some irate father or boyfriend.' Janet sniffed. 'I heard plenty of tales about Jim Martin's son when he was growing up. Had a thing for the ladies from what I could tell and I don't think he really cared which lady it was.'

Jude wondered at Janet's incredible skill for both keeping up with and remembering so much tittle-tattle over the years. Malvern End was a small village, but the Martins' farm was in Leigh Sinton, five miles away on the other side of Malvern Link. How on earth did she know about the people who lived out that way? She seemed to have it spot on so far.

'You knew him, Janet?' Mrs James was clearly interested.

'My cousin had a house that backed on to one of their fields. She was a terrible a gossip, Anne was. God rest her soul.'

Jude caught Mrs James' eye and gave the smallest of smiles at the irony of these words.

'Although I don't remember ever meeting Jim Martin and Griff Gould, I felt like I knew them because Anne would always tell me all about their latest arguments and escapades. It was like waiting for the next episode of *The Archers*.' Janet leant her elbows on Jude's newspaper that still hadn't been rung through the till. 'If they weren't quibbling about the boundary lines of their properties, they were objecting to overflowing ditches or overgrown hedges.'

'It seems such a shame for two neighbouring farmers to have fallen out like that,' said Jude. Although she loved her farming life, she knew that it was made easier because of the people she surrounded herself with. Jim was a widower with David as his only son, and Griff had never married. They could have provided each other with such valuable support and friendship and yet they couldn't be in the same room as each other without sparring.

'Anne told me that it had all gone bad when Jim married the love of Griff's life.' Janet was really getting into her stride now but this particular piece of gossip made Jude want to listen. The animosity between the two neighbours was clear but now here was a possible reason as to why it was so deeply set. 'Griff never got over the betrayal and never found anyone else to marry. Anne said that when the poor woman died of sepsis, so young too, both men were equally torn apart by it.'

'Gosh, how awful,' said Jude.

'It was,' said Janet, clearly pleased that her story was getting a reaction. 'Anne heard an almighty row between them soon afterwards, each blaming the other for her death.'

Janet stopped and pulled a face to emphasis the weight of this information.

Jude thought back to the anger and hatred she'd witnessed between Jim and Griff and the things Frank had told her, how they'd been pitching themselves against each other for as long as anyone could remember.

'It sounds like a terrible tragedy,' said Mrs James who was clearly enjoying the soap opera. 'What made them think they could blame each other?'

'It was the way the sepsis spread. Pam, that was Jim's wife, she fell on Griff's farm and cut herself pretty badly on an old piece of machinery. The wound became infected but they didn't seek medical help until it was too late. I suppose Griff was angry with Jim for not acting sooner and Jim thought Griff was to blame in the first instance for having dangerous rubbish lying around.'

It was such a sorry story and Jude found herself feeling equally sad for both men. It must have been so hard for Griff to live next door to the woman he loved who was married to someone else. It was a good enough reason for him to have harboured a deep hatred for both Jim and David for so many years.

'I can't help wondering what Pam was doing round at Griff's farm,' Janet said.

For as long as Jude had known Janet Timms, she had always had an effortless way of moving from facts, or at least a version of them, to speculation and insinuation.

'You don't think there was still something going on between her and Griff, do you?' Mrs James leant further across the counter.

'Stranger things happen all the time,' said Janet. 'And if there was something going on, then who's to say whether David was actually Jim's son.'

'Sorry, Mrs James, but could I pay please?' This was territory that Jude did not feel comfortable in. 'I don't want to be late for Sebbie.'

'Of course, dear.' Mrs James finally scanned Jude's shopping and passed her the credit card machine. 'See you again soon.'

Jude left the two women chattering about David Martin and whether or not Jim was actually his real father.

It was an interesting thought but Jude dismissed

it. She had seen David and Jim standing side by side and, although David was much taller and slighter than Jim, their facial features had definitely been carved from the same gene clay.

More interesting to her was the renewed reminder that David Martin had been a seasoned philanderer. Also that Griff had a real reason to hate Jim, and perhaps David too as the product of the love Jim had stolen from him. Where he and the Martins were concerned, feelings were deeply embedded like a pool of molten lava that had the capability of erupting with the merest catalyst.

David had been bullish in his drive to get the planning permission approved for the development on the Martins' farm. The note he'd written to the as yet unidentified person he was hoping to manipulate proved this. Perhaps he'd already had his reply and felt confident enough in the outcome of the planning meeting to taunt Griff. Griff already hated him so something like this could have been an instant spark to his bubbling anger, already on the verge of exploding.

'And what about Jim?' Jude muttered to herself as she opened the door of the car and threw her shopping onto the passenger seat. He hadn't wanted the development to go ahead either and he felt let down and used by his son. Jim had certainly been distraught by David's death, and his grief and shock were visceral and raw: there was no acting at play there. But was it possible this was more than the grief of losing a son? Could his sense of grief have been magnified exponentially with the guilt of having been the one to snap and attack his only child? Olivia had said she'd been to check on him but the timing of her alibi had been unclear so he wasn't ruled out completely.

Jude's bap lay untouched on top of the newspaper as she locked the car door and set off down the road towards the village primary school.

Everyone was a suspect. They all had means and motives and yet no evidence had so far come to light that would help weed out the killer from the rest.

That was when Binnie called.

'Jude, are you busy?' she said as soon as Jude answered.

'I'm just picking Sebbie up. What's up?'

'I had our lip-reading expert take a look at that video of Zander's. And it raises some very interesting questions.'

12

Jude waited just outside the school playground whilst Binnie told her what David had been so annoyed about on the day he'd been killed.

'There's not much to go on but he was definitely unhappy about something,' Binnie confirmed. 'We've got him saying "That's not what we agreed," and, "That's half as much again." Then he turns away from the camera so there's a bit missing. The last thing we got is him saying, "You're getting greedy."'

'You're right, it isn't much but it is interesting.' Jude had assumed David had been talking to Olivia so she tried to put her on the other side of the conversation, filling the gaps. 'Could Olivia be the one supplying him with the marijuana?'

'It's possible, of course, although I think she'd be daft to jeopardise Zander's reputation like that. If the two of them are as close as Tara said they are then I think that is unlikely.'

'They certainly don't need the extra money,' said Jude. 'Any update on whether it was definitely Olivia talking to David?'

'She's claiming she had no recollection of the conversation,' said Binnie. 'We've asked everyone but nobody can shed any light on it. It was filmed not long before you were all due to take your sheep into the ring so everyone was busy.'

'Me included,' said Jude. 'So if it was Olivia he was talking to then what else could it have been about? That blackmail note we found about the development plans?'

'I can't see how Olivia would fit into that scenario though. Can you?'

Jude couldn't but she filed that thought away for the time being. 'Perhaps it wasn't Olivia. Maybe someone else was in her pen for some reason and David was talking to them. Taking out the people we can see elsewhere in the shed, that just leaves Jim, Griff and Penny.'

'None of whom are admitting any knowledge of the conversation,' Binnie reminded her. 'And don't forget they weren't the only people at the show that day. David could easily have been talking to someone who had nothing to do with the Kerry Hill lot.'

Jude sighed. That certainly threw a wide net over thousands of people. And yet he had been right next to Olivia's pen and so she had to be the most likely candidate.

'Mull it over and see if you come up with anything,' said Binnie.

'Will do. Look, I've got to go now. I can see children already coming out of school and I don't want Sebbie to be the last one in the playground again.' Jude started to walk towards the school gates.

'Absolutely not,' said Binnie. 'You go. Are you around tomorrow, though? I have a day off if you want to meet for lunch.'

'That would be a nice treat,' said Jude. 'You can come to the farm if you like?'

'Only if you let me bring food,' said Binnie.

'Deal!' Jude smiled as she switched her phone off and dug it deep into the leg pocket of her cotton combat trousers.

As soon as Sebbie spotted his aunt he left his teacher behind and came flying across the tarmac to wrap his little arms around her legs.

'Aunty Judy, I had a terrible day today. Kai

wouldn't sit by me in music and then Layla told me I wasn't good at running in PE.'

'Oh dear. That does sound terrible but would it cheer you up if I told you there were Maltesers in the car and I planned on fish fingers and waffles for supper with baked beans and extra ketchup?'

Sebbie broke free and did a little dance of joy in the middle of the playground, all the worries of his day instantly dismissed with the promise of his favourite food.

Jude scooped up Sebbie's abandoned backpack and passed it to him before taking his gloriously squidgy hand in hers. Together they walked out of the playground and headed back to the Land Rover which was still parked outside the post office. Jude opened the door for Sebbie to climb up into his booster seat and then she clipped his seatbelt on. She closed the door and was about to get into the driver's seat when she heard the tinkle of the shop bell and turned to see Marco coming out armed with two string bags of groceries.

'Treating yourself.' Jude pointed to the bottle of red wine that was pushing against the knotted green string of the bag.

'Clara's coming round later to watch a film.'

At the mention of Clara's name, Jude's heart involuntarily – and rather annoyingly – flipped as she imagined the two of them cosied up on Marco's sofa together.

'Oh,' she said. 'I didn't realise you two were...' She felt awkward, as though she were trespassing on territory she had no right to be on. Marco wasn't hers. He never really had been so he could date whoever he wanted to. Of course he could.

So why did the thought of him with Clara make her feel so nauseous?

'Oh, no.' Marco blushed. 'It's nothing like that. We're just friends. Friends sharing a film and a bottle of wine.'

The relief was instant and physical which discombobulated Jude.

She shook her head to make light of both her outer misunderstanding and the inner turmoil it had created. 'Sorry,' she blundered. 'I just... Well, enjoy the film.'

'You're welcome to join us?'

Jude looked at him and suddenly knew with complete certainty how much she wanted to go to his house to share a bottle of wine with him. How very much she wanted to curl up on the sofa and laugh together at a funny film. But she also knew that Clara was not involved in her mind's scenario. She wanted

Marco to herself. He was the only man other than Adam to ever have ignited her in this way and yet she had built a defensive dam of excuses and half-reasons to stop herself from getting carried away with feelings that she wasn't sure she had room in her life for.

The thought of Marco and Clara together had created a small but significant crack in the dam and it seemed that it was all that had been needed for the pressure to cause the whole thing to collapse. The unexpected outpouring of realisation took Jude by surprise and she stepped backwards, away from Marco.

'Jude?'

'Sorry. That sounds like fun but I can't make it tonight.' She feared that her face was a complete giveaway and so she turned away and climbed into the safety of her car.

She wound the window down just enough to stick her hand out and give what she hoped was a friendly, nonchalant wave goodbye. 'Have fun this evening, and enjoy the film.'

Jude was aware that Sebbie was chattering away in the back of the car but she had no idea of a single word that he was saying.

She was listening to another voice in her head. And it was saying one thing on repeat.

You're in love with Marco. You're in love with Marco. You're in love with Marco.

* * *

It had been a long and exhausting day and by the time Lucy came back from work Jude felt spent both emotionally and physically.

'Sebbie's eaten,' she said. 'But I'm afraid I haven't cooked for us. Do you mind just having freezer food tonight?'

'Actually, do you mind if I take Noah out to the pub? It feels like we have hardly had a moment to talk recently and I want to pin him down on a few points of the wedding.' Lucy held her palms together. 'Sebbie is running on fumes so he should be out for the count by seven-thirty which would give you a nice quiet evening to yourself.'

'Of course,' said Jude. 'That's actually exactly what I could do with.'

Lucy hugged her sister. 'I'll pay you back tomorrow. I've got the whole day off so I'll cook us something nice and we can have a catch up over a leisurely lunch. I'm sure Noah and Frank can cope for a few hours without you.'

'Binnie's got the day off as well and she's coming over.'

Lucy grinned. 'Perfect, we can be ladies who lunch.'

'Lovely. Just don't expect me to wear my twinset and pearls. And there's no way I'm learning to play bridge until I retire.'

'Like you're ever going to give up farming.' Lucy kissed the top of Jude's head and went to pour herself a glass of water. 'You and Noah are the same. You'll both be driving your mobility scooters over the fields to check the sheep when you're ninety.'

'If I'm still able to be hands on around here when I'm that age then I have no need for bridge.'

'Fair point.'

* * *

Just as Lucy had predicted, Sebbie was tucked up in bed and fast asleep before half-seven. Jude changed into her pyjamas, poured herself a glass of cider and sat in front of the telly with the four dogs at her feet. She flicked through the channels but nothing was interesting enough to drag her mind away from the thing it most wanted to focus on. Her newly exploded feelings for Marco Ricci.

As the cider relaxed her and she gave herself permission to explore how she felt, Jude realised that there was nothing stopping her any more. She'd been creating barriers that had never truly existed and the time had come for her to take a hatchet to every one of them. When she got into bed that evening she looked at the photo of Adam that sat on the little table next to her. It had felt wrong to think of loving another man when she had promised herself to her husband for life. But life had chosen to give them only ten precious years together before death snatched him away.

'You'd be happy for me, wouldn't you?'

Jude knew what he would say. He would tell her that the most important thing to him had always been her happiness. He'd said it to her time and again and then, when he knew the cancer had progressed to a point beyond hope, Adam had talked to her about life once he was no longer in it. He had told her to find someone else and she had dismissed him, not ready to listen then. But she was ready now and the words he'd gifted her all those years ago wrapped her up in a blanket of certainty.

'You'd like him,' she said to Adam's photo. 'He's a good'un.'

As she closed her eyes, Jude felt a lightness of relief that she had finally allowed herself the release to let Marco in. As she drifted into a happy sleep, she imagined heading down to see him in his cottage the next day and telling him that she was ready to give him what he wanted. Because Jude now knew with her whole heart that it was what she wanted too.

* * *

Like a divine metaphor, Jude was woken by the sunshine streaming through her window and instantly she remembered why she had slept with a smile on her face.

She wanted to jump out of bed and head straight over the fields to see Marco but it was too early and she had animals to tend to first.

As she made herself a morning mug of coffee, Jude found that she was quietly humming to herself.

'You're in a good mood today,' said Noah as he joined her in the kitchen. 'It must be the thought of spraying the sheep today.'

Spraying the flock to keep away flies was vital to help prevent the nastiness of eggs being laid and maggots hatching on the skin of the animals. Jude loved working the fields with Noah and the dogs, rounding the sheep up and treating each one. She had, however, temporarily forgotten that they had scheduled it in for that day.

'Do you think Frank might be able to help out?' she said. 'There's something I need to do down in the village and then I'm having lunch with Lucy and Binnie. Or we could do it tomorrow?'

'I'm sure my dad will be only too happy to help with the spraying.' Noah poured himself a mug of coffee. 'What are you doing down in the village that's so urgent?'

Jude averted her gaze just in case Noah could read her face like the front cover of a gossip magazine. 'Actually, I'm going to see Marco about something.'

'Is that why you were humming to yourself when I came in?' Noah chuckled.

'Can't I just be humming because it's a sunny morning and I've got a lunch date booked in that doesn't involve me preparing food of any description?'

'Jude, you know I think you deserve whatever it is that makes you this happy on a Wednesday morning.'

Noah came to stand next to her. He put his hands on her shoulders and turned her to face him. 'And for what it's worth, Adam would say the exact same thing. Nobody deserves to hum on a Wednesday more than you do.'

'Thanks, Noah.' Jude rested her head against her old friend's chest and let him hug her for a moment before she pulled away. 'Right then, we'd better get on and make the most of the best part of the day.'

* * *

Jude felt an intoxicating mix of excitement and nerves as she went through her morning jobs. With Noah's encouragement she was now even more sure that she was doing the right thing but it was still early and she had to be patient.

She let the Runner ducks out of their stable and checked the rest of the paddock animals were okay. Then she headed over to the orchard at the end of the garden to see to the Bantam hens she kept in henhouses under the apple and pear trees. Whilst she gathered up the daily haul of small but delicious eggs and boxed them up to go in the honesty box at the end of the drive, she could not stop thinking about Marco. What would he say when she told him how she felt?

Jude glanced at her watch. It was only seven. Still early but perhaps by the time she went inside and cleaned herself up, had a bit of breakfast with Lucy and Sebbie, it would be a decent enough hour to go down to the village. She could walk Sebbie across the fields to drop him off at school and pop round to Marco's cottage afterwards.

Sebbie and Lucy were both equally on board with Jude's plan when she put it to them. Lucy hardly ever had the opportunity to enjoy a leisurely morning shower and Sebbie loved walking to school but there was rarely a morning where they managed to get themselves organised early enough to make it happen.

'I have a couple of things to do in the village,' Jude said to Lucy as she and Sebbie put their shoes on. 'I'll see you when I see you.'

'Thanks, Jude.'

Sebbie ran ahead of her, his backpack bouncing jauntily on his back as he crossed the yard and opened the gate into the first field.

'Come on, Aunty Judy,' he called over.

Jude smiled and picked up her pace to try to match her young nephew. As they walked, they chatted about all the things that interested Sebbie the most. The farm itself was always a hot topic and Jude was constantly hopeful that he might be keen to take it on when he was old enough. She and Adam hadn't had children so succession of Malvern Farm either meant Sebbie or it would have to be sold off.

'Wouldn't it be cool if we could have dinosaurs on the farm?' Sebbie looked at Jude, his little rosy cheeks bursting with innocence as he found a way to link his second biggest passion to the farm.

'Don't you think that would be a bit scary for the sheep?' Jude asked.

'No, because we wouldn't get the meat eaters, we'd only choose dinosaurs that are herbivores. Did you know that means they only eat plants?'

'You're absolutely right.'

Sebbie carried on filling Jude's morning with dinosaur facts as they left the farmland and walked down the path that led down into the village. As they passed Marco's cottage, Jude glanced up at his bedroom window and saw that the curtains were open which meant he was already up and about.

They carried on until they got to the school in the middle of the village and Jude waited as patiently as she could in the playground, chatting to some of the parents of the other children until the bell rang.

'Have a good day.' She kissed Sebbie goodbye. 'And watch out for any stray velociraptors hiding under your chair.'

Sebbie laughed and ran off to join the line of children standing in front of their adored teacher, Miss Elgar.

With the distraction of Sebbie removed, Jude's nerves took over and she found her mouth drying out and her palms becoming sticky as she walked back to Marco's cottage.

'Don't be so daft,' she told herself. 'Pull yourself together and get on with it.'

Before she could chicken out, Jude marched up to the front door and pushed the doorbell. She waited for the sound of bare feet padding down the hall to open the door but all was quiet inside.

After psyching herself up for her big moment, Jude felt a crush of disappointment. She had seen his blue Renault 4 parked on the road outside the cottage so she supposed he was either somewhere in the village or had set off on one of his early morning hikes. These often lasted for hours, especially if he took his sketch book with him, so there was little point in hanging around waiting.

Jude walked back down the garden path and let

herself out of the gate just as Clara was coming out of the cottage next door.

'Morning, Jude,' she said. 'If you're looking for Marco, I saw him heading out a little while ago. He had his backpack on so I assumed he's gone off on one of his sketching expeditions.'

'I thought that must be it,' said Jude. 'It doesn't matter, it wasn't anything important. How was your wine and film evening? Sorry I couldn't join you.'

'It was fun, thanks. Anyway, I'd better get going. I'm already late for work.'

As Jude watched Clara get into her car, a seed of something unappetising drifted into the deeply ploughed furrows of Jude's mind. Had she imagined it or had Clara flushed a little when Jude had mentioned her evening with Marco?

Clara drove off and Jude turned to walk back to the track that ran behind her fields. The treacherous seed began to push roots down and Jude started imagining what might have happened between Clara and Marco whilst she had been on her own in the farmhouse planning on how best to tell him that she loved him.

Had she left it too late? The thorny doubt that was growing quickly in her mind twisted around the excited expectation she had woken up with and threatened to suffocate it.

'Stop being so bloody melodramatic,' she said to herself. 'It was just a film and a bottle of wine, Marco told you that himself. Wait until you have a chance to talk to him before you start jumping to conclusions based on nothing but a smile.'

Jude took out her phone and sent Marco a message before she had a chance to think too much more about it.

> Morning. Hope you had fun last night. Just been round to see you but obviously you're not home. Assume you're out either walking or sketching. Wondered if we could meet up today when you're back? There's something I want to talk to you about. J xx

* * *

With her morning plans somewhat scuppered and no desire to waste time dwelling on things whilst she waited for Marco to get back to her, Jude pulled her work clothes on and went out to help Frank and Noah with the sheep spraying.

It was exactly the distraction she needed and

Noah knew without a single word from either of them that she didn't want to talk about why she had swapped a morning with Marco for a field of sheep.

Spraying sheep was definitely not a three-person job but Jude was happy to be out there with the animals and she enjoyed the methodical practice. With Floss taking things easier these days, it was down to Ned and Alfie to bring the sheep into the pens. Frank was waiting with the fly repellent strapped to his back and nozzle in hand ready to give each animal a dose. Two strokes up the back and one across the rump painted them blue and gave them the coverage they'd need to hopefully last the rest of the summer.

Jude then scanned their ear tags to log each individual medical record and the animals were let out to enjoy the pasture fly-free.

It wasn't exactly the morning she'd been hoping for when she'd woken up but Jude enjoyed her work and by the time she went in to clean up for lunch she had reclaimed some of her earlier bonhomie.

There was an enormous amount of food as both Binnie and Lucy had been busy in their kitchens that morning and they decided to take everything out to the garden to enjoy a spot of the al fresco whilst the weather was so glorious.

The garden at the front of the farmhouse was a

tranquil haven with views out over the orchard towards the hills.

Jude had thought of talking to Binnie and Lucy about Marco but she decided that she would keep it to herself until she knew exactly how things stood between them. She kept glancing at her phone to see if there were any messages from him but it remained stubbornly empty.

Once lunch had finished, the lazy afternoon spent sipping spritzers and picking at the remains of a pavlova felt decadent and whilst Jude was thoroughly enjoying it, she couldn't help feeling a little guilty. It was very unlike her to be idle at the farm when there were jobs to be done, but everyone needed a bit of a treat now and again.

'What time is it?' Lucy asked as they debated whether or not to pour another drink.

Binnie picked up her phone. 'Two forty-five,' she said.

'Bollocks,' said Lucy. 'I'll have to go and fetch Sebbie from school.'

She reluctantly got to her feet and Jude started to follow, but Lucy stopped her.

'No need for us to call it a day. I'll be half an hour, you two stay put and we can carry on when I get back.'

'Good plan.' Whilst Lucy left the garden, Jude sat back in her chair and looked at Binnie who had her phone against her ear.

'Everything okay?' Jude asked when she'd finished.

'Fancy a trip to Leigh Sinton to get some answers?' Binnie replied.

'Jim or Griff?' Jude was instantly intrigued.

'Griff just left me a voicemail to say he has some urgent information to pass on to me but he wants to do it off the record.'

'About David?'

'He didn't say. I just tried calling back but he isn't picking up so I thought we could take a drive out there.'

'I'll get myself ready,' said Jude.

* * *

There was no sign of Griff when Jude and Binnie pulled up outside his farm.

'I can see why he was so anti any development on Jim's farmland,' said Jude as she looked out across the fields. 'It's beautiful here and that lane we've just driven down would be a nightmare if there was a constant stream of building vehicles going up and down it.'

'Let's go and see if he's in,' said Binnie.

Binnie knocked on the front door but all was quiet. Whilst she tried a second time, Jude walked over to the window and used her hands to shield her eyes from the sun's glare as she looked inside. Some-one, she supposed it was Griff but she could only see the back of his head, was sitting in an armchair.

'Binnie, he's in there.' Jude rapped on the window but Griff didn't move. 'It looks like he's out for the count. There's a whisky bottle on the table next to him.'

As Binnie came over to take a look, Jude saw that there was something else there too. A little orange pot had been tipped over with what looked like white tablets spilling from it. Suddenly, Griff's utter stillness seemed very much more sinister and it made Jude's blood cool.

'Griff,' she shouted, banging on the window with more desperation. 'Binnie, we've got to get in there.'

'Shit.' Binnie ran back to the door and tried the handle. 'It's unlocked,' she said.

The two women ran into the house and round to the room they had seen Griff in. As soon as they arrived it became sickeningly apparent that whisky and tablets weren't the only thing they had to worry about.

One of his wrists had been sliced at the artery and blood had pooled on the carpet beneath.

'Oh crap.' Jude rushed forward to see if there were any signs of life.

Binnie had dialled the emergency services on the way in and was already talking to an operator.

'I don't know exactly what he's consumed but there's a pot of benzodiazepines and a bottle of whisky... I don't know, someone is checking for signs of life now.' Binnie looked at Jude who shook her head.

She knew that when an artery was severed, if the heart was still beating it would force blood from the wound in rhythmic spurts. Griff's limp arm was covered in what looked like very fresh blood, but the wound itself had run dry.

'He's already dead,' she said.

13

If the benzodiazepines, whisky bottle and sliced wrist weren't strong enough clues that Griff had chosen to take his own life then the note on the table seemed to make things pretty conclusive. On a single sheet of cheap A4 printer paper was a simple handwritten message in a scratchy cursive font.

I am David Martin's killer.
I can't live with what I did.
I am sorry. This is my justise.
Griffin Gould

Jude went to pick the note up and felt the thin paper crease beneath her fingers.

'Stop,' said Binnie. 'This is now a crime scene. We can't touch anything.'

'Sorry.' Jude let go of the paper. She was still crouched on the floor next to the body and stared at the table, taking as many details in as she could. The note, with the final word incorrectly spelled. The almost empty whisky bottle and glass. The sedatives, spilt from an American-style drugs pot. The surgical-style scalpel.

'It doesn't make sense to me,' she said. 'Why only cut one wrist? If he wanted to kill himself then surely he'd have done both.'

'With that amount of alcohol and drugs in his system perhaps he passed out before he had a chance to cut the other wrist,' Binnie suggested.

'No.' Jude pointed to the blade on the table. 'If he'd passed out then the blade would have fallen on the floor. And look at which wrist has been cut.'

'His right side,' said Binnie. 'Which would only make sense if he was left-handed.'

'Exactly,' said Jude. 'But we know he was right-handed because you checked all the suspects after David was killed. And if he didn't cut his own wrist, then who did?' Jude looked around the room. There had been no sign of anybody in the house when they'd entered, and she hadn't seen any other vehicles in the farmyard. 'It only takes a couple of minutes for a person to bleed out from a severed artery. Could we have arrived just as someone was in the process of killing Griff? Perhaps we disturbed them before they finished the job and they scarpered before we could get a glimpse of them.'

Binnie took her phone out and put in another call. 'It's DI Khatri here. Listen, I'm at Heath Farm in Leigh Sinton, owned by Griff Gould, a suspect in the David Martin murder case. I need a team up here ASAP, he's been found dead and there's a chance the murderer is still in the vicinity. I have no description but they could be on foot and covered in blood.'

Jude was already on her feet and heading for the door.

'Where are you going?' Binnie said.

'There's a good chance the murderer is still close by. We'd have heard if anyone had driven off and the place is surrounded by fields so they'd be out in the open if they left on foot.'

'So you're going to hunt them down on your own?' Binnie made it sound as though Jude was being reckless but Jude knew it was the right thing to do if they were going to catch the killer before they got too far away.

'If we're right then whoever killed Griff almost

certainly murdered David too. Why else would they try and frame Griff for it? And we know that if someone kills twice, then they are very likely to do it again.'

Jude didn't wait for Binnie's reply before heading out of the house and searching for signs that someone had recently made a hasty departure. Looking across the fields bore no fruit so Jude turned her attention to the collection of barns and out-buildings.

'Anything?' Binnie asked, coming to stand next to her.

'I can't see anyone out in the fields but they could be hiding in one of those sheds, or they might still be in the house somewhere.'

'Yeah, well if they are then there's a good chance they'll have their eye on us, ready to attack if we get too close.' Binnie stood with her hands on her hips. 'The team are on their way and they're trained prop-erly for this sort of thing. We need to stay out here until they arrive.'

Jude didn't argue. It was pointless as Binnie was right. Out in the yard, they could be on sentry duty to make sure anybody who might still be lurking couldn't escape.

Although nobody came out of the house or the

outbuildings before the police arrived, someone did walk up the driveway with a thunderous look on his face.

'Jude, DI Khatri, what are you pair doing here?' Jim asked.

Jude looked down the rutted track and thought how easy it would have been for Jim to have left Griff's house by the back door whilst she and Binnie were completely focused on the dead body they'd just stumbled across. The driveway was long but it twisted round a bend and he would have been safely out of sight before Jude had come out of the house. He wouldn't have needed a vehicle to get from his farm on the other side of the road at the end of Griff's drive. But if he was escaping a murder scene then why not carry on until he was safely back home?

At that moment, Jude heard the sirens. It meant the help they'd called for would soon be with them. Help that Jim Martin would have known they'd summon. If they turned up whilst he was still walking away from the farm, he would be the instant chief suspect. But if they discovered him going towards the scene of the crime then it would be infinitely less suspicious.

Except, if that had been his plan, it hadn't worked as Jude had instantly marked him as the most likely candidate. He had all the motivation to want Griff dead. The rot of years of anger and hatred had peaked when Jim blamed his neighbour for David's murder. Had he come to take his revenge, planting a suicide note that told the truth he was so sure about? If so then was Jim right? Had it been Griff who'd killed David?

'Jim, I'm going to need you to stay here with us.' Binnie took control of the situation, instantly picking up the role of on duty detective.

'Why? What's he done now?' Jim was red in the face and he wiped sweat from his brow with the back of his hand. 'I was right, wasn't I? You found proof that he was involved in my David's death? He's had it in for me ever since I married my Pam.'

'Mr Martin, please stay calm. My colleagues are on their way and when they arrive I will be able to talk to you properly.'

'I knew it. Did he do it himself, or was it Ffion Davies and her fancy husband?'

'You mean the Proctors?' Jude wondered why Jim had brought them into the conversation.

'Griff's definitely got something on them. Did you know they sold him that winning ram for next to nothing?'

Jude nodded. 'I'd heard about that.'

'I reckon he'd have gone for ten thousand guineas if they'd taken him to market. I've not seen a gem like that in all my days rearing Kerries. So it got me thinking. The only way they'd have let that animal go is because Griff was blackmailing them or something.'

'What are you inferring, Mr Martin?' Binnie asked.

'I'm saying that if Griff didn't kill David himself then perhaps he knew who did and he's trying to get rich by keeping their secret.'

A police car and ambulance arrived at the farm at the same time and Binnie went to speak to the paramedics.

'Why's there an ambulance?' Jim said. 'What's happened?'

Jude watched his reaction. He was either a very good actor or he genuinely had no idea what had happened to his neighbour and nemesis.

A uniformed officer that Jude recognised as a friendly man called Nige, came over to speak to her.

'Jude, good to see you. I gather you were with DI Khatri when the body was found?'

'Body?' Jim looked appalled. 'Whose body? What happened here?'

'Oh, I'm sorry,' Nige faltered. 'I assumed everyone here would know why we'd been called.'

'This is Jim Martin, Griff Gould's neighbour. He just came round to talk to him about something.'

'Is it Griff?' Jim looked over at the house. 'Has something happened to him?'

Jude's phone rang as Nige tried to placate Jim without being able to give him the details he wanted. With a sudden jolt of the heart, she saw it was Marco calling and stepped away from the others to answer. So much had happened since she'd sent him the message that morning. It all seemed wholly inappropriate now, given where she was and what had happened in the house behind her.

'Sorry it's taken me so long to call you,' said Marco. 'I had my phone off so that I could really focus on the scenery. I'm trying out a new style which I hope will be popular with Malvern's tourists.'

'That's okay, it's ended up being a bonkers sort of day anyway.'

'You okay? You sound distracted.'

'There's actually a lot going on at the moment. If you're around later then perhaps I can come down for a drink and tell you about it then?'

'Of course. I'll be home all evening so just come whenever you like. Actually, there was something I wanted to talk to you about as well.'

Despite herself, Jude tingled at the thought of an evening with Marco. 'I'll come around seven then.'

'Perfect. See you then.'

Jude put her phone in her pocket and turned back to the scene outside Griff's farmhouse. Another two squad cars had arrived and uniformed officers were moving in to search the barns.

Jude assumed that others were in the house, going from room to room in case anyone was still inside. Binnie had gone to guard the crime scene whilst they waited for the forensics team. She was Jude's ride home so there was nothing she could do except wait.

Nige had taken Jim off and Jude was on her own so she sat on the corner of a low stone wall and let her mind drift back to what she'd seen in the room where Griff had died.

The more she thought about it, the more she felt sure she was right and that Griff had not taken his own life, but someone had gone to great lengths to make it look as though he had. Not just that but they were also framing him for the murder of David Martin. Maybe someone who knew what it was that Griff had been about to tell Binnie and wanted to stop him?

On the surface, Jim Martin seemed to be the obvious suspect. He had motive and he was the only one so far who had the means to do it. If it had been anyone else then where had they gone? The only way the single wound to the right wrist made sense was if Jude and Binnie had disturbed the murderer, in which case they'd have had to escape quickly. The fields around the farm were open for miles with nowhere to hide. If they'd gone down the driveway by foot then Jim would have met them coming the other way. The high hedges on either side would have offered them no easy place to hide. And there was no quick getaway to be had as there had been no sign or sound of a vehicle.

Jude tried to retrace the steps of the killer. Someone had come to the farm. How? Either they'd walked, they'd come by some sort of invisible, noiseless car or Griff had driven them there himself. Was that an option? It would explain the lack of another vehicle in the yard.

Whoever had come to the farm must have drugged Griff, significantly enough for him to lose consciousness so they could slit his wrist. Jude had noticed on the label stuck to the yellow pot that each tablet contained 10mg of sedative which seemed liked a pretty high dose. She guessed that, especially when mixed with alcohol, it wouldn't take too many tablets to have knocked him out. But how had they got Griff to take the tablets? He obviously wouldn't have taken them voluntarily but maybe someone crushed the benzodiazepine into his whisky.

A quick search on her phone showed Jude that this couldn't have been the case as the tablets were not soluble so they would have left a gritty and obvious residue at the bottom of the glass. Had something else been used and the tablets left there as a red herring? If that was the case then whoever had done it was seriously blinkered if they thought the post-mortem wouldn't pick this up.

Perhaps he hadn't known what he was taking. Jude tried to think of a situation where this would make sense – if he had a headache maybe and the killer had persuaded him that the tablets were nothing more than paracetamol. But then how would they have known that Griff would need painkillers? It was all very flaky.

Binnie came over. 'I'm sorry about this, Jude. I can't leave yet but once someone has taken your statement, you're welcome to drive my car back to the farm. I can get a lift with Sami.'

She passed Jude her car keys.

'Thanks,' said Jude. 'I'll stay here for now and see how things go.'

'Okay. I'll send Sami over soon.'

Binnie hurried off and Jude turned her thoughts to the note. The writing was scratchy and unusual, probably quite difficult to fake unless someone had been practising. Again, if someone had tried to fake the note then they were playing a dodgy game as handwriting specialists were trained to pick up the smallest anomalies. Time would tell if the writing was a match to Griff's or not, but if it was then how could someone have made him write such a thing?

It was possible that he had written the note himself as a true confession of his guilt, Jude supposed. When he'd told Binnie he had something important to tell her, perhaps it had in fact been to free himself of his guilty secret. Had he bottled it last minute and decided to take his own life rather than face up to the consequences of his actions? There was something about the misspelling of the word justice that somehow gave it a whiff of authenticity.

Jude felt that suicide was unlikely given what she'd seen and yet it was not impossible. He could have picked up the scalpel in his left hand and chosen to only cut one wrist before setting the blade back on the table for a reason that they might never know. But the pot of tablets bothered her. They were not UK prescription drugs or they would have come in blister packs. So how had Griff managed to get hold of them? Jude had no doubt that anyone who knew their way around the dark web would be able to get their hands on any type of medication they wanted. But Griff had barely even known his way around the simplest functions on his own phone so the idea that he had cracked the deepest crevices of the web's underworld seemed ridiculous.

Jude realised that this might well also be further indication that Jim hadn't been the one who had killed Griff. They were of the same ilk and Jude couldn't imagine either of them mastering illegal drug purchases.

'Hi there, Jude,' said Sami, coming to sit down next to her on the wall. 'How are you doing?'

'I'm going over a few things in my mind that just don't make sense,' said Jude.

'Binnie told me that you were the one who initially doubted that we're looking at a suicide?' Sami picked at the moss growing on the wall next to him. 'It's a pretty convincing set up with the note and everything but I think we're all on the same page in thinking that something fishy happened here today.'

'I think someone has gone to a lot of trouble to set a scene and then blown it by not finishing the job properly,' said Jude.

'You mean they only cut his right wrist?'

'That was the first mistake, yes. But there are others as well. The sedatives, for example. They're obviously not prescription but where would someone like Griff, with his archaic views on technology, have bought illegal medication?'

'Could he know someone with the right connections?'

Jude raised an eyebrow. 'An old stalwart of the farming community like Griff? I can't see it myself although of course it's always a possibility. But why bother? I mean, if he was going to slit his wrists anyway, why did he need the benzodiazepine? He'd have known that death would be quick without it.'

'Good point,' said Sami.

'And why today? He'd just left Binnie a voicemail to say he wanted to talk to her about something but then apparently killed himself before he had the chance.'

Jude felt sure that the timing wasn't a coincidence. If someone knew that Griff was about to spill whatever piece of vital information he had then they may have killed to stop him.

'It is always possible that the message was left to make sure Binnie brought the police round here and they would find his body with the note,' said Sami.

Jude rubbed her eyes in frustration. 'Ah yes, that note,' she said. 'How did that come about if he didn't write it as a suicide note.'

'Forgery?' said Sami.

'It would be tricky writing to copy.' Something else dawned on Jude then. 'Did you see it?'

'Only Binnie and the paramedics have been allowed in until forensics have finished. Why?'

'It's just that the note was written on A4 printer paper so if Griff did write it then the paper would match that in his printer.'

'There can't be that many different types of printer paper out there but I suppose it's worth checking.' Sami took out his pocketbook and made a note. Jude knew that his body cam would be recording their conversation but he'd obviously thought of something that he wanted to highlight.

'It felt like really cheap, flimsy stuff and it might sound odd to you but it was a different shade of white to the one I use at home, for example. I think it should be easier than you think to tell if it's the same as the stuff in his printer and if it isn't then that obviously means it was written elsewhere.'

'Interesting,' said Sami. 'So let's say that Griff didn't do this himself. Who do you think did? Jim Martin?'

Jude sucked in a deep breath. 'He was in the vicinity and clearly had strong reasons to want to kill, but if it *was* him then he is a very convincing actor.'

'We've both met plenty of those over the years so I'd say that certainly isn't a reason to discount him. And with a son like David, known for dabbling in at least marijuana, there's every chance there were other illegal drugs – like non-prescription knock-out pills – lying around the house.'

Jude knew Sami was right. Just because Jim hadn't acted like a killer when he turned up on the farm, didn't mean he wasn't one. If the police found nobody else at the scene then surely that not only made him a suspect, but the chief one too.

'The only thing is that there doesn't seem to be any blood on Jim,' said Sami. 'I would have thought that if you cut one of the main arteries in someone whose heart was still pumping, it would go off like a water pistol and there'd be blood everywhere.'

'There was, I saw it.' Jude thought for a moment. 'Jim has lived his entire life around animals. I bet he's slaughtered a few in his time so he would know exactly what to expect. If he stood behind, worked fast and got out of the way then there's every chance he could have avoided the spray. Especially if he was wearing a pair of gloves.'

'I hadn't thought of it like that,' said Sami. 'Then I think we have our first suspect. Nige has taken him down to the station so we'll see if he breaks.'

'It's a shame we never got to find out what it was that Griff wanted to tell Binnie.'

Another car arrived and two people got out. As Jude watched them suiting up in white forensic suits, she imagined what Griff's important piece of information might have been. It was of course possible that he had known who killed David. But it could equally have had something to do with the production or dealing of hash that David had been involved with. Maybe he knew something that linked the two crimes together.

'Jude, do you mind if I take an initial statement from you?' Sami asked. 'Got to dot all the i's and cross every t or Binnie will have me on desk duty for a month.'

It wasn't the first time Jude had been called on to make a statement and she felt relieved to get it out of the way. She had always had a brilliant eye for spotting the small details and was blessed with a strong memory so she could give a clear account of what she'd noticed on arrival at the farm, and how she and Binnie had found the body. She answered all Sami's questions and watched as he jotted the odd thing down in his pocketbook.

'Thanks for that,' he said when he'd finished. 'Very useful as always.'

'Binnie's given me her car keys so I can get home but I don't want to leave her stranded.'

'Don't worry about her. She won't want to leave until everybody else does, you know that. DI Khatri is here for the duration and there are plenty of people who can get her back to the station. I can drive her over to the farm later to pick the car up, you head off.'

'Are you sure?' Jude felt bad for leaving and yet there was nothing else she could do there. Besides, the afternoon had started to seep into the evening and she wanted to get home so she could tidy herself up before going down to see Marco.

'Go. It's fine.'

With that, Jude took her leave and headed back to her farm.

14

'You're looking nice,' said Lucy when Jude walked into the kitchen, ready to head down into the village.

'I look clean, that's all.' Jude smiled. 'You're just not used to it.'

'I'm glad you're going out after the afternoon you've had. You look like you could do with relaxing for a bit, you're all jittery.' Lucy stared at her sister and narrowed her eyes. Jude felt as though she was being opened up so that Lucy could see right into her inner thoughts. 'Oh my goodness, this is a date, isn't it?'

'I'm just going round to Marco's for a couple of drinks.' Jude felt herself flush and was grateful to Noah who clearly hadn't already told Lucy her secret.

'No you're not. You're wearing your best top, I can smell perfume and is that mascara I see? This is not a few drinks with a friend, these are all the signs that you're finally ready to take things further with Marco.'

Jude couldn't deny it; there was little point as Lucy knew her well and had sussed her completely. 'Don't make a big deal about it. I just thought it was worth having a conversation with him to see if he still wants, you know, something more from me.'

Lucy threw her arms around Jude and hugged her tightly. 'Of course he does, any idiot can see that. You're the perfect fit for each other, we've all been telling you that for the past two years.'

Jude hoped that Lucy was right and that she wasn't about to make a huge mistake and ruin the friendship that she held so dear.

'Right then, blow in my face so I can check your breath.'

Jude did as she was told and held her hands out so Lucy could check her stubby fingernails passed the cleanliness test.

'Am I good to go?' she asked.

'You, my gorgeous sister, are perfect to go.' Lucy kissed her on the cheek. 'Have fun.'

It was only two days before midsummer and the

sun was keen to make the most of it. Although it was almost seven when Jude set out to walk over the fields, it was bright enough to be the middle of the afternoon. She sucked in deep lungfuls of summer air to try to take the edge off her heightened state of expectation but by the time she arrived at Marco's front door, the nerves had well and truly kicked in.

As soon as Marco opened his front door and Jude caught a familiar whiff of his cottage – oil paints and linseed mixed with his citrusy shower gel and fresh coffee – she relaxed. He was her safety and she belonged there with him.

'Jude, what happened?' His face was full of concern. 'You sounded so distracted on the phone, I've been worried about you all afternoon.'

He ushered her into the sitting room where a bottle of her favourite red wine was already opened and breathing.

'Here.' He poured her a generous glass and handed it over. 'Now tell me everything.'

Jude took a mouthful of wine and felt it ease her muscles as she relaxed back into the soft sofa cushions.

'There's been another murder,' she began.

Marco listened without interruption as Jude told him about her afternoon at Griff's farm. She left

nothing out and it felt so good to be able to offload
her thoughts and feelings in the warmth and protec-
tion of Marco's sitting room.

'Bloody hell,' said Marco when she'd finished.
'You must be really shaken after seeing that. And
they didn't find anyone else on the farm apart from
Jim Martin?'

'No.' Jude took another sip of her wine. 'They
searched every inch of the house and outbuildings
but there was nobody there.'

'So either Jim killed him or someone else managed to make a very sneaky escape somehow whilst
you and Binnie were in with Griff.'

'That's about the shape of things at the moment,
yes.'

Jude had had enough of talking about murder
and wanted to lighten the mood. 'So that was my day.
But tell me something lovely, how was your sketching
trip?'

'Fruitful,' said Marco. 'It was such a glorious day, I
walked for miles and did some sketches for a couple
of new paintings. Then I people-watched up on the
ridge. I thought I'd try and use pictures of walkers,
cyclists, joggers, dogs, kite fliers, basically everyone
who uses the hills as the starting point for my next

series of greetings cards. It's not exactly fine art but it does bring in good money.'

'That's a great idea,' said Jude. 'And you're so good at it too.'

Marco smiled at her and rested his head back on the sofa. For a while they just sat together in easy silence sipping their wine and enjoying being in each other's company. It seemed like the perfect time for Jude to bring up the topic of conversation that she had really come to talk to Marco about. And then she remembered that he'd mentioned on the phone there was something he had wanted to ask her. Maybe their stars had finally aligned and he had the same thing on his mind.

'Was there something that you wanted to talk to me about?' she asked. 'Earlier on the phone, you mentioned it.'

'Oh.' Marco looked across at her. 'There was something but it can wait. I'm not sure it feels all that appropriate given what you've been through today.'

Jude sat up so she could turn to him properly. 'I'm fine, honestly. What was it?'

Marco also sat up so they were facing each other, knees touching in a subtle way that sent sparks shooting up Jude's leg.

'It's a little bit awkward to be honest as we both

know I've made it very clear to you in the past that I wanted things between us to become more than friendship. And we also know that you haven't felt the same.'

Jude could hardly breathe as she listened to him, waiting for her moment to tell him that things had changed and that she was ready for him now.

'Well, I think it's time for me to move on.' Marco's words hit her like a charging bull. 'You know that Clara and I have always got on well, and last night when we watched the film together, we had so much fun.'

Everything shifted horribly for Jude in that moment and she suddenly felt the red wine sour to vinegar in her stomach, making her feel nauseous. When he said he'd had fun last night with Clara, what exactly did he mean? Jude wanted to know and yet the thought of it was like a knife in her heart.

'So you and Clara, ey?' Jude tried to keep her voice light and a smile on her lips, worried that Marco could see straight through her. 'You do have a lot in common, and she lives next door so that's got to be handy.'

'Nothing's happened yet. It only really occurred to me last night that I might want to ask her out on a proper date. But I wanted to ask what you thought first.' Marco looked at her, searching her face for what? Her opinion? Her agreement? Her blessing?

Jude's phone gave a welcome ping of distraction and she was grateful for the excuse to look away. It was a text from Lucy.

> Hope you're having a good time.

> Don't do anything I wouldn't do.
> And by that I mean don't come
> home tonight!

> Love you. L xx

Jude felt tears threaten as she read the message and swallowed down a lump of something unwelcome. She tapped out a quick response.

> Make an excuse to want me home
> and come and get me.

Jude hit send and turned back to Marco. 'Sorry about that. Just Lucy.'

Marco pulled one foot up onto the sofa and tucked it underneath him, leaning a little closer to Jude as he did so. This made Jude even keener to get out of the cottage and back to the farm where she could lick her wounds and then follow Marco's example and move on.

'So?' he asked. 'What do you think? Should I ask Clara out on a date?'

The question hung in the air between them for a moment whilst Jude tried to think of an appropriate reply. What was she supposed to say? Tell him to go for it and say goodbye to her chances of finding her own happiness with the man she'd only just realised she was in love with? Or throw herself at him and beg him to reconsider?

Marco had moved on, he'd just told her that. He didn't feel the same way about her as he once had and more than that, he had transferred those feelings to someone else. Someone kind and sweet who would give him everything he deserved. Jude had seen them together and knew they were perfect for each other.

'She's lovely,' said Jude. 'And if that's what you want then you should go for it.'

'Really?' asked Marco.

Jude was saved the pain of having to repeat herself as Lucy had seen Jude's text and was calling her.

'Sorry, I should get this.' Jude flicked her phone on. 'Hi, Lucy, everything okay?'

'Tell him there's a sheep needing your help and

Noah and Frank are both out. I'm in the car and will be with you in a couple of minutes.'

'Oh bugger.' Jude had never been so grateful for her sister's knack of understanding her completely. 'Thanks for letting me know, I'll see you in a minute.'

Jude put her phone down and looked at Marco. 'There's a sheep stuck in one of the hedges and Noah and Frank are both out so Lucy's coming to pick me up. I'm so sorry.'

Marco looked disappointed that their evening was about to be cut short. 'The joys of farming, ey?'

Jude nodded and put her wine glass down on the table. 'No such thing as time off.'

The doorbell rang as Jude was putting her trainers back on. She was glad to leave her tattered evening plans in Marco's cottage as he kissed her goodbye and closed the door on their chance of building a new relationship together.

'Do you want to tell me about it?' Lucy asked as they drove out of the village.

'He told me he's moved on,' said Jude. 'And he wants to ask Clara out on a date so I guess that's that. I've blown it. But it's probably for the best as it means I can concentrate on the farm.'

'He said that to you?' Lucy sounded surprised but also a little cross at this.

'Yep.' Jude had learned over the years that when her emotions threatened to take over, she could avoid the fallout by being brisk and to the point. 'That's the size of it. He asked me what I thought about Clara and if he should ask her out.'

'You told him that you loved him and his response was to tell you that he wanted to ask another woman out on a date?' They'd just pulled into the driveway of Malvern Farm and Lucy turned to look at Jude, her face a picture of angry incredulity. 'And then he asked for your blessing?'

'Well, not exactly. I hadn't quite got around to telling him how I feel which was lucky, really. Imagine if I'd got in first.'

Lucy unexpectedly slammed her foot on the brake making Jude lurch forward and look around for a stray pheasant or rabbit that had run into the car's path. There wasn't one.

'For God's sake, Jude.'

Jude wasn't sure why her sister's fury had suddenly turned on her.

'What?'

'Are you really that stupid? Rrrhh!' Lucy growled. 'I'd shake you right now if I thought it would do any good.'

Jude felt herself flush with a budding anger of her

own. She'd had the shittiest of days and had been banking on sympathy from Lucy, not whatever this was.

'Hey. That's not fair. What have I done exactly?'

'You've done what you've been doing for the past couple of years. You've tried to sabotage your own happiness.' Lucy sighed and her voice softened. 'Marco isn't in love with Clara, he's in love with you. Everyone can see it, just like we've all known that you've been in love with him pretty much since the first day he arrived on the farm.'

'He used to be,' said Jude. 'But not any more. Didn't you hear me? He wants to ask Clara out.'

'Didn't *you* hear you? He wanted to know what you thought about him asking Clara out. Can't you see what that means?'

'It means he trusts my judgement and wants to run an important decision past a good friend.'

Lucy covered her eyes with one hand and shook her head. 'No it doesn't, you poor, silly fool. It means he was giving you one last chance to change your mind. He was hoping that you'd tell him not to ask Clara out because you are completely nuts about him and want him for yourself. Which is exactly what you should have said.'

Jude stared out of the windscreen at the woodland that ran up one side of the driveway. Was Lucy right? Had she really misjudged the situation that badly?

'But he told me how well they got on and that they had a really fun time together last night.'

'Did that fun time end up becoming a *fun* time?' Lucy surrounded the second *fun* with finger quotation marks.

'If you mean did anything happen between them, then no it didn't. Marco made it clear that nothing like that has ever happened.'

Lucy held her hands up in despair. 'And the fact that he offered you this piece of information wasn't an instant giveaway? He was testing you, Jude. In his usual, thoughtful way he was letting you know that he hadn't been unfaithful to his hopes that you might one day want to take things further with him. He was giving you one last chance to fall into his arms before he gave up completely and moved on.'

Jude thought back to the conversation she'd had with Marco. He had been looking at her pretty intensely. She thought about the Three Counties Show and how he'd stayed with her when everyone else had gone home. The little Kerry Hill lucky charm, or love token as Tara had called it, was sitting next to her bed and she remembered the fizzy feeling she'd had when she'd opened it.

'I messed up again, didn't I?'

'Yes.' Lucy was already reversing back to the field entrance on the other side of the drive. 'But it's not too late to put it right.' She executed an impressively speedy three-point turn and was heading back down to the village before Jude had a chance to object.

Jude wasn't sure whether the butterflies swooping around her insides were due to the speed Lucy was driving, the wine she'd already drunk or the thought of testing her sister's theory by laying her true feelings out at Marco's feet. They went past the village shop, closed for the night and past the school with all the lights switched off. The little row of stone cottages stood around the last bend in the road, just before the village gave way to fields and woods.

Lucy slowed down as they approached the bend and Jude closed her eyes and took in a couple of deep breaths to still the butterflies.

'Oh, Jude.' Lucy said and Jude opened her eyes. 'Sweetie, I'm so sorry.'

They had stopped outside Marco's cottage where the front door was open and Clara was heading inside armed with a bottle of wine. Lucy had been wrong. Marco didn't want her. He must have called

Clara before Jude had even got to the end of his front garden.

'Jude...'

The door of Marco's cottage closed and Jude was already picturing what they were doing inside together. It was far too easy as it had only been a few hours since she'd pictured that very scene in minute detail; except then it had been her and not Clara in the role of leading lady.

'Just go home.' She turned her head away to look out of the side window so Lucy couldn't see the tears that were making her eyes damp.

'I'm sorry,' Lucy repeated. Then she turned the car back around and they limped home with their tails firmly between their legs.

15

Jude found that the best way to stop a broken heart from taking over her life was to keep herself busy. It hadn't been the first time she'd employed this philosophy and whilst it didn't take the pain away, it helped control it.

Keeping busy wasn't hard for Jude. Between her farm, her family and the double murder investigation, she found plenty to occupy her body and mind.

That Friday, just a week after the terrible happenings at the county show, Jude and Frank were out together with Pip and Alfie in one of the fields watching the lambs born that spring.

'It'll be time to wean them off their mothers soon.' Frank leant onto his shepherd's crook and sent his seasoned eye across the field, silently assessing the animals one by one. 'They're looking good, Jude. Not a bad year, this'un.'

Jude smiled at him. She'd learned over her years on the farm what to look out for and she agreed that it was a particularly good batch of lambs. They were fun to watch when the weather warmed up and they were getting fatter on the last of their mothers' milk along with the lush grass of the early summer. Alfie was lying next to Jude with his ears pricked and body tense, ready to round the sheep up as soon as he was called to do so.

'Easy,' Jude warned him and he rested his head dejectedly on his front legs, ears still pricked in case his time would come soon. Pip, who was older and had never been trained to run with sheep, had already fallen asleep in the sun.

'You alright, Jude?' Frank asked. 'After that terrible business at Griff's farm, like.'

'I'm okay, thanks. It was horrid though.'

'Shows that you never know what's going on, do you?'

'In what way?'

'I mean Griff being the one that killed David after all.'

'I don't think that's been decided yet,' Jude pointed out.

'Wasn't there a note or something from him, saying it was him who done it?'

'How did you know about that?'

'I heard it from Laurence Palmer who lives that way. With Griff dead and Jim being held by the police, there's nobody looking after all them sheep. Laurence has been helping out but he has his own flock to be dealing with so he called me up this morning to see if Noah or I could help out.'

'Noah said he was heading over there today,' said Jude. 'I'm glad he can help. Mind you, if they don't charge Jim with Griff's murder, he'll be out later today and back on the farm himself.'

'I hope so. Can't picture it, you know, Jim Martin being a killer. He's a tough old boot but not a bad man. Mind you, I could say the same about Griff. Just can't see him killing David or finishing himself off either. I don't much care for what was in that note.' Frank stretched out his back. 'And another thing. Farmers like Griff would never have taken on that ram from Batters Farm if he wasn't going to see it through to lambing.'

'What do you think will happen to all his sheep now?' Jude asked.

'I s'pose they're going to have to be moved before too long. Can't keep relying on the likes of Noah and Laurence.'

'Does Griff not have any family who would want to take over the farm?'

'There's talk of his sister's boys coming back to it but I don't know for sure what's been decided.'

'I suppose if they don't want the farm then the sheep will be sold off. I bet several of the farmers from the show would like some of those Kerry Hills. Maybe Zander Pettiford will buy the lot so he can introduce them back to the wild.'

'Pah.' Frank snorted. 'Like those show sheep would look the way they did if they'd been reared out in the wild. No. And I'll tell you another thing. They didn't even come directly from Zander's fancy farm.'

'What?' Jude felt her eyebrows crease at Frank's bold statement. 'How can you know that?'

'Because I know Jane at the show who handles all the movement papers for the livestock. I went over to see her and have a bit of a natter and we got talking about Zander Pettiford. He had to declare where the sheep had been prior to the show, same as everyone else did, and where they were going to be taken back to after it was over. We all know that Zander lives at Greener Days Farm – stupid name he gave it.'

'And the papers show that the sheep came from elsewhere?' Jude found this very interesting indeed as, if it were true, then this could be a significant clue in the murder investigations. Zander's brand revolved very much around the fact that he was trying to prove rewilding was the way forward and that top, show-quality sheep could be reared in this way. Whilst Jude didn't dispute the fact that the Kerry Hills could well thrive in the wilds of Zander's farm, it would be difficult to keep an eye on the animals Olivia put aside for showing. It would be far easier to have them housed somewhere more in keeping with traditional sheep farming.

Jude could imagine how denting this would be to Zander's brand and credibility if it came out – not only that he'd bred his top sheep away from his wild farm, but he'd also lied about it so publicly.

'Where is he keeping them?' Jude asked.

'No idea,' said Frank. 'Jane would know though. Why? Do you think it's important?'

'It might be,' said Jude. 'It's as well to give Binnie Jane's details so she can at least check it out.'

If Frank had known about the true home of Zander's sheep then it was very possible that Griff did too and maybe even David. And if they had threatened to tell his adoring public what was going on, then perhaps Zander had been forced to keep them quiet.

'Who else knows about this?' Jude asked.

'Ooh, I dunno. Not many, I wouldn't think. Jane isn't one to gossip to folk. Specially nobody who might want to cause trouble.'

'Did Griff know?'

'Hard to say for sure but I reckon if he did then he didn't get it from Jane.'

'But she told you,' Jude pointed out.

'We've always enjoyed a joke together,' said Frank. 'It's why I went to see her. I s'pose she thought it would tickle me. Time was she was sweet on me, back in the day.'

Frank grinned, revealing two deep dimples above the line of his beard. 'Maybe she still is.'

Jude punched him playfully on the arm. 'You should ask her on a date.'

Frank choked on his laughter. 'Not sure what her husband would have to say about that.'

Jude had never thought about it before but perhaps Frank did want a new partner to share his golden years with. Noah's mum had died several years ago and Jude wondered if she ought to nudge him gently on to the dating scene again. This thought only served to remind her of her own failed love life and she pushed the thought firmly away.

'If you wouldn't mind giving me Jane's details, I think Binnie would be very keen to look into this second farm of Zander's.'

'Jane won't like that I've spilled her secret,' said Frank.

'If you tell her you thought it was useful in a murder investigation or two then I'm sure she'd understand.'

Frank prodded his crook into the ground several times, making Alfie sit up tall again, ready for duty. 'I suppose she would.'

They started to make their way towards the farm-yard together, happy that all the sheep in their care were well. Alfie looked back over his shoulder, annoyed that he had been denied a good run out with the sheep.

'Wouldn't it be something if that stuck-up pop star turned out to be a real villain,' said Frank.

'It would certainly do more harm to his clean-living reputation than housing a few sheep on a different farm.'

'I reckon Jane would like the chance to see that happen too, as it goes. I'll give her a ring as soon as I get back to my cottage.' Frank's phone was as mobile as anybody else's and yet it spent most of its life plugged into a charging cable in his kitchen. Noah and Jude had tried many times to persuade him that it would be better off in his pocket so that he could call them in an emergency or vice versa but he was both set in his ways and increasingly forgetful.

'I'm going to get a sandwich if you're interested,' said Frank when they got back to the farmyard. 'And we can give Jane a ring whilst you're there.'

Jude was very much interested in a sandwich and she was also keen to hear what Frank's old flame, Jane, had to say about the farm where Zander kept his show sheep so she walked with him back to the little pink cottage.

Inside, nothing much had changed since Noah had moved out and passed the cottage on to his father. It was an old worker's cottage that comprised a central living space with a bedroom off to the right and a bathroom to the left. The ceilings were low and the windows small which made it quite dark inside even on such a sunny day. And yet Jude had always thought that this just made the cottage even more cosy and homely.

'Have a seat,' said Frank as he went to pick up his phone. 'I'll see if Jane's in.'

Jude moved over to the sofa that was pushed up

against the wall below one of the windows and sat down with the dogs at her feet. Frank dialled Jane's number and Jude noticed that he entered each individual digit rather than search for her by name. He seemed to know the number by heart.

With nothing to focus on, her mind went straight away to Marco and Clara which was less than useful so she took her own phone out and forced her attention back to the investigation.

> Did you know that Zander Pettiford's 'wild' sheep are not so wild?

She texted Binnie.

> Apparently they live on a second farm, Frank is just trying to get an address. Don't you think that's interesting? I bet Zander wouldn't want his fans to know what a fraudster he is.

Binnie must have had her phone in her hand because a reply pinged back instantly.

> That is interesting.

There was a pause but Jude could see Binnie was still texting and waited for the next message to come through. Frank had got through to Jane on the phone and was talking about someone called Peter who she assumed was Jane's son.

Binnie's text arrived.

BINNIE

Puzzle for you.

Benzodiazepine found in Griff's stomach was not from tablets but a liquid form.

No trace in the whisky left in the bottle or the glass and no sign of an empty vial at the house.

JUDE

100% someone else must have killed him then.

Jude waited whilst the bouncing dots told her that Binnie was writing a reply.

BINNIE

Also, paper from Griff's printer doesn't match suicide note. I think we can safely say that we are looking at murder. No evidence it was Jim though, we've let him go. Text me when you have an address for that second farm.

JUDE

Will do. x

Whilst Frank chatted to Jane, Jude thought about the administration of the benzodiazepine. Binnie had said that it was in Griff's stomach so that ruled out someone injecting him. If it hadn't been in the whisky he'd been drinking, then how had he ingested it? Could it have been mixed in with some food or dropped into water? She didn't know anything about the drug, what it tasted, looked or smelled like so she didn't know if this was possible. There hadn't been any sign of food on the table or anything other than the whisky. And that had been clear.

How someone had managed to drug Griff was not the most important question anyway. Who had done it was the ultimate mystery and in order to find that out, she needed to think about why he had to die. Whereas David's death had probably been a spur of the moment act of anger or fear, whoever had killed Griff had gone to great lengths to package his death up as a suicide. They had made mistakes, big ones too that would have been picked up even if they had managed to finish the job and cut both of Griff's wrists. But that didn't take away from the thought required to carry out the deed.

Jim had been released but that didn't remove him from her sights completely. He had been the only person found at the scene for one thing, he had motive but he would have had to have been incredibly clever to have carried out a crime like that and not pick up any sign of it on his body or clothing.

If not Jim, then who?

Maybe someone else who thought Griff had killed David and wanted revenge for his death. But if this was the case then who had loved David enough to kill his killer? Jim came easily to mind but perhaps there was someone else: maybe a secret affair that had ended tragically. Jude pictured Tara, Olivia and Ffion. Could one of them have been in love with David Martin? Tara had once had a fling with him but that had ended really badly – there had been no love between them when Jude had seen them together in the shed that night. Olivia and Ffion had nothing but dislike for him either so perhaps Jim really was the only one to have revenge on David's behalf as a possible motive for killing Griff.

This brought Jude back to the idea that Griff had known too much. He had certainly wanted to tell Binnie something that he said was important and she'd already played with the idea that he'd either seen who'd killed David or knew who was growing the cannabis that David had been selling. Was it linked in some way to the note that had been found at the show, written by David to try and blackmail someone into helping push the development plans through? Perhaps the secret that David had been using as leverage had been the key to his death. And maybe Griff had tried to use the same thing.

Jude thought about the ram that Ffion and Carl had sold to him. Everyone knew that this was bizarre behaviour and Jim had been convinced it meant that the Proctors were using it to buy Griff's silence. According to Jim, that was the reason he had gone to Griff's farm on the day of the murder, to confront him about what he was being bribed to keep quiet about. Was it possible they'd sold him the ram at a bargain price because he had known something that would cause them problems less fixable than the money issues they'd hoped to bridge with the sale of the ram?

And then there was the odd way that Ffion had been acting when Jude had visited Batters Farm. She'd had a strong feeling that there was something in the house that Ffion was hiding. Could it be that there was a secret cannabis farm in the attic? If Jude had gone inside, would there have been any evidence of weed?

Or was their secret even darker than that? Were either of them David Martin's killer?

'Actually, Jane, before you go could I just ask you a small favour?' Frank was finally getting to the point of his phone call. 'We had a chuckle at the show last week didn't we, about that Zander Pettiford making such a fuss about his wild sheep when you'd seen that they hadn't even come from his farm.'

There was a pause as Jane obviously answered him.

'Don't fret. It's only that I was thinking of this murder business and who might have wanted to kill people around here. I suggested to one of the investigators—' he winked at Jude '—that if Zander perhaps wasn't as organic and wild and all that as he wants everyone to think then perhaps he might be very keen to keep it quiet.'

Another pause.

'That's it. Anyway, I know the detectives would be very grateful if I could pass on the address of the other farm so they can go and have a look at it.'

Frank gave Jude a little thumbs up.

'No hurry. I'll hang on for you, Jane.'

He held the phone away from his mouth and whispered, 'She's checking her records.'

Jude returned his thumbs up as he put the phone back to his ear.

Jude's attention had gone full circle and was back at Zander Pettiford. Would he really kill if someone threatened to reveal him for the fraud he was?

And then another thought struck Jude. Was it possible that the second farm wasn't only being used to house pedigree show sheep? Could Zander be the grower of cannabis? He'd definitely developed a taste for it during his time with The Spods. The entire band had if the tabloids were anything to go by. And hadn't the band folded when Coby Tyler died of an overdose? Not hash maybe, but the drug link was definitely there.

For some reason this made Jude think of the Instagram video clip with David in the background talking to someone. He had accused them of being greedy and not sticking to some deal they'd agreed on. When Jude had first seen the clip, she'd assumed he'd been talking to Olivia as he was standing right next to the Greener Days Farm pens. Binnie had pointed out that it would be a very risky business to grow weed on Zander's farm and that they had more than enough money as it was.

But things could look different if the drugs were grown away from Greener Days and on a small-holding that wasn't in either of their names.

Although Zander had earned a lot of money from his days in The Spods and was still bringing money in from sponsorship and books, he had an expensive life. Greener Days couldn't have been cheap to buy or run, and he loved his luxuries. He'd also been keen to tell everyone about his wonderfully philanthropic nature and how he paid for his mother to live in the best care home money could buy. Perhaps when it was all added together, his money didn't stretch as far as it needed to and so a little side hustle was necessary.

'Thank you, Jane.' Frank was writing something down on the back of an unopened envelope lying on the counter. 'That's kind of you and I promise I'll only mention this to the people doing the investigation. No point in churning up more mud than necessary, is there?'

Frank passed the envelope to Jude who looked at the address. Hope House, Goodrich, Herefordshire.

'Right you are,' said Frank. 'Cheerio then.'

He tapped the screen and then held the phone out for Jude to see. 'That's properly off, isn't it? Only I've been caught out before and gone for a pee with the phone still on in my pocket. Luckily it was only Noah on the other end but I can't be too careful now.'

Jude smiled. 'You're definitely okay this time.'

'Got what we needed, anyway.'

'Yes. Goodrich. That's in the Wye Valley, not far from Ross where Greener Days Farm is located, isn't it?'

'That's it,' said Frank. 'Just a bit further downstream.'

Jude knew the area; she'd driven past on her way to Abergavenny only a few days previously. Was it a coincidence that everywhere her investigations wanted to take her were all clustered so close together? She sent the address to Binnie and went over to the kitchen unit to help Frank make some sandwiches for lunch.

'Ham and mustard okay?' Frank asked.

'Perfect. Thanks.'

Jude buttered the bread whilst Frank took a small

gammon joint from the fridge and started to slice
wafer-thin ribbons onto a carving board.

Binnie had already replied to Jude's text by the
time the sandwiches were ready.

> Hope House is a smallholding. 2.5
> acres registered to Lorna
> Routledge, bought six years ago.

Jude wondered who this Lorna was and what
connection she had to Zander or if it stopped at
merely being his sheep's landlady. It wasn't un-
common for people with a little piece of land to rent
it out for a farmer to graze animals on.

'Are you going to eat or just spend your lunch
break staring at that thing in your hand?'

'Sorry, Frank.' Jude put her phone away and sat
down with him to eat her sandwiches. 'I was thinking, I might take a trip over to Ross tomorrow.'

Frank was bent over his plate with a sandwich in
his mouth and he looked at Jude over the top of his
glasses.

'If you can manage around here without me.'

Frank chewed his sandwich slowly and swallowed before answering. 'You know what Noah
would say if you told him.'

Jude did know what her friend and self-appointed guardian would say. He hated it when she got tangled up in murder investigations and with fair reason seeing how many dicey scrapes she'd gotten herself into over the years. But this was different. She wasn't putting herself in any danger, she just wanted to talk to Olivia and have a sniff around Greener Days. And if her day happened to take her to Goodrich as well then she might have a little peek at Hope House to see what was going on there.

16

The roads were fairly quiet the following day as Jude drove through the pretty market town of Ledbury on her way through Herefordshire.

Olivia was expecting her at Greener Days Farm as Jude had called the day before with the perfect excuse for wanting to pop over and see her at the farm. She'd pretended that she was keen to find out more about the process of rewilding with a view of turning a portion of her own farm over to it.

Although she had no intention of setting bison or beavers wild on her land and wasn't going to be persuaded that good, fertile farmland was best served by returning it to nature, she was interested in having a proper conversation on the topic. But of course that wasn't her main reason for wanting to go and visit Greener Days.

The entrance to Zander Pettiford's farm was secured with high wrought-iron gates and several CCTV cameras pointing at them. Jude had to get out of the Land Rover to ring the security bell which buzzed whilst she waited for someone to answer it. Tall larch trees ran alongside both sides of the tarmac drive, set back enough to make the sweep up to the currently hidden house feel stately rather than dark and foreboding.

Jude expected a voice to come through the speaker underneath the keypad of the security system. Instead, Olivia herself came out of the pretty brick gatehouse tucked in behind a low hedge on the other side of the gates which were swinging open.

'Welcome to the farm,' she said with a welcoming smile. 'I thought we'd head up to the main house to chat then I can take you to have a look around.'

'Thanks for having me, I really appreciate it.' Jude felt like a poor relation from a Dickens novel standing there at the threshold of such grandness. 'Shall I leave the car where it is or drive us up?'

'Why don't you just pull in over there and then we can walk up together?' Olivia indicated a gravelled area opposite the gatehouse and Jude got back in her car so she could drive through the gates and park up.

'I was so pleased you called,' said Olivia as Jude got out and locked the car. 'You said you were thinking about rewilding a chunk of your farm. Is that right?'

Jude felt a fraud lying to Olivia's face when she was being so accommodating but she had to keep up the pretence now that she was at Zander's farm.

'I'm toying with the idea but I don't know anyone else who's done it, apart from you and Zander of course.'

Jude and Olivia started to make their way up the driveway together. Past the larches, Jude could see a young mixed woodland to the right of them and an open field full of tangled bushes and tussocky grass on the left, leading right down to the River Wye.

'There are a few estates in the country that have fully rewilded successfully but the first thing I would say to you is that, whilst I am infinitely proud of what we're achieving here at Greener Days, it isn't for everyone and it isn't for every type of land.'

'I know the land on the Knepp Estate was not fit for traditional farming which was why they first insti-gated the rewilding programme.' Jude had made sure she'd done a little homework on the topic to make her interest seem real. 'Is it the same here at Greener Days?'

'It was actually visiting Knepp with Zander a few years ago that made him want to do something similar with his land. When he first bought the farm, it was traditional mixed arable and sheep.'

Jude realised that Olivia hadn't really answered the question but she didn't push her on it and she suspected that this was because, unlike the first big rewilding project at Knepp, there had been nothing unfarmable about Zander's land when he'd bought it.

'Tell me more about how it works,' said Jude. 'Is it really just a case of leave the land and see what happens when you let nature and carefully chosen animals take over?'

Olivia laughed. 'In a way yes, but then I have a couple of extra issues that I need to consider.'

Jude cocked her head in question.

'Zander Pettiford and his adoring public,' Olivia said with obvious affection. 'You should know that for all his bluster and nonsense, Zander really is trying to do what's right both for the environment and for me. He's one of the good ones.'

'I got that from what I saw of him at the show.' Jude actually thought that Zander was a bit of narcissistic shit-stirrer who had a narrow-minded view on farming that was opposed to pretty much every other farmer Jude knew. But she kept that to herself.

'You know that we grew up together?' Olivia took Jude through a double gate that cut through a thick yew hedge. 'I'm an only child, same as Zander, so we kind of adopted each other as brother and sister.'

They had come out into the farm's formal gardens which looked like a troop of National Trust gardeners were in full-time employment there.

'Wow,' said Jude. 'This is impressive.'

'It was always Zander's dream to live in a big house.' Olivia looked a little embarrassed of the grandeur of the gardens, not to mention the red-brick house with huge windows and multiple chimneys.

'And yours to be in the countryside.' Jude remembered the conversation she'd had with Tara about Olivia and Zander's inner-city childhood.

'When you live in a two-bedroom flat in the middle of Sheffield with people squeezed in all around you then it's normal to dream.' Olivia paused by the front door and took a bunch of keys out of her pocket. 'It's just not many people are lucky enough to see those dreams coming true.'

She pushed open the door and they stepped into

a large boot room with a long bench running down one side and shelves of shoes with coats hung above on the other. Olivia sat down on the bench and unlaced her trainers whilst Jude kicked hers off without bothering to untie them.

'Let's have a drink first and chat through the ideas for your farm and what I've learnt from taking this place on. Then we can go and have a look at the land so you can see how it's all starting to come together.'

'This is really kind of you,' said Jude.

'I've been looking forward to it,' said Olivia. 'Zander's friends aren't all that interested to be honest, and the farmers I've met around here aren't very keen on a celebrity neighbour nor the fact that we've decided to rewild.'

'Why did you?' Jude asked. 'Sorry, that sounded blunter than I meant but I'm interested in what made you make such a big leap away from traditional farming methods.'

'The official PR line is that Zander is dedicated to making farming more sustainable for the planet and has a passion for the natural environment.' Olivia had brought Jude into what was clearly a very modern, and no doubt expensive, take on the clichéd farmhouse kitchen. 'Clearly now you're here you can see the irony of that.'

'This room is incredible,' said Jude. 'But I suspect this is a side of the farm that Zander doesn't tend to show on YouTube?'

'You mean you haven't seen every video?' Olivia said.

'I'm not that great with social media, I'm afraid.' Jude gave an apologetic shrug. 'By the time I sit down in the evening, I'm already half asleep.'

'I'm just teasing you.' Olivia took out a box of little plastic pods and passed it to Jude. 'Coffee, or tea?'

Jude knew that these things went into a fancy coffee machine but she'd never used one herself and marvelled at the casual way Zander had such a wasteful machine in his life when he was supposed to be all about saving the environment.

'Just regular tea for me please.' Jude went for the safe option.

Olivia made the drinks and indicated to a high table running along the side of the kitchen where a full-width window overlooked the garden. Jude perched on one of the bar stools there and accepted her mug of tea.

'Despite the fact he's a very visible public figure, it's all actually very carefully orchestrated and Zander's very private when it comes to personal stuff. We both are,' said Olivia as she sat next to her. 'I think I can trust you, that's why I agreed to having this chat and showing you round. I just have to make sure though that what we talk about and what you see here is kept between us.'

Jude saw an element of worry in Olivia's eyes and realised for the first time that the dream life might not be exactly what she'd had in mind when she'd been lying on her bed in the Sheffield tower block. The big house and country living had come at a cost. High security, high scrutiny, high intrusion, high caution.

'Of course,' said Jude.

Olivia slid a sheet of paper across the table towards Jude. 'I'm so sorry to have to ask you this but it's standard for everyone who comes into the house. Zander had his lawyer draft a simple document of silence. It's just a precaution.'

Jude tried not to let the surprise show on her face. A document of silence? The very idea made her feel decidedly uncomfortable.

'You want me to sign this?'

'It's just to make sure you don't leave and decide to tell everyone that we use coffee pods and our salad comes pre-washed and in plastic bags.'

Jude smiled to try and make light of what was a

bizarre situation. 'You mean you don't grow your own organic rocket?'

'You'd be surprised what the bloody tabloids would like to get their vampire teeth into. Something as minor as coffee pods could ruin Zander's reputation and credibility.'

Jude thought about the movement of Zander's show sheep from Hope House and not his wild farm. If Zander was worried enough about keeping his eco-persona clean that he had a legally drawn up form created for every visitor to Greener Days, what would he do to keep Hope House a secret?

Olivia put a rollerball on top of the piece of paper. 'Zander asked the lawyer to keep it short and jargon-free so that it's easy to digest but we'd both really appreciate you taking a look. Really, I should have done this down at the gatehouse, that's Zander's rule. But I didn't want to scare you off straight away and I trust what I saw of you at the show. You weren't gossiping and elbow nudging like some of the other farmers when Zander was around.'

'I don't see the point in gossip,' said Jude. *Unless it contains something of interest in a murder case,* she added to herself.

Jude picked up the pen and read the document. Olivia was right, it was very short and very simple.

She was signing to say that she respected the privacy of Mr Alexander Pettiford and all those working at Greener Days Farm, Ross-on-Wye. Once the document was signed, she would not be able to pass on the details of any element of the farmhouse, its inhabitants or staff, or the grounds of Greener Days Farm. Interesting that no mention was made of Hope House, further proving that this was a place they wanted to keep secret. Except that no piece of paper she signed, no matter how legally binding, would stop her from passing on anything she thought Binnie would be interested to hear about.

Jude carefully read every word and then again to make sure she hadn't missed anything and then she signed and dated at the bottom where Olivia had drawn an x.

'Thanks for doing that,' said Olivia. 'I really hate asking people but Zander is a stickler.'

'I don't mind. I'm just really grateful you're letting me pick your brains. I find the whole rewilding thing fascinating but it's such an enormous commitment.'

'It is.' Olivia looked out of the panoramic window across the lawn and waved at a gardener who was pushing a wheelbarrow towards one of the flowerbeds. 'It is hugely satisfying but you're right. There's no point doing this unless you are fully committed as it's very much a long-term plan. We've been slowly moving things over for almost seven years now and we've still got a long way to go before the new woodland areas really start to take over.'

'But it's worth it?' Jude had thought there'd been a little catch in Olivia's voice.

'Jude, I'm going to be completely honest with you as I'm not part of Zander's publicity team and you're not here to be impressed. You're here to learn and I'd hate to bullshit you into making decisions that potentially wouldn't be right for your own farm. In return I am trusting you not to share my thoughts further than this room.'

Jude pointed to the folded sheet of paper in the table. 'I have just signed the Official Secrets Act.'

Olivia's face relaxed into a smile. 'I suppose you have. Well then let's get brutal. Whilst rewilding has definitely got its place in our countryside, for most farms it's probably not the right option and I would encourage you to think carefully about what it is you want to be doing and why you want to do it before you set aside any big portion of your land to use in this way.'

Jude hooked her heels over the foot bar of the stool she was sitting on so she could lean forwards and prop her elbows on the table. 'I suppose it's an environmental pull that makes any farmer want to return land to the wild.'

'Sure,' said Olivia. 'That's why Zander was so adamant we did it here at Greener Days.'

Jude noticed how Olivia had mentioned Zander on his own and not as a paired decision with her. 'Am I sensing that you didn't agree with him?'

Olivia paused to sip her coffee before answering. 'It wasn't what I thought he'd bought the farm for, let's say. When we were growing up we both dreamed of peace and space. I remember saying to him once that one day I would own my own tree. In those days I imagined just the one tree in a garden with a swing attached to the branches, and now look at us.' She pointed to the wide palette of greens outside the window. 'Zander made all of this happen.'

'Not just Zander,' Jude pointed out. 'You took yourself to agri college and got yourself the job at Jim's farm. You earnt your own first step out of Sheffield.'

'Actually, Zander paid for me to go to Hartpury,' said Olivia.

'Maybe, but you put all the work in to win the place, get qualified and find a job.'

Olivia nodded but it was quite clear that she felt as though she owed everything she had to Zander.

Jude didn't mention the fact that the same could be said in reverse and that if she hadn't bought that first guitar for Zander then he would almost certainly never have joined The Spods.

They sat in the kitchen for a little whilst longer until they'd finished their drinks and Olivia gently talked Jude out of the idea of rewilding. Or at least she would have if Jude had ever been serious about it in the first place. Whilst Olivia was clearly very happy at Greener Days and loved being the custodian of the land there, Jude got the firm impression that if it had been her choice, they'd have kept farming in a more traditional way.

'Right then.' Olivia stood up and took the two mugs over to the sink. 'Let's go and have a tour.'

They re-trainered their feet and went out of the other side of the house into a very smart yard where several shiny vehicles were lined up. Even the tractors looked like they'd just been cleaned or were only there to take part in a photo shoot for a farm machinery catalogue.

'We'll take the buggy.' Olivia took Jude over to a solar panel-covered shed where the only mud-splattered vehicle was housed. It was a funky, angular cross between a quad bike, a golf cart and a Tonka toy with metallic blue paint and *Kandi* written across the front.

Olivia pulled the thick charging cable out and hung it on a hook, gesturing for Jude to jump in. Once the engine had been started, the inside of the cab lit up with buttons and screens.

'This is fancy,' said Jude as Olivia drove out of the shed and into the yard.

'Zander was gifted it,' said Olivia.

'Wow, that was generous.'

'Product placement. His Instagram is a great platform for advertising so he gets offered all sorts of things.'

Jude raised her eyebrows. Zander no doubt could afford to buy as many of these things as he wanted and yet there were so many farmers out there struggling to make ends meet who'd love handouts like he was enjoying.

The farm itself was beautiful and there was something thrilling about being out in the midst of the young saplings, more established woodland and riverside grasslands. It may not have been the best use of fertile farmland as far as food production for the nation went – and the food supply would collapse very quickly if too much land was purposed in this way – but nature was clearly thriving all around them.

'It's stunning,' said Jude as a herd of deer galloped across a meadow in front of them. 'I'm interested in how you chose the animals you keep here.'

'We used Knepp and the work they've already done to help us decide what to home here. Deer obviously, pigs and a small number of wild ponies.'

'And the Kerry Hills.'

'Ah yes, well they were Zander's choice. Our primary school took us to a city farm once and they had a couple of Kerry Hills. They were the first sheep either of us had ever seen and Zander fell in love with them. We both did. It was one of the reasons I was so delighted to get the job with Jim when I left college. When I used to talk about owning a farm, he said he'd buy me a hundred of them.' She shrugged. 'Not the obvious choice for a project like this maybe, seeing as they're naturally hill sheep, but they seem to thrive out here.'

Jude thought about the second smallholding that Zander had been using to keep some of his flock separated from the wild rest. Having seen the setup at Greener Days, she could see why they'd want an easier way to rear show sheep in a much more contained setting. But why not make it clear to his followers? He had a brilliant opportunity to showcase farming from all angles and she was sure that this wouldn't make any dent in his ratings. In fact, she wondered if making himself more authentic would actually grow his popularity.

Suddenly, there was a loud buzzing sound and Olivia tapped the touchscreen on the dashboard. A security camera image of the front gate popped up on the screen and Jude could see a car waiting there.

'Hello?' Olivia said.

'Hi, love. Special delivery for you.'

'Hi, Tara. Thanks. I've actually got Jude Gray here with me and we're out on the buggy. I'll buzz you in and we'll meet you at the house.'

'Gotcha,' said Tara. 'I've brought bara brith with me.'

Olivia tapped the screen again and Jude saw the gates swing open to let Tara drive in.

'Sorry,' said Olivia. 'I didn't think she was coming until this afternoon.'

'Don't worry at all. I'll say a quick hi to Tara and then get out of your way.'

'You don't have to do that.' Olivia bumped the buggy through the woods and pointed out a group of red-haired Tamworth pigs snuffling through the leaf litter. 'I'm sure Tara would love to catch up with you.'

'It's nice that you don't live all that far from each other now.'

'Yeah, although she won't stop teasing me that I made it all the way to the border but haven't quite earnt the right to cross over into Wales.'

'It must be lovely to have her close enough to just pop in,' said Jude.

'It really is,' said Olivia. 'Penny too. They've always been so kind to me, Clive as well when he was still alive. I spent so much time at their farm when we were at college and Zander was away with the band.' Olivia let out a gentle laugh. 'I think Penny and Clive felt I needed a dose of proper parenting when they found out my dad was a waster and my mum had left us to it. Penny still mothers me now, to be honest. She was there at the Three Counties making sure I was fed and watered, the sheep too. I swear she spent as much time with my sheep as she did with her own.'

The woodland ended then with a gate and Jude jumped out to open it and let Olivia drive back into the yard where Tara was already waiting. Whilst Olivia put the buggy back in its shed, Jude walked over to say hello to Tara.

'This is a nice surprise,' said Tara. 'I didn't expect to see you here.'

'Olivia kindly offered to give me a tour of the estate. It's impressive, isn't it?'

'It's certainly that.' Tara made it sound as though impressive wasn't a quality she found particularly worth having. 'What did you think of the solar field?'

Olivia had taken Jude right to the edge of the estate where an enormous number of solar panels had stretched out over the old pastureland.

'I can see why people think it's a good idea,' she said.

'Very tactfully answered,' said Tara with a smile. 'When Ffion saw it she called it a bloody monstrosity that was zapping the life out of farming.'

'Bit harsh maybe,' said Jude.

'You know what she's like. She's a millionth-generation farmer who still loves the old ways. You went to see her the other day after you'd been in to see me and Mam, didn't you?'

'Yes.' Jude decided to seize the opportunity to bring up Hugh and see if Tara knew what the deal was. 'I met her brother too. He seemed very nice.'

'Who's very nice?' Olivia asked coming to join them.

'Alright, Liv?' Tara kissed her friend on the cheek. 'We were just talking about Hugh Davies, Ffion's brother.'

'I've never met him,' said Olivia. 'He's not a farmer, is he?'

'No and I don't think his father has forgiven him for not wanting to take over the farm despite the fact Caitlin, that's the sister, is really keen to run it herself. He's still totally old-fashioned like that.'

'What does he do?' Jude asked.

'He's some bigwig in rural planning for Hereford-shire, bringing in more money than he would if he was still working on the farm, especially if he was sharing it with Caitlin.'

All talk of Ffion's family stopped then as a black motorbike, so quiet that it had to be powered by electricity, sped into the yard.

The rider, clad in black leathers, took his helmet off to reveal Zander Pettiford.

'Ladies.' He greeted them with a nod. 'This is a nice surprise.'

'Not sure I can say the same,' Tara scowled at him 'I thought you'd be out.'

Zander held his hands up in surrender. 'Can't we just let bygones be bygones? I know I did a dickish thing telling people about your baby.'

'Dickish?' said Tara. 'Try damaging and unforgiv-able. Do you know how awful it was to have all that dragged up in a police interview?'

'I was upset. I still can't believe Liv went to work for him knowing what he was capable of.' Zander looked as angry as Tara did. 'And then you both hid it from me all this time.'

'Don't try and turn this around,' said Tara. 'What you did was far worse.'

Zander looked to Olivia for support but she shrugged. 'Zan, she's right. You owe her a proper apology.'

Zander pouted for a moment and then his face creased into a smile. 'I'm sorry, Tara. Look, I've been offered a couple of tickets to see Taylor Swift in London. They're yours if you want them.'

Tara wavered and Olivia swooped in with a counter offer. 'If you throw in travel and a hotel room then you might have a deal.'

'Fine.' Zander put his palms together in a prayer position. 'Tara?'

'Apology accepted.' Tara grinned. 'Liv, I assume you'll be coming as my plus one?'

'Of course.' With the row smoothed over, Olivia turned back to Zander.

'How was Lorna?' she asked.

Zander looked at Jude. 'I've been to see my Mum. She's not well but I've made sure she's in the very best nursing home.'

Jude already knew this as he'd been very vocal about his own kindness and consideration. What she hadn't known though was that his mother was called Lorna. And that was something that was really very interesting, given the name on the deeds for Hope House.

'She was as well as can be expected,' said Zander. 'Thank goodness we can afford the best care. Now, I'm parched. Liv, fancy brewing a cuppa?'

'I'm afraid I gave you an empty promise when I said I'd brought a special delivery,' said Tara. 'Ma baked a batch of bara brith for me to give you and I just realised it's still at home on the kitchen table.'

'Not to worry, there's half a lemon cake inside,' said Olivia. 'Are you joining us, Jude?'

'Thanks for the offer but I'd better get back to the farm.'

'Will we see you at the Cheshire Show on Tuesday?' Tara asked. 'Liv and I have decided not to take our sheep this time but Ffion and Carl are still going so we thought we'd go and support them.'

'I'm not sure I can make it but I'll double check the diary.'

'Wait, there's another chance to show the Kerry Hills and we're not going?' Zander didn't look very pleased at this.

'After what happened at the Three Counties, neither of us have the appetite for another show so soon,' said Olivia.

'I suppose so.' Zander looked petulant as he put his helmet back on. 'Stick the kettle on, Liv.'

He switched the motorbike back on and zoomed off at full speed to put it away in the shed next to the farm buggy.

Jude watched him go with interest, hardly any sound coming from the bike despite the rate it picked up speed.

'I hope all goes well on Tuesday,' she said. 'Thanks again for showing me round, and lovely to see you both.'

'I'll drive you back down to your car,' Olivia offered.

'Don't worry, I can walk if you let me know how to get out.' Jude's mind was whirring with a new possibility that Zander's bike had offered her.

'The gates will open when you drive up to them. Lovely to see you.'

Olivia and Tara waved as Jude set off down the driveway to her Land Rover. As soon as she was far enough away she took her phone out and fired off a text to Binnie.

Zander has an electric motorbike. Quiet, fast and small enough to hide out of the way somewhere – possible way of getting away from Griff's farm in a stealthy hurry? Could have been down the drive and off before Jim had even left his farm.

17

In the main, Jude had liked the other Kerry Hill farmers she'd met at the Three Counties Show. Zander was hard to warm to, but the only one she had taken a proper dislike to was David Martin, and it seemed she wasn't alone in this feeling. And yet there she was, driving alongside of the path of the River Wye, trying to work out which one of them was capable of murder. Calculated, premeditated murder in its coldest form.

Was it possible that Zander had been the one to drug Griff and cut his wrist, disappearing quietly and quickly from the scene on his electric motorbike? If so, then why? Maybe just because Griff had discovered his lies about his not so wildly reared wild Kerry

Hills, or perhaps there was a bigger secret lurking at Hope House. Something that Olivia may or may not be involved in or even aware of.

And then there were the Proctors and Ffion's mysterious brother, Hugh Davies. Jude would need to do a bit more digging around where he was concerned. David had been trying to blackmail someone into helping push through the development plans for his farm and Tara had just told her that Hugh was something to do with rural planning in Herefordshire. The wrong county for the Martins' farm but had David thought it was still worth a try?

There had definitely been something very strange about the whole situation when Jude had been to visit the Proctors at their farm. Ffion hadn't wanted her to go into the house and Jude had wondered at the time if that was because there was evidence of illegal marijuana production or supply. When Ffion had come outside and found Hugh talking to Jude, she'd been very quick to whisk him away on what seemed like a flaky pretence of helping her with her paperwork. Jude thought it was a strong possibility that he was the thing that Ffion had been trying to hide in the house. She knew that Jude was aware of the blackmail letter that David had sent and that someone with clout in planning applications would be deeply suspicious. Had she been keeping Hugh away from Jude to stop her making that connection?

It couldn't have been Ffion though who'd killed Griff. Binnie had told her she had an iron-clad alibi along with Tara and Olivia: all three of them had been at a market together and there were plenty of people who could corroborate this. None of them could have been the one to administer the drugs and cut Griff's wrist and yet that didn't mean they couldn't have played a part in his murder. Each of them had someone very close who could have worked with them, possibly to cover up either the accidental killing of David Martin, something else that they didn't want Griff sharing – or possibly both these things. Zander, Carl, Penny, Jim and Hugh had no alibis that indisputably took them away from the scene of the crime.

Penny. That name in particular was bothering Jude. Penny and Tara.

'Bara brith,' said Jude to her steering wheel. 'Tara said Penny had made a batch but she'd left it at the farm.' And yet Jude had been offered bara brith when she'd gone to see the Watsons. She'd complimented Tara on her baking only to be told that they always bought it from the farm shop as neither of them were skilled in the kitchen. There was something else too. Olivia had mentioned that Penny mothered her and looked after her all the time, spending as much time in Olivia's sheep pen as she did her own at the show. What if Penny had been there when Zander had been filming his Instagram video and it had been her, not Olivia that David had been talking to?

The satnav on Jude's phone told her that she was approaching her destination and the lane started to narrow. Jude knew that Zander and Olivia were occupied back at the house but she decided to park the Land Rover out of the way as she so often did when she didn't want to alert people to her whereabouts. That was the curse of such a recognisable vehicle. Instead of taking the left turn as instructed, she drove further down the road until she came to a lay-by where she pulled in.

The land around her was quiet when she got out of the car. No traffic noises or other human sounds to destroy the peace of the countryside. There was a little rustling from the overhanging branches of a row of huge oak trees next to the lay-by, and the scurrying of a couple of squirrels as they raced up a gnarly trunk. Otherwise the world was still.

Jude walked back along the road and turned up

the track that her satnav had pointed her towards. It was rutted from years of various wheeled vehicles compacting the ground on either side of a grassy ridge.

She passed a large Tudor manor house with intricate designs created through a combination of patterned brickwork and black beams. The windows were cross hatched with lead and the many chimney stacks twisted upwards from multi-gabled roofs. It was a beautiful building but Jude cringed at the thought of trying to upkeep a house like that with the listed building restrictions it would certainly have slapped on it.

The manor house's gardens extended for a little way and then gave way to a patch of woodland that had a couple of pig shelters and a small collection of Gloucester Old Spots in. Just beyond that, at the end of the lane was Hope House, a brick cottage that looked as though it had seen better days, but was charming, nonetheless.

There was no sign of life as Jude walked over the gravel drive but she had her excuse ready if anyone should surprise her. She had gone for a walk and somehow got herself lost. Could they tell her how to get back to the Cross Keys pub where she'd parked her car please?

It suddenly occurred to her that someone like Zander Pettiford may well have installed security cameras at the house and she cursed herself for being so stupid. She'd already walked brazenly up the drive and knocked on the front door and Zander could be sitting in the kitchen at Greener Days watching everything.

She glanced around but there were no obvious cameras that she could see and the doorbell was old-fashioned and definitely not connected to the internet. She decided to hedge her bets and carry on with her low-level reconnaissance as, if there were cameras, she'd already have been spotted and the game was up anyway.

As she'd expected, nobody answered the door and the cottage remained silent. Jude looked through the front window and saw that the living space inside was very sparsely furnished with a double seater sofa and coffee table only. No television, no pictures on the walls, no signs that this was anyone's loved home.

She walked around the side of the house, past a triple garage that was much newer than the cottage itself. The back garden was surrounded by over-grown hedges. Although the grass had been recently mown and there were a couple of heavy wooden benches sitting on the paved area that ran along the length of the house, it was obviously a garden that was pretty much left to its own devices.

From her position at the corner of the house, Jude scoured the hedges and ran her eye along the roofline of the house in case there were cameras out there but she found nothing so stepped into the garden and made her way down the path to a gate in the furthest hedge. On the other side was a paddock that Jude estimated to be about two acres, the exact size of the land that was owned by Lorna Routledge and used by Zander Pettiford. There were six Kerry Hills in there, all with their heads down, nibbling the grass.

Jude wanted to get into the house to see what it was being used for as it definitely wasn't being lived in, but it was far too risky.

She was just looking through one of the back windows when she heard the crunch of tyres on gravel as a car pulled up. Glad that she was at least in the back garden so wouldn't be spotted straight away Jude looked quickly to see if there was any chance of hiding herself should whoever had just arrived choose to come around the back. The worrying conclusion was that if this happened she'd be well and truly stuffed.

A garden hoe was propped against the side wall

of the garage but Jude wouldn't be able to get to it without being seen, and even if she did, then what? If she used it she'd only be adding assault to the list of crimes she'd already committed.

With her heart pumping twice as hard as was good for it, Jude flattened herself against the brick wall hoping that she was invisible should anyone look out of one of the windows. To her absolute dismay she heard the unmistakable sound of footsteps coming around the side of the house. Jude turned her head, waiting to be discovered and failing to think of a single good reason as to why she should be hiding round the back of Hope House.

But the footsteps stopped short of the garden on the corner where the garages stood. Jude hardly breathed as she heard the scraping sound of stone on stone followed by a garage door sliding opening.

Jude thought about edging to the corner of the house to see if she could get a good look at the garage without being seen. Perhaps if the person inside was away from the door or at least with their back turned, she might be able to sneak past and make a run for it. But whoever had gone into the garage clearly wasn't there to linger. Before she'd even had a chance to think her plan through properly, the garage doors were clanked back into place and Jude could do nothing but cross her fingers and pray that whoever was there would not come into the garden. If they went into the house she would be safe for the moment but would still have to wait for them to leave before she could make her move. And who knew how long that would be?

The slam of a car door and the sound of retreating tyres on the gravel made Jude breathe a tentative sigh of relief that this time, her prayers had been answered.

She waited until the car had gone and her heart had started to slow down again before she moved. The air that had seemed so peaceful earlier now rang with a dangerous silence as she moved along the side of the house and poked her head around the corner to make sure she was really alone again.

She went over to the garage doors and tested them to see if she could get in but they were locked. Sure that the scraping of stones must have been someone uncovering a key, Jude looked around for a suitable hiding place. The shed was sitting on a concrete footing and there was a border of large pieces of decorative rock surrounding it. One of them must be a cover for the key, but which one?

Jude started with the one closest to the garage door but there was nothing underneath and she replaced it. She tried several more with no luck and was about to lift another when the sound of a car coming up the road made her freeze in alarm. She imagined for the second time in the space of less than ten minutes that she was about to be discovered. Only this time she was in an even more precarious situation seeing as she was trying to break into the garage and uncover the secret of what it was being used for.

The car drove on past but it had already torn away the remainder of Jude's nerves and she decided that it was time to leave. She made sure all the stones were back in their correct places and then she power walked out onto the road and back to her car.

Jude thumped the steering wheel in frustration. She had been close to getting into the garage, she knew it. The key had to be under one of the rocks and she'd have found it if she hadn't let her jitters get the better of her.

'Go back and finish the job,' she said to her reflection in the glass of the dashboard. 'Or you'll spend all evening regretting it.'

Jude took a few deep breaths and put her hand on the door handle to get back out. A fraction of a second before she pushed the door open, she was abruptly halted by the sound of another approaching vehicle. She waited to see if it was going to drive past but it didn't. It slowed as it approached the lane up to Hope House. Jude's Land Rover was tucked well off the road in the lay-by and she couldn't clearly see the car though that meant she was almost certainly invisible to them too.

Once it had turned up into the drive, Jude got out of her car, resting the door gently back in place without slamming it closed. Then she walked a little way down the road, keeping herself tucked into the treeline so she couldn't be seen. Finding the perfect spot where she could remain out of sight and yet get a good view of the entrance of Hope House's drive, she waited.

Before long, the car came back out and Jude recognised it instantly. It was the fancy hybrid Range Rover she'd seen Zander driving when he and Olivia had arrived at the Three Counties Show. The windows were blacked out so she couldn't see who was driving but Jude knew it had to be either Olivia or Zander and that their visit to Hope House was almost certainly linked to the visitor who had just been inside their garage.

* * *

Jude got back to Malvern End just as Lucy and Noah were leaving the farmhouse with a very small pirate between them sporting furry ears under a red headscarf.

'Aunty Judy,' said the pirate. 'Look at me. I'm Steady Eddie the pirate hamster from *Pie-Rats*. Mummy did my face paints.'

'You look very cool. Is that my stripey T-shirt you're wearing?'

'Yes. Mummy said it's too small for you anyway so she said I was allowed to borrow it.'

'Oh did she, now?' Jude looked at her sister who gave her a sheepish shrug.

'Are you coming to the school barbecue with us?' Noah asked. 'You could do with a break.'

'The theme is pirates but you don't have to dress up if you don't want to,' Sebbie said. 'Miss Elgar said there's going to be ice creams, a bouncy castle and lots of games.'

'Sounds exactly like my sort of thing,' said Jude. 'You go ahead and I'll meet you down there. I've got a few things I have to take care of first.'

Lucy shot her a look that said *Make sure you do* before she and Noah walked off, holding one pirate hamster paw each. Once they'd gone, Jude went into the farmhouse, said hello to the dogs and then went into the office space to switch on her laptop.

Whilst she waited for it to kick into gear, Jude pushed herself back into the office chair to think. There was no doubt in her mind that Zander Pettiford was using Hope House as a base for selling marijuana. His history showed that he had a contact list full of people in the music industry who were known for using the stuff so it was an easy way for him to get some extra money. She wondered if Zander had been the one to supply David with his own stash and a little extra to sell on to friends and acquaintances. Each person in the chain making a profit from something highly illegal. But at the Three Counties, the two men had behaved as though they'd never met before. Was that just an act or had David been getting his hash elsewhere?

'Olivia?' Jude wondered aloud. 'She knew David from her time at Jim's farm.'

Olivia could have been dealing back then to make a little extra money whilst Zander was still starting out with The Spods. Maybe she'd carried on despite the money Zander was giving her because she didn't like being so beholden to him and his fortune and wanted to have something of her own to fall back on.

Jude knew that she was jumping the gun again,

something she had a habit of doing when she was frustrated. She was assuming that Hope House was being used as a base for marijuana dealing but what proof did she have exactly? Nothing other than a hunch and a snippet of a one-sided conversation between David Martin and someone whom she had assumed was Olivia. Although it could just as easily have been Penny, or any number of people who had made up the footfall of the Three Counties Show that day.

She needed more. She needed to get into the garage at Hope House and find out exactly what it was being used for.

In the meantime there was another line of enquiry she was keen to pursue and that was her reason for logging on to the internet in the first place.

She typed *planning officers corruption cases uk* into the search bar and was instantly hit with page after page that served to prove that it was a very real problem. The use of bribery in a discretionary planning system that lacked the necessary safeguards was rife if the articles were anything to go by.

She then ran a search on Hugh Davies and had to dig a bit deeper to uncover an article of interest. Although it contained nothing to suggest he had personally taken bribes, it did link him to a locally explosive new development on the fringes of Hereford. A large construction company had managed to get controversial planning permission to put sixty new houses on farmland and Hugh had been the one who had ultimately signed it off.

Jude wrote down the name of the company, Plover Homes, and then typed it into the search bar. A fancy sales website came up and she could see that they specialised in rural developments within the counties of Herefordshire, Worcestershire and Gloucestershire. As well as houses to buy and upcoming projects, the menu offered a button for those interested in talking to them about developing land they owned. When Jude clicked on it, there was a page of information for rural land owners that included details on planning permission and when this might be granted for agricultural land. It also gave case studies of farmers who had made significant money by selling some of their land off for development.

For someone like David Martin, this could have been very alluring indeed. Jude wondered if Plover Homes had been involved in his plans for development. She searched for other construction companies in the area but none of them seemed to fit the bill as well as Plover Homes, and there was the previous link that they'd had with Hugh Davies which Jude found very interesting.

Jude decided she could lose nothing by giving them a quick call and seeing what she could uncover so she pulled up a number and fed it into her phone.

'Good afternoon,' said a chirpy voice, 'Plover Homes, development department. You're speaking to Gabriella, how can I help?'

'Oh hello, I was wondering if you might be able to offer me a little advice,' said Jude adopting a version of her voice that sounded far from her own. 'I'm a farmer looking to develop some of my land and I was hoping to talk to someone about what the process might be.'

'Lovely,' chirruped Gabriella. 'Can I start by taking a name?'

'Yes, it's Ju—' Jude stumbled on her name realising she didn't want to use her real details. 'Julie Pounder.'

'Is that Miss, Mrs?'

'Mrs.'

'And the address of the farm in question?'

'Laybrook Farm in Colwall.' Jude gave the address and postcode of the farm that Frank had recently given up the tenancy of. If anyone from Plover Homes wanted to get in touch in the future

then the new tenants would just have to fob
them off.

'And is this the best number to reach you on?'
Gabriella asked. 'Ending 879?'

Bollocks! She hadn't thought of that. Oh well, if
anyone called her she'd have to just tell them that
she'd changed her mind.

'Yep.'

'Lovely. Can I ask how you heard about us?'

'It was actually a friend of mine, David Martin
from Leigh Farm in Leigh Sinton. He said you were
helping him with his application.'

'Oh yes. Such a nice man. We were all devastated
to hear about his sad passing.'

Bingo! David had been in conversation with the
construction company that had previously had controversial work approved by Hugh Davies. In her
mind this helped Jude link together several of the
mysteries surrounding David's death. The note he'd
written asking someone to help with his planning
application. David had told them he knew about the
issues with their farm's finances and the way they'd
been making extra cash. Although Hugh himself was
no longer farming, his family was and she knew that
Ffion was definitely having trouble with money. And
hadn't Ffion been overly distressed at the Three

Counties Show? She had not been a fan of David's by any stretch of the imagination so it was unlikely she'd been overtly saddened by his death, unless she had been involved with it, of course. Or had her reaction been to do with the blackmail letter that had been discovered?

'Hello? Julie, are you still there?' Jude was pulled back to her call with Gabriella.

'Just about.' Jude tried to make her voice sound a little glitchy by moving her hand backwards and forwards across her mouth. 'But it's a really bad line. I'm afraid I'll have to call back another time.'

She clicked the *end* button and called Binnie to update her on what she'd discovered.

18

Jude walked through her fields to get to the village and could hear the laughter and music a long way before she reached the school.

To her utter dismay, the first people she saw as she came out onto the road were Marco and Clara carrying bags of shopping. Jude was used to feeling her heart soar when she saw Marco and seeing his face light up when he saw her. It was a mule's kick therefore to feel nothing but nausea and to see his easy smile slip from his face only to be replaced by awkwardness.

'Hello, Jude.' Clara was the only person who seemed happy at the unplanned meeting. 'Are you heading to the party at the school? It sounds like they're having a great time.'

Jude forced a smile; after all, none of this was Clara's fault. It was Jude who had misjudged things so badly at every turn when it came to Marco. 'Yep. Lucy and Noah took Sebbie down earlier but I'm hoping there might still be a hot dog or something left for me.'

'How was the stuck sheep?' Marco asked.

'The what?' Jude was momentarily wrong-footed until she remembered the excuse she'd made when she'd wanted to get out of Marco's house quickly the other night. 'Oh, she's absolutely fine. Just tangled herself up in the hedge. It happens all the time.'

'Even when they've all been sheared?' Marco knew she had been bullshitting him.

'Sometimes.' Jude gave what she knew was a watery smile. 'Anyway, I'd better go and find the others. Don't want all the ice creams to disappear.'

Marco nodded and Jude passed them to head to the school with a heart full of lead. Things were even worse than she'd thought. Apparently she had not only lost the chance to carve out a relationship with Marco, she'd also broken the friendship that had been so very, very dear to her.

'Stupid cow,' she muttered to herself as she kicked a stray pebble along the pavement.

'You okay, Jude?'

She looked up and saw Kerry coming towards her in her standard uniform of a rugby shirt tucked into a pair of jeans.

'Hey, Kerry. Where are you heading?'

'Lucy put me down on the list to do face painting at Sebbie's school. I'm supposed to be there in ten minutes but then I saw you coming so I thought we could go in together.'

'It was kind of you to volunteer to help out,' said Jude, although she knew that Lucy could be very persuasive and Kerry was always keen to please.

'I don't mind. It's nice doing things, keeps my mind off my results.'

They had reached the front gates of the school which were wide open and being manned by two dads Jude recognised from the playground. They were sitting at one of the school tables which had been dragged outside as a makeshift front desk.

'Two tickets?' one of the dads asked.

'Yes please.' Jude took her purse out of her pocket, glad that she'd remembered Lucy telling her to bring cash.

'I didn't realise I had to pay.' Kerry looked stricken and Jude held her hand up.

'You're definitely not paying.' Jude handed over the cash for the tickets and she and Kerry walked under a low-flying string of plastic bunting into the playground.

'Actually, I was hoping I might see you today,' said Jude. 'I was thinking about David Martin and how your brother used to see him at the pub sometimes.'

'Oh yeah?' Kerry looked instantly wary.

'I just wondered if he'd ever mentioned seeing a woman called Olivia Cook with him?'

'Ent she that fancy one who's shacked up with that Zander Pettiford?' Kerry asked.

'That's her.'

'Don't know why she'd be hanging around with David Martin and my brother.'

'She wasn't always fancy,' Jude explained. 'Before Greener Days, she worked at Leigh Farm with Jim and David for a couple of years.'

'No wonder she left when something better turned up.'

'You think Zander Pettiford is a better bet?' Jude pulled a face.

'Not his biggest fan?' Kerry grinned. 'I think he's

pretty fit, myself. But then I guess you're looking more at his farming than his body, aren't you?'

'I just try not to look at any of it to be honest,' said Jude.

'So why are you asking about this Olivia girl?'

'Just interested in piecing a few things together,' said Jude.

'You think there's something in the whole hash thing with David then?'

'There might be.'

'Did you tell that policewoman who it was who gave you the lead?' Kerry looked as shifty as she always did when she talked about Binnie. She'd been conditioned to mistrust the police and it was a point of view that would take some time to shake off.

'I had to,' said Jude as she scoured the packed school field, searching for Lucy, Noah and Sebbie. 'But she said that it wouldn't impact Jamie's chances of an early release at all.'

'I know.' Kerry broke into a wide grin. 'We had a call from him yesterday. The hearing went well and they're setting a date for his release.'

'That's brilliant news,' said Jude.

'I was thinking he might be able to get a job with you up at the farm. He's a hard worker and he won't do anything stupid, I promise.'

'Oh, Kerry, we can't afford to pay anyone else, I'm afraid.' Jude was genuinely sorry that she couldn't offer to help as she knew how much Kerry adored her brother.

Kerry looked at her. 'This ent cos he's bin inside, is it? Cos I swear those days are gone and he's a changed man now.'

'No!' Jude shook her head. 'Between Noah, Frank and me, we can get most things done and then we get Spud in when needed. You know that.'

'Sorry.' Kerry looked contrite and Jude was reminded of how young she still was despite her outward appearance. 'I just don't want him doing anything stupid and getting in trouble again, 'specially when he's on parole.'

Jude squeezed Kerry's arm. 'With you looking out for him, he wouldn't dare.'

Kerry grinned at that. 'That's true enough. Look, there's a coconut shy. I used to be good at that but I always thought it was a bit crap that you won a coconut. I mean, what does a kid want to do with one of them?'

Jude pointed at the pile of miscellaneous prizes on the table next to the stall: obviously the result of a mass clear out of the village's cupboards. 'I think you might get to choose something from there instead,' she said. 'If you've still got it, that is.'

'Oh, I still got it.' Kerry rolled up her sleeves and Jude took a pound coin from her purse to give to Greta, the mother of one of Sebbie's friends who'd been roped into running the stall.

'There you go.' Greta passed Kerry three wooden balls. 'Stand behind the skipping rope and good luck.'

Kerry was clearly taking the whole thing very seriously, not wanting to let herself down in front of Jude after her big boast. She drew back her hand and aimed the ball which shot through the air and clean past the three coconuts propped on stands a few metres away.

'Just getting my eye in,' said Kerry, taking aim with the second ball.

This time it found its mark with such force that the coconut was sent flying into the orange netting that had been set up behind it.

'Bravo!' Jude clapped. 'Can she make it two out of three?'

It turned out that she could and a second coconut was callously dispatched and sent to join his friend on the grass at the foot of their pedestals. Kerry turned around in triumph.

'Told ya.'

'Well done,' said Greta. 'Two hits means you get two prizes.'

Kerry went over to rifle through the jumble on the table whilst Jude helped Greta retrieve the balls and reset the coconuts.

'Here you go.' Kerry passed Jude a book. 'I thought I'd better choose something for you, seeing as you paid for me to have a go.'

There was a mischievous smile on Kerry's face and Jude saw why when she turned the book over to look at the cover.

'*My Greener Days* by Zander Pettiford,' Jude read. 'Very funny.'

'Thought you'd like it. And I got this for Sebbie.' She held out a little resin figure of a border collie with her head cocked to one side and the tip of a pink tongue protruding from her open mouth. 'I thought it looked just like Pip.'

'It really does,' said Jude. 'He'll love it.'

Jude pushed the book into the depths of her bag and she and Kerry went off to find the face-painting table.

* * *

The school barbecue continued through the afternoon and involved a steady stream of entertainment on the makeshift stage that had been set up. Jude felt a pang of nostalgia as she watched the children perform various pirate-themed songs and dances that they'd prepared with their teachers.

It was a world she understood having spent four years earning her teaching degree and several years in the classroom before she gave up completely to take over the farm. And yet it was a world she now felt a little detached from. She no longer worked in schools and had been denied the opportunity of watching the children she and Adam had planned on having climb their way up through the classes until it was their turn to ring the school bell on their last day there.

At the end of a long afternoon, Jude helped tidy things away with Noah whilst Lucy took an over-sugared, overexcited, overtired Sebbie home for a bath.

By the time she and Noah were walking back to join them, she felt dead on her feet and ready for a bath of her own.

That night, Jude had a headache that rattled her brain as she tried to sleep. She went downstairs and dug around in her bag for a paracetamol. As well as the box of painkillers, Jude also found the book that

Kerry had chosen for her and shook her head with a wry smile. She looked at the staged picture on the front of Zander Pettiford in immaculately clean clothes, standing with one foot propped on an old stone trough. He was holding a shepherd's crook, although Jude imagined he'd never once used it to pull a sheep out of a muddy ditch or catch a ewe who needed a prolapse dealing with. Jude picked up a glass of water that was still on the table and swigged a little to help her swallow the tablets. Then she opened the book and flicked through the thicker pages of colour plates that were dispersed throughout. The later ones of Zander at Greener Days didn't really interest her but she did pay more attention to some images of him with the rest of The Spods in their heyday. There was no doubt that he looked the part on stage with the coloured lights bouncing off his guitar and a sea of adoring fans in front of him. There were pictures of them headlining Glastonbury, Reading and Leeds, The Isle of Wight, all the biggest festivals in the country, and abroad too.

Jude propped herself against the kitchen dresser and turned the pages.

Under one picture there was a caption that read:

Madison Square Garden – it was here that we realised we'd finally broken out in America.

Jude had obviously known that Zander's band was a big deal, but she wasn't really all that switched on to the world of celebrity and hadn't realised quite how big they were. If Coby Tyler hadn't died then perhaps they'd still be touring and making albums. But, as so often happened, fate had other ideas and Zander Pettiford was now more well-known for his views on farming than his rock and roll lifestyle.

Jude looked at a picture of the band in a hotel room on tour in Japan and wondered about the surrealism of their lives. They had the fame, the money, the adoration and they seemed to be having a great time on the surface. But when Jude picked apart the scene, she noticed the empty vodka bottle lying on its side under Coby Tyler's chair. The packet of Rizlas sitting on Zander's knee and the glassy look in his eyes. He was holding a bottle of whisky at such an angle that, if it hadn't already been half empty, it would have been pouring down the side of his leg.

And whilst Zander was off touring the world, getting off his face on whisky and weed, Olivia had finished her agricultural course and was working for Jim Martin. Jude found that she was more than a little interested in the two lives that had started off in a council estate and ended up on a vast country estate.

There were only two photos of Zander as a child and these were by far the most authentic pictures in the book as they were the only ones not taken with a professional camera. One was of Zander playing his first guitar, the guitar that Olivia had stolen money to buy him – Jude wondered if that little detail had made it into the book.

The other was of a young Zander and Olivia, perhaps seven or eight years old. They were standing in front of a Christmas tree together, arms wrapped tightly around each other and grinning madly into the camera. It was the only photo of Olivia in the whole book and Jude wondered if that was a decision Zander had made because he knew how much she hated being in the limelight.

Beneath the photo was the caption:

Me and Liv at the school Christmas disco.

Kerry had given the book to Jude in jest and yet Jude felt somehow compelled to dip into it. She was still standing in the kitchen in her pyjamas and her headache was refusing to shift, so she refilled the water glass and took it and the book up to bed with her.

The rest of the house was quiet as Jude closed her door and switched on her bedside lamp. Then she settled herself back on her pillow to read the first chapter.

Chapter 1 – My Early Life

Life was hard growing up in a council flat in Sheffield. Not bad necessarily but definitely hard. I don't wish that things had been different for me back then because I'm a firm believer in playing the hand you've been dealt, but that doesn't mean I don't understand the value of the privilege I now enjoy.

It's that understanding that made me take on the project at Greener Days because I think those of us in a position of privilege with the chance to do something good should use it wisely.

A lot happened before I took over the farm though, some of which you may already know about but plenty that you won't. I thought a lot about whether to include details of my childhood in this book and in the end I decided that my early days and the people who filled my world then shaped me into the person I am today so it was important to start with them.

My mum was a single parent and a real inspiration to me, she still is. She worked hard every day of her life doing several jobs at a time to bring in enough money to keep the two of us ticking over. I suppose you could say that she is responsible for my strong work ethic. There was always food in the house and she made sure the bills were paid and I had a school uniform that fitted, but it meant that I never really saw her.

I don't know what I'd have done or the kind of life I'd have forged for myself if it hadn't been for my best friend, Olivia, who lived with her dad in the flat next to ours. She was everything to me growing up, more than a friend really. We used to say that we were like sister and brother but with none of the bad bits. I can't remember ever fighting with Liv, not once. I'm sure we must have done at some point but I truly can't remember. It was as though we knew we both had so much going on in our lives that was trying to trip us up, we needed to be each other's safety nets, and that meant there was no room for arguments.

The chapter went on to talk about how fundamental the two women had been in Zander's life and why he was now so grateful that he could pay them back by looking after them. This made Jude's eyebrow raise as she thought of hardworking Olivia doing the lioness's share of the work on the farm, whilst Zander dealt with the publicity side of things.

The tone of the book was a little grating as it was clearly written with Zander casting himself as a hero and saviour of those around him. It was, however, fascinating to read and it was only after the first few chapters that her eyelids started to tell her it was way past the time they should have been closed.

For want of a better solution, and having been brought up to never turn the corner of a page down, Jude put a clean sock in the book to mark her place and switched the light off.

Before she slept though, her brain processed the gist of what she'd read about Zander and Olivia's upbringing. The facts about Olivia were sparse, deliberately so, but he did say that her father had cause to leave before she left school, so Olivia moved in with

Zander and his mother for the last year of her A levels.

Zander had already left school and was making a bit of money as a guitarist. By the time Olivia left school, The Spods had been formed and he had enough to send her to Hartpury agricultural college.

If Zander painted himself as the hero of his own life then he definitely thought of Olivia as his heroine. And that made Jude wonder exactly how far he would go for her in a dangerous situation. If Zander had thought David and Griff were threatening her in some way, would he think it was his job, as her saviour, to stop them both in any way possible?

Jude felt that the answer to this could very believably be yes.

19

The next day was Sunday and Lucy had made arrangements for Granny Margot to join them for a full roast lunch to celebrate her birthday. The invitation had been extended to Gerwain, along with Binnie, Sami, Kerry and of course Frank. Jude felt Marco's absence as it wasn't all that long ago that he would have been a natural addition to the party too.

Nobody was entirely sure how old Granny Margot was and she pretended that she herself had lost count of the years. As the manager of Perrins House, Gerwain had the means to find out but he kept his lips firmly sealed on the subject.

'That was delicious.' Granny Margot set her knife and fork down on her empty plate.

'Another slice of pork?' Lucy offered.

Granny Margot patted her rounded stomach, clad in a pair of violet linen trousers. 'I couldn't eat another bite, I'm afraid.'

'You have to have a bit of space.' Sebbie looked at her earnestly. 'I made you a birthday cake with real cream for pudding.'

'Did nobody ever teach you that you can be as full as a hay-barn after harvest and you'd still have space in your pudding tummy?' Granny Margot tickled Sebbie on the stomach and he dissolved into fits of giggles.

'Don't wind the boy up, Margot,' said Frank. 'He'll get indigestion.'

'Oh don't be such a stick in the mud, Frank. He's okay.'

'How about we all let our food settle for a bit and come back for cake and coffee in a little while?' suggested Jude. 'Sebbie, you can get down from the table and find something quiet to do if you like.'

Sebbie, who was penned into the corner of the full dining room, wriggled out of his chair and disappeared under the fully extended table. Jude felt a scurrying by her leg and looked down to find his head popping up next to her.

'Well that's one way to get out, I suppose,' she said.

'Now then, I've been waiting to ask you all the big question.' Granny Margot wiped her mouth and folded the paper napkin onto her plate. 'What's the latest news on the murder investigation?'

'I'm not sure you should be quite so keen to gossip about such things, Margot.' Frank looked at her over his glasses.

'Oh hush. I'm not gossiping, I'm assisting in the clue solving. Now let's clarify facts to make it easier for everyone, shall we?' She looked around the table and then carried on before anyone could put in a formal objection. 'David Martin was killed at the Three Counties in a murder that would suggest a crime of passion or something similar. There were eight suspects including Griff Gould who became the second casualty. That means there are now seven suspects in Griff's murder, one that must have taken a fair bit of planning to commit. Am I right so far?'

'You're doing very well,' said Binnie.

'Drugs were found in David's possession suggesting that there may be a link with his death, but he was also busy upsetting people left, right and centre with talk of developments on the Martins' farm, disgracing Zander Pettiford and trying to blackmail someone in a position of authority.'

'You are very well-informed in all this.' Sami looked at Jude suspiciously.

'The grapevine at the care home carries all sorts of interesting pieces of information my way,' said Granny Margot without batting an eyelid. 'Like the fact that Ffion Proctor's brother is a member of the planning department at Hereford Council and has been responsible for pushing at least one dubious large-scale planning application through.'

Jude raised her eyebrows at this; she hadn't seen Granny Margot since she'd discovered this particular piece of information. She cast a surreptitious glance at Lucy who was busy trying not to catch her eye.

'I assume you've already made a connection between the note and the blackmail,' said Granny Margot.

'We're aware that it's a possibility,' said Binnie.

'But are you also aware that Hugh Davies would have had a very good reason to have taken a bribe at the time the planning for the houses near Hereford went through?' Granny Margot picked up her cider glass and took a sip to whet her whistle before she delivered the punchline. 'I did a little digging of my own and I discovered that the year the planning went through, 2019, was the same year that the Davies family farm was struck down with a catastrophic number of TB cases.'

Jude remembered Ffion telling her about the TB disaster that had ripped its way through the cow herd and the farm's cash reserves. 'Ffion said they were on the brink of selling up,' she recalled.

'But they didn't,' said Granny Margot triumphantly. 'And where do you suppose the sudden injection of farm-saving money came from?'

'A backhander from Plover Homes,' said Jude.

'Now don't go jumping to conclusions.' Binnie pushed her plate away and rested her arms on the table.

'I'm not jumping anywhere,' Granny Margot retorted. 'I'm just laying down the facts. I'm also interested in the relationship between Jim Martin and Olivia Cook. I know she worked for him for a while and I wondered how much they saw of each other now. Frank, you know Jim.'

Frank itched the skin beneath his beard. 'I know that he had a very soft spot for Olivia when she was on the farm. Said she was one of the best workers he'd ever had and there was a feeling from many that he hoped she'd make a good match for David.'

Jude had been staring into the bowl of apple

sauce as she listened, deciphering the information and storing the useful bits away.

'Did David want that for himself?' she asked.

'I don't suppose any of us could know what that boy wanted.' Frank shook his head. 'He was trouble and Olivia did well to keep clear of him if you ask me.'

'What about Zander?' Lucy asked. 'Do you think she'd be better steering clear of him too?'

'That's a hard one, isn't it?' Frank pushed his glasses up his nose to look at her. 'If you ask Jim he'd say that he's a useless townie trying to play at being a farmer and making Olivia do all sorts of stupid things on that farm of his.'

'Isn't that what you think too, Dad?' Noah patted his father on the back playfully. 'Sounds exactly the words you'd choose.'

'Maybe,' said Frank. 'But there's no doubt he's looking after her, is there?'

Jude thought about the book she was reading and agreed. 'He's an interesting character,' she said. 'I can't work him out at all. I suppose that comes from developing a celebrity persona. He's trying so hard to make the public like him that I think it sometimes backfires. It's a shame, really. He's actually done some pretty cool things.'

Kerry let out a single loud guffaw. 'Oh my God, Jude. You're reading that book I won on the coconut shy, ent you?'

'What book?' asked Sami.

Jude refused to feel embarrassed about doing a little extra research. 'Zander's biography, and yes, actually I am reading it. I thought there might be something interesting to the case in it.'

'And is there?' Binnie asked.

'I've only read the first few of chapters and so far he's just talking about his childhood. It sounds pretty dismal and he definitely relied on Olivia a lot. It went both ways too – she moved in with them for a bit when her dad went away suddenly.' She looked at Binnie. 'I got the sense that he was serving a stint in prison.'

Binnie pulled a face to show that this was the first she'd heard of it. 'I'll run a check.'

'How would that be useful?' Sami asked. 'I mean, it must have been years ago so surely it can't have anything to do with what we're investigating.'

'Thanks for volunteering.' Binnie gave Sami a look. 'See what you can dig up tomorrow when you're back at the station.'

'See what happens when you go out to lunch

with your boss?' Sami rolled his eyes at Granny Margot who had been quietly taking in everything.

'I don't know about that,' she said. 'I was always my own boss and I rather liked it that way.'

'Is this what you lot always do when you get together for a posh lunch?' Kerry asked. 'Try and solve murders and stuff?'

'Not always,' said Jude. 'But we do seem to have a bit of a habit of it.'

Sebbie came rushing in then waving a piece of paper with a picture of what looked like a bunch of flowers drawn in wax crayon.

'This is for you, Granny Margot. It's a birthday card.'

Granny Margot pulled him into a hug and admired the card as though it were a genuine Monet. 'It's absolutely marvellous, darling. You are such a clever pickle. Now, didn't you mention something about a birthday cake?'

* * *

'I don't know why I'm surprised that lunch turned into a breakdown of the murder case I'm leading,' said Binnie as Jude walked her and Sami out to the car when it was time for them to go home.

'Sorry about that,' said Jude. 'I hope it didn't put you in a difficult position.'

'Not really. Nothing was discussed that hasn't already found its way into the public domain somehow anyway. There are some new pieces of information that aren't so public yet that you might be interested in though.' Binnie jerked her head back to the farmhouse. 'As long as none of it makes its way inside to the judge and jury in there.'

Jude smiled. 'I assume Granny Margot would be the one wearing the white curly wig in that scenario.'

'I think it would suit her,' said Sami.

'I'm only telling you because you have a habit of spotting things and making connections that we don't,' said Binnie. 'We've had further analysis back of the content of Griff's stomach. The whisky he ingested was not the same as that found in the bottle and the glass we found on the coffee table at his house. According to the experts, they were completely different and it's suggested that the one he actually drank came from a much more expensive bottle.'

'Further proof that someone had put a lot of thought into his murder.' Jude thought back to the Stockman's Bar and hearing Griff tell everyone how much he enjoyed a good glass of fine whisky. Had someone else noted this and used it to tempt Griff to let them come in on the pretence of talking? Perhaps someone who knew Griff was about to spill the beans to the police about something and who wanted to persuade him to change his mind.

'Whoever was at Griff's farm must have sat him down with a nice whisky, probably already laced with the sedative,' said Jude. 'Perhaps they went to see him on the pretence of trying some persuasion or bargaining. The fact that he managed to get the Proctors' ram makes me think that he wasn't above a bit of favour swapping.'

'What do you mean?' Sami asked.

'I mean that Ffion and Carl would not have got rid of their ram if they had a choice.' Jude crossed her arms in front of her and leant against the stone cider press that stood in the yard next to Binnie's car.

'Griff definitely had something over them,' said Binnie, 'and I think that Ffion's brother taking bribes from Plover Homes is a very plausible explanation.'

'What if Griff's demands didn't stop at the ram?' Sami suggested. 'What if he got greedy and wanted more?'

Binnie shook her head. 'There's one big problem. They all now have confirmed alibis for the time of Griff's death.'

'Who?' Jude asked. 'I know that Ffion, Olivia and Tara were all at the market but what about Carl and Hugh?'

'Hugh's is pretty flaky to be fair,' said Binnie. 'He went to see a property but the owner was a no-show so can't confirm this. Secretarial records match this.'

'That's more than flaky,' said Jude. 'It's barely worth taking any notice of.'

'Not on its own. But he was placed elsewhere before and after which means if he had done it he'd have had to have been driving with some welly to get to Griff's farm, butter him up with whisky and kill him before getting to his next appointment.'

'Doable though?' Jude asked.

'Just about.'

'What about Carl? You said he'd gone on a long walk on his own.'

'We now have CCTV confirmation of his story,' said Binnie. 'He went on a hike in the Wye Valley and we have camera footage from the car park that shows his pickup arriving and him getting out with a small backpack and walking boots on. He returns three hours later, opens his pack to tip his picnic rubbish in the bin and then gets back in the car.'

'Are you sure it was just the picnic rubbish?' Jude asked.

Binnie took out her phone and opened a file. She found the part in question and handed the phone to Jude who used two fingers to zoom in on the bin. She hit the edit button and adjusted the speed to make it run as slowly as possible. When she watched Carl throw his rubbish away, one piece at a time, she saw an apple core, sandwich box, crisp bag and chocolate bar wrapper but that was it. No whisky bottle or empty benzodiazepine bottle, no blood-soaked clothes and no used surgical gloves.

'Looks like he really did just go for a hike,' said Jude, who was watching him now return to the pickup and get inside. 'But I still think he and Ffion are hiding something. When I went to see them, she was definitely keeping me out of the house for some reason.'

'Then let's go and pay her another visit, just a social one,' said Binnie. 'Can you come up with a plausible reason why you might pop in and say hi?'

'How are you fixed on Tuesday?' Jude asked. 'I know they won't be at the farm then as they're taking some of their sheep to the Cheshire Show.'

'We don't have a good reason to go into an empty house with no search warrant though.'

'It won't be empty,' said Jude. 'Whenever they go to a county show, Ffion's sister stays at the farm to look after the animals. I thought it might be quite interesting to talk to her, and also she might be more agreeable to us going inside for a surreptitious snoop.'

'I'm all for that.' Binnie opened her car door. 'See you on Tuesday. I'll come and pick you up in the morning.'

'I'm working.' Sami looked dejected at the thought of missing out on a bit of out-of-uniform sleuthing.

'You wouldn't be able to come anyway,' Binnie pointed out. 'Jude and I are just being sociable. If you came then it would turn into a police procedural and we can't have that.'

'Whilst we're in that neck of the woods, how do you feel about breaking into the garage at Hope House?' Jude asked. 'Zander and Olivia are going to be in Cheshire supporting the Proctors so we should be able to have a mooch undisturbed.'

'We'd be skating on thin ice.' Binnie looked decidedly dubious at Jude's suggestion.

'You said yourself that we won't be able to go in legitimately without a search warrant and we both know we haven't got any evidence for that.'

Binnie leant against her car door. 'Which means we can't gain access.'

'But who would know? The key is hidden under a rock so we wouldn't have to break the lock.' Jude thought she saw Binnie showing signs of wavering. 'We could be in and out in minutes. Take a quick look around, see if there's anything in there and if there is I'm sure you could pull some strings to get that warrant. If you know for sure it would be worth it.'

Binnie let out a long sigh. 'Against my better judgement, okay then.'

'See you on Tuesday then.' Jude grinned at her.

Binnie and Sami got into the car and Jude waved them off before returning to the remainder of the birthday party.

Once the rest of the guests had left and the party had been tidied away, Jude picked up Zander Petti-ford's book and carried on reading it. There was nothing of particular interest in the chapters she read which took her as far as the forming of The Spods. But before she closed the book she flicked through the coloured plates again and was drawn to the image of the band with Zander cradling a bottle of whisky. Jude knew nothing about whisky but she as-sumed it was an expensive brand and made a note of the name, Bowmore. When she found a similar bottle online, she learned it was retailing for over a thousand pounds and seemed to be widely viewed as a whisky for the connoisseur.

Zander Pettiford was clearly a man who knew his whiskies. Had he used this to his advantage and taken a bottle round to Griff's house that he knew he wouldn't be able to resist?

Or had Hugh sourced the whisky? It might have been difficult but he'd had the opportunity to make a trip to Griff's and fudge the records in the diary. Perhaps Ffion and Carl had played their part somehow too.

Jude had a lot more puzzle pieces to fit together than when she'd woken up that morning but this didn't help her see things more clearly. She had more reasons to point the finger of suspicion, and yet that finger was still constantly moving.

There were many players in this mystery and one of them at least was a cold-blooded killer capable of planning a murder in meticulous detail. As long as they were still out there, Jude knew that anyone else who might be in a position to uncover their secrets was in danger.

20

Monday dragged for Jude. It was a day of no movement in the case and very little in the way of new information.

Binnie called with details of Griff's will which was mostly straightforward and uninteresting: everything had been left to his sister's two sons with a clause to say that the farm was to be kept as agricultural land whether they farmed it themselves or got a tenant in. The only exception was that all of his Kerry Hills went to Jim Martin, an inclusion that had been inserted just a few days after the Three Counties Show, which definitely was interesting.

Jim and Griff had been staunch enemies for pretty much their entire lives by the sound of it, and there had certainly been no love lost between them at the end. So why had Griff left the sheep to Jim?

There weren't all that many of them; like Jude, Griff had a range of different breeds on the farm, but there was the inclusion of the Proctors' show ram which should be worth a considerable amount of money if it went to market. Jude wondered if it was simply that Griff knew his pedigree sheep would be well looked after by his neighbour, or maybe that it was his way of finally burying the hatchet on his deathbed. But the timing of the inclusion meant that there must be something more in it. Perhaps Griff had felt compassion for Jim at the brutal loss of his son and wanted to do something nice for him without the awkwardness of Jim knowing what he'd done. Or was it an act of guilt? His way of assuaging his conscience about something that he could never admit to in life.

Jude had asked Binnie about David's will as well but as far as they could tell, he hadn't made one which meant that the Martins' farm would return to Jim as David's legal next of kin.

It seemed a coincidence that both deaths meant the same man was set to gain significantly. But then Jim hadn't really gained. He'd lost his son and with that the only natural successor to his farm. And would he have even known about Griff's will?

Jude wondered about the future of Jim's farm with no succession plan and suspected that on his death it would be the end of the line for yet another family farm. The only people these days who could afford to buy farmland were not those best equipped to become its custodian. It would most likely end up in the grubby hands of a big corporation who had no interest in best food production practices and just wanted land to access carbon credits. It was hard not to be constantly angry with the powers that be who continued to allow the desecration of traditional British farming. But Jude had a murder case to focus on and she was itching to get on with the planned trip to Abergavenny and Goodrich.

Binnie offered to drive as her little hatchback was far less conspicuous than Jude's bluebell-coloured County 110 Land Rover. It was also a much thriftier beast to drive out to the Welsh borders.

Jude had the foresight to pick up a can of fleece fixing spray and a bar of Tony's chocolate to take with her on the pretence of visiting Batters Farm to drop them off and wish Ffion and Carl good luck.

As expected, it was a woman who looked so much like Ffion that she had to be her sister, Caitlin, who opened the Proctors' front door when Jude knocked on it.

'Oh hi, I was hoping to catch Ffion before she went to Cheshire,' Jude said. 'Is she in?' She bent down to stroke Tom who'd come out to say hello to the visitors.

'No, I'm afraid she and Carl drove up last night.' Caitlin looked apologetic. 'I'm Ffion's sister, can I help?'

'Oh, that's a shame,' said Jude, hiding the fact that it was actually exactly what she'd been banking on. 'We came to wish them luck.' She held up the fleece fix and chocolate. 'Bit late for these, I suppose.'

'It's never a bad time for chocolate.' Caitlin took the gifts. 'I'll give them to Ffion when she's back. Who shall I tell her they're from?'

'It's Jude Gray. We met at the Three Counties when we were both showing our Kerry Hills.'

'Oh yes, Ffion told me all about you. You're from Malvern, aren't you?'

'That's right.'

'You didn't come all this way just to drop off some fixing spray, did you?'

'No. Actually my friend Binnie and I had to pick something up from Monmouth so I thought I'd quickly pop in to say hi to Ffion and wish her and Carl good luck.'

Binnie was primed to ask if she could go in to use the loo in the hope that Caitlin would invite Jude in to wait for her and they could have a subtle snoop around. There was no need for further subterfuge though.

'Now that you're here, why don't you come in for a cuppa. I was just about to make one anyway and I always love talking to other farmers.'

'If you're sure,' said Jude. 'That would be lovely.'

'Brilliant.' Caitlin whistled for Tom who ran back inside, checking over his shoulder that everyone else was following him in.

The inside of Batters Farm was as oppressive and dismal as the outside. Heavy, nicotine-stained wallpaper lined the hallway, peeling in places and textured with a pattern last fashionable a good few decades earlier. The carpet was a dark brown, obviously laid to hide any muddy footprints and there was a slightly stale smell to the place, but no undertone of cannabis.

'Excuse the mess,' said Caitlin as she took them into the kitchen which was much friendlier, with warm terracotta tiles, a large Welsh dresser and old range cooker. One corner was heaped with cardboard boxes and a big dog bed took up another. 'Ffion would love to get busy with some redecorating around here but she and Carl don't have the time.' She pointed to the boxes. 'Those have been there since they moved in a couple of years ago.'

'It's lovely in here,' said Binnie.

'The kitchen's not too bad, I suppose. The rest of the house is pretty grim though. But then she's not living here for the house, is she?' Caitlin pointed to the large window that looked out over the farm's pastureland full of contented Kerry Hills. 'And once they start making a bit of money from those sheep of theirs, they can pay for a deep clean and new carpets and curtains. A lick of paint and it'll be a new place.'

Jude wondered if the state of the house was the only thing that had made Ffion reluctant to invite her in on her previous visit.

'It's a shame they had to let that ram go,' said Binnie. 'He could have been a nice little money earner for them.'

At the mention of the ram, Caitlin's smiling mouth locked and she was instantly wary.

'Don't worry.' Jude decided to hedge her bets and play a dodgy game of pretending they knew more than they did. 'No need to say anything, we know what happened and completely understand. Any of us would do the same if we had the opportunity to save our farms. A friend of mine had TB on his farm. It nearly crippled him.'

'Worst time of our lives, that was,' said Caitlin. 'I was still at school and I came home to find Dad in floods of tears. I think it's the only time I'd ever seen him cry.'

'Ffion said that's why she'll never have cattle on her farm,' said Jude. 'We haven't had any at Malvern Farm since I've been there and until there's a proper answer to the TB problem, I have to say I'm not at all tempted.'

'I don't blame you,' said Caitlin. 'Are you mainly Kerry Hills or do you farm other breeds as well?'

The conversation turned to the farms that the two women lived and worked on and they shared an amiable chat about the pitfalls and joys of their industry. When Binnie asked to use the loo, Jude knew that she'd take the opportunity to suss out the rest of the downstairs and she kept Caitlin talking to give Binnie time.

When Binnie came back, Jude kept expecting Caitlin to ask her what she did for a living but Binnie was doing a great job of keeping up with the conversation and Caitlin obviously assumed that she was tied up in farming somehow too. No doubt that would change when she told Ffion about their visit.

'I hope the show's going well,' said Binnie.

'You decided not to take your sheep this time?' Caitlin asked.

'The Three Counties was my first ever show and I'm not sure I'm ready to do another one so soon afterwards,' Jude confessed.

'It wasn't the best one to cut your teeth on, that's for sure.' Caitlin picked up the teapot and topped up the three mugs on the table. 'It's dreadful what happened there, and then to Griff Gould too. Even though she had no love for either of those chancers, Ffion's been really shaken by the whole thing. I did wonder if she'd go ahead with the Cheshire Show herself but she needs to really establish Batters Farm as a top Kerry breeder this year.'

'They've had such bad luck,' said Jude. 'First that nonsense with the hair dye and then finding the note that David wrote. Cheeky bugger, trying to blackmail Hugh. It's just a shame that Griff found out about it and made her virtually give him the ram to keep him quiet.' Jude felt her nails dig into her palms a little as she tried to keep her voice light and not like she was digging for truths.

'Yeah, well thank goodness that's all over now and

we can get on with helping Ffion build up her flock.' Caitlin took a sip of her tea, unaware that she'd just unwittingly confirmed what Jude and Binnie had suspected. 'She and Carl work so hard, you know.'

'It'll come good for them,' said Jude. 'It's still very early in their journey.'

'I know you're right but it's been hard for Ffion to stay positive when everything seems to be against her right now.'

'Let's hope the show is going brilliantly and things start going their way a bit more.' Binnie tipped her mug up to finish the dregs of her tea. 'Well, I guess we should be heading off, Jude.'

Jude glanced at her watch. 'Gosh, yes. It was so lovely to meet you, Caitlin, after all the amazing things Ffion has told us about you and the family farm.'

'Thanks for the tea.'

Caitlin and Tom came out into the yard to wave them off, and Jude and Binnie drove away from Batters Farm knowing two things they'd only suspected when they had arrived. The blackmail note that David had written shortly before he died had been meant for Hugh Davies, and the reason Griff had been virtually gifted the Proctors' prize ram was because he had also discovered the truth behind the development-planning backhander Hugh had accepted.

'I think Caitlin has just confirmed two reasons for murder,' said Jude as Binnie turned out onto the road back to Ross. 'But do you think it's enough? I mean, I can see why Ffion or Carl would have snapped if confronted by David and his plan to manipulate Hugh. David was an arse and he would definitely have taunted them with the knowledge he had about Hugh's previous susceptibility to a bribe.'

'Blackmailing Hugh wouldn't have done David any good,' Binnie said. 'He works for Herefordshire Council so wouldn't be involved in the planning application that David wanted to put through for his farm in Worcestershire.'

'Perhaps the Proctors pointed this out to him and he threatened them.' Jude could picture the scene. Cocky, egocentric David expecting Ffion and Carl to conjure the impossible and bullying them with threats. It would be easy for one of them to snap and pick up the closest thing to hand, in this case a pair of sheep clippers. 'Ffion and her family are fiercely proud of their farming heritage and would want to protect it at all costs.'

'I agree.' Binnie pulled the car's visor down as she

was driving directly into the late morning sun. 'But enough to murder twice?'

Jude thought about it. She could certainly see how David was capable of pushing the right buttons to make anyone snap and impulsively lash out. But Griff's murder was a different kettle of fish altogether. He had clearly known about the bribe and how the Davies' family farm had managed to survive despite the devastation of TB wiping out the bank account in one swoop. Caitlin had confirmed that this was why he had become the owner of the most impressive Kerry Hill ram anyone in the field had come across for many years.

But would Ffion, Carl, Hugh or even Caitlin go as far as putting together such an intricate murder plan?

'Unless Griff had more beans to spill than just the fact he knew about Hugh and the planning application he pushed through,' said Jude. 'Perhaps he saw something the night David died and decided to keep it as currency rather than share what he knew with the police.'

'You think he saw who killed David?'

'Possibly. It's a much stronger motive to kill again. And perhaps that was what Griff wanted to tell you.

Maybe his conscience got the better of him and he decided to come clean.' Something else seemed to fit with this theory too for Jude. 'That could be the reason he left all the Kerry Hills to Jim in his will. It could have been his way of saying sorry for not coming forward with what he knew sooner.'

The discussion about wills and motives had taken Jude and Binnie over the Welsh border and back into Herefordshire where they traced the River Wye down to Hope House.

'It's up that track there,' said Jude as they approached. 'I checked for cameras the last time I was here and I'm pretty sure it's clean. No trees to hide them in and there were none around the house, but you might want to park the car in the lay-by up ahead anyway. I know Zander and Olivia are at the Cheshire show but that doesn't mean whoever came and let themselves in before won't be back again.'

'Good thinking.' Binnie drove past the track and parked in the same place that Jude had left the Land Rover a couple of days earlier.

They got out and walked the short way down the lane and up the track to the entrance of Hope House. Before they tried their luck at finding the key to the garage, Binnie went up to the front door and knocked loudly. There were no lights on inside and when Jude peered through the window, there was no sign that anyone had been there.

'I wonder if Zander's mum ever did live here or if it was always supposed to be a hidden asset for anything they don't want to be linked to Greener Days,' said Jude.

'Imagine having that kind of money,' said Binnie. 'Well there's nobody there now so let's go and have a look in this garage and see if there's anything worth breaking in for.'

Jude showed her the row of rocks that she thought the key to the garage was hiding under but they checked every one and found nothing.

'Dammit! I was sure it would be here.' Jude looked around to see if she was missing something. 'Whoever went inside when I was hiding round the corner definitely had to move something because I heard it.'

There were no other rocks or planters or anything else moveable that looked as though it was made of stone and Jude felt as though it had been a wasted trip when Binnie called her over to the water butt attached to the drainpipe coming off the roof of the garage.

'Look at this.' She pointed to the bricks it was resting on.

'It can't be under there,' said Jude. 'Nobody would be able to slide the entire water butt out of the way.'

'They wouldn't have to, look at the brick in the middle.'

Jude did as Binnie said and noticed that it was marginally lower than the others which meant it wasn't taking any of the weight as it wasn't touching the butt. As though she was playing an odd version of Jenga, Jude slid the brick out with a scraping sound that matched the one she'd heard before. There, in the dip of the brick, was a single key.

'Bingo,' said Jude. 'Well done, Binnie. Only one key though so which do you think it fits?'

There were three garage doors and the key fitted into the first lock perfectly. The metal door clattered as Jude rolled it up. She hoped that nobody was close enough to hear it but there was no going back now.

The inside of the garage was big and opened into one large space. It was full of the things that Jude would have expected to see there. A petrol lawn-mower and a cluster of garden tools. Several bales of hay that would be used for the sheep, a metal feed bin that Jude assumed contained sheep nuts or something else that needed to be kept away from rats, and a couple of red tubs containing sheep lick. White show halters were hanging from a hook and there was a set of electric clippers sitting on top of a table which were weighting a piece of paper down to stop it from blowing off when the door opened.

Jude went over to take a look and saw that it was a note, handwritten on a piece of paper surrounded with a pattern of green ivy leaves and a rough edge down one side that showed it had been torn from a notebook.

Left in usual place. Sorry but didn't bring enough to fulfil the extra you asked for so left overpayment for you. Will bring the remainder as soon as I can and collect money then.

'I recognise that paper,' said Jude. 'Tara Watson has a notebook just like it.'

There may have been any number of things that Tara might be dropping off in Zander Pettiford's garage for payment and Jude tried not to jump to the conclusion that her mind was presenting her with.

'What did you leave?' Binnie whispered as though to herself. 'And where exactly is your usual place?'

There were cupboards running along the far side of the garage and Jude went over to investigate them whilst Binnie focused on the hay bales and feed bin. The first only contained a mix of iodine sprays and fleece fix but the second one was far more interesting. A set of battery-operated scales sat next to a box of plastic bags ranging from small to tiny in size. There was an envelope containing a wad of fifty-pound notes, as well as rolls of tape and a little brass bowl with a pouring lip on it.

Jude picked the bowl up and gave it a sniff. The smell was faint but it was definitely there. A pungent, earthy smell of dried marijuana.

'Gotcha,' said Jude at the same time as Binnie gave a gentle whoop of triumph.

Jude turned to see her standing over the metal feed bin holding up a large packet of something wrapped in brown parcel tape. Binnie had her back to the open garage door and Jude's smile at finding concrete evidence turned to horror as someone suddenly rushed in, taking them both by surprise. Binnie turned around just as Penny Watson flew at her with the hoe that Jude had seen leaning up against the wall of the garage.

'No!' shouted Jude, rushing towards Penny but

getting there too late as she heard the metal of the sharp weeding head connect with Binnie's skull.

Binnie crumpled to the ground and Penny stood over her, shaking with the enormity of what had happened.

'Oh Lord. What have I done?' Penny whispered. She'd turned as white as a ghost and her eyes had taken on the full horror of the situation as she stared down at Binnie.

Jude grabbed the hoe from her hands and tossed it away before dropping to her knees next to Binnie. There was a large gash across her forehead and her eyes were closed but she was still breathing.

'Binnie,' Jude shouted. 'Binnie, can you hear me?'

To her intense relief Binnie's eyes opened and she tried to sit up.

'What happened?' Binnie asked. She touched her forehead and looked at the blood that came away on her fingers. Penny crouched down as though to help but Jude didn't trust her in the slightest.

'Get away from her,' she shouted.

Penny stepped back and Jude managed to help a wobbly Binnie to her feet.

'I didn't know it was her,' said Penny. 'Or you, Jude. What are you even doing here?'

Jude knew she had to take control.

'We were fetching something for Olivia.' Jude hooked her arm around Binnie's waist so that she was taking a lot of her weight. 'As were you, no doubt. I'm guessing the money in the cupboard is meant for you.'

Penny's eyes flicked to the cupboard at the far end of the garage. 'I didn't know that you had dealings with Olivia.'

'We all like to keep things quiet, don't we?' said Jude, moving towards the open garage door. 'And I assume we both want to keep it that way.'

Penny squinted at her, trying to work out whether Jude was to be trusted. If Jude was going to get Binnie out safely and have a chance of restraining Penny too, she knew she had to tread carefully and not give her cause to come after them.

'We've got what we came for and I need to get my friend checked over so I'll leave you to lock up and put the key back,' said Jude.

She took another step towards the door, struggling under Binnie's weight but strong with determination. Penny watched them leave and then went over to the cupboard to collect her money. Jude knew she had to act fast and as soon as she was clear of the garage door, she propped Binnie against the side of the garage, reached up and pulled the door down, twisting the key in the lock just as the sound of hammering came pounding on the other side.

With shaking hands, Jude pulled her phone out to make the emergency call. Whilst she was talking to the operator, Jude saw Binnie's eyes roll back in her head and she caught her just before she collapsed.

21

Jude sat on a chair at the hospital waiting for news to come out of the operating theatre. She had accompanied Binnie in the ambulance and watched all the beeping, flashing machines that showed she was still alive whilst a paramedic used a bag to get air into her lungs. As soon as they arrived at Hereford A&E, a team of medical professionals were waiting to rush Binnie straight into theatre whilst Jude was ushered to a plastic chair and offered a cup of tea.

She'd let the tea go cold as she stared into the cardboard cup, her focus bypassing the brown liquid and searching the floor for answers. Someone had told her that the blow to Binnie's head had caused an acute subdural haemorrhage and that she was undergoing an operation to remove the blood clot on her brain. What she didn't know and what she certainly didn't want to ask Dr Google was what the prognosis was, the chances of survival, the quality of life Binnie might expect if she did survive. These were questions she desperately wanted answered and yet she knew that only time would be truly honest with her.

'Jude!' Sami rushed into the waiting area, his face as worried as she knew hers must look. 'Any news?'

Jude shook her head. 'Nothing. She's still in surgery, they said it could take anything from one to four hours, depending on the size of the bleed they find.'

She looked at her watch, expecting it to be already near the two-hour mark but discovered that she had only actually been sitting in the waiting room for about thirty minutes. Sami took a seat next to her and leant forward to rest his elbows on his knees.

'I can't believe she's in there,' he said. 'Not Binnie Khatri the invincible.'

Jude leant over and took his hand. 'You're right, Sami. She *is* invincible and therefore any minute now someone in scrubs is going to walk through those doors and tell us that she's out of theatre and will make a full recovery.'

Sami squeezed her hand. 'I hope you're right.'

They sat in silence for a while, each lost in their own thoughts, until Sami's phone pinged and he checked his messages.

'Penny Watson has admitted attacking Binnie. She'll go to prison,' he said.

Jude nodded. It was good news but it didn't help the surgeons who currently had their fingers or instruments, or however it worked, inside her best friend's head.

'They've pinned the cannabis production on her too,' said Sami said. 'Apparently she didn't deny it although they've yet to search her farm. She's saying that Tara had nothing to do with it, didn't have a clue. I don't buy that though. How can someone grow drugs under your nose and you have no idea it's going on?'

Jude found she didn't really care. She didn't care about the drugs or who was involved and in what capacity. She didn't even care about the murders that had taken Jude and Binnie to Hope House in the first place. All she cared about was what life would look like when they finally had news about Binnie.

Jude just wanted to sit in silence and wait but

Sami obviously dealt with stress in a very different way and he wanted to talk.

'Do you think Penny killed David Martin and Griff Gould?' he asked. 'She's shown she definitely has a violent streak.'

'I don't know.' Jude picked at the edge of her fingernail, knowing that it was going to hurt but relishing the distraction of the pain.

'I suppose it could have been any one of them,' said Sami. 'Penny, Tara, Zander, Olivia, they must have all been mixed up in this so all would have had plenty to lose. Perhaps they were in it together, but who do you think was the brainbox behind Griff's murder? I mean, that took some planning, didn't it?'

'Sami, stop.' Jude clamped her hands to her forehead. 'I don't know who killed David and Griff and I don't know exactly what parts they all played in the whole marijuana thing but right now I don't care. I'm sorry. I know you're worried too but until I know Binnie's going to be okay, I just can't...'

Jude ran out of words and felt the comfort of Sami's arm wrap around her shoulders and pull her in for a hug.

'Sorry, Jude,' he whispered. 'I don't know when to stop when I'm frightened.'

'I know.'

They sat like that, glued together in their fear, waiting for news. Jude fielded calls from Lucy and Noah offering to come and lend their support, and Sami took a call from another colleague but they told everyone else not to come. There was no point in a whole crowd of people hanging around; they would call if there was news.

Eventually, a man came to find them who introduced himself as Mr Lavin, the neurosurgeon who had carried out Binnie's craniotomy and removal of the haematoma. Jude and Sami jumped to their feet.

'Is it done?' Sami asked.

'Is she going to be okay?' Jude added.

'It's early days but the operation was a success.' Mr Lavin smiled and right then, that smile meant everything to Jude. That smile meant it was good news. It meant he believed Binnie was going to be okay and it meant she could ease off a little on the worry scale. 'She's in intensive care whilst her brain has a chance to start the healing process but we are confident that she has a very good chance of recovery.'

Jude's heart swooped and bubbled at this piece of golden news. She grabbed the surgeon's hand and pumped it with both of hers. 'Thank you so much.'

'Can we see her?' Sami asked.

'She'll be groggy for a while yet,' said Mr Lavin. 'I would suggest you head home now and come back in the morning, see how she's doing then. In the meantime, if anything happens that you need to know about, someone will give you a call.'

Mr Lavin disappeared back through the double doors and Jude and Sami looked at each other, beaming in delight. Sami opened his arms and Jude hugged him tightly, grateful for an outlet for the intense feelings of relief that had taken over from the huge strain of the past couple of hours. As she pulled away, their faces touched for the briefest of moments and Jude felt Sami's lips gently brush hers. It was a surprise but not an unpleasant one and it was far from being a romantic gesture on either of their parts. It felt more like the release they both needed to acknowledge their shared joy that had come after inwardly fearing the worst.

'Jude?' Marco's voice cut through the moment and she instinctively stepped away from Sami's embrace.

'Marco!' she said. 'What are you doing here?'

'Lucy told me what had happened and I just thought I should be here to see if you were doing okay.' He looked awkwardly at Sami. 'I did try calling but your phone was off.'

'Yeah, I switched it off to stop the constant beep-ing.' Jude was embarrassed to have been caught in what must have appeared to be a highly inappropriate clinch. 'The surgeon has just been out to see us, Binnie's going to be okay.'

Marco smiled a wide, genuine smile that still had the power to disarm Jude entirely. 'That's brilliant news. Are you allowed in to see her?'

'No, actually we were told to go home and come back in the morning.'

'Oh, right,' said Marco. 'I can give you a lift if you like?'

Jude looked at Sami.

'I have my car with me but thanks for the offer,' he said.

'Jude?' Marco asked, and although nobody was outwardly making her pick between them, to Jude it felt as though there was more to the question than just a case of whose car she travelled back to Malvern in. A week or so ago Jude would have thought nothing of accepting a lift from Marco. She would have enjoyed the comfort of being in his presence, saying only what they needed to and letting an easy silence fall when no words were required. But so much had changed and the situation had become a lot more complicated since she had realised her true feelings for him. Not to mention the fact that he was now dating someone else and had just caught her in a dubious embrace with Sami.

'Actually, I could do with heading straight to work. I want to catch up with what's been happening whilst we've been in here,' said Sami.

'I'd love a lift.' Jude tried to make it sound as though this wasn't just because it would be easier on Sami. 'It'll give us a chance to catch up. It feels like we hardly see each other these days.'

'Great. That's settled then.' Marco's smile seemed genuine as Jude and Sami gathered up their things and the little party made their way out to the car park. When it came time for them to part ways, Jude gave Sami a quick hug and followed Marco over to his sky-blue Renault 4. It was small and old with rattles and creaks but Jude loved travelling in it.

'Thanks for coming over,' she said as she buckled herself into the passenger seat.

'I'm glad to hear Binnie's going to be okay.' Marco turned the key in the ignition but before he put the car in gear to get the old thing moving, he turned to Jude. 'And I'm glad I was here to take you home. You're right, we haven't seen each other properly since that night when I told you about Clara and I've missed you. Things aren't weird between us, are they?'

Jude knew that they were weird and that they'd continue to be a little bit weird until she had moved on in the same way Marco had. But she also knew that she valued his company far too much not to try and get that easy friendship they'd enjoyed back on track.

'No, not at all,' she said. 'I think I was just a bit surprised to see Clara heading into your house that night. But you know how much I love our friendship and I've really missed you too.'

Marco's brow furrowed. 'You mean the night the sheep was stuck and you had to go home early? You saw Clara then?'

Jude realised her mistake. 'Um, yes. I thought I'd forgotten my jumper so Lucy turned round and we saw Clara. But then I found my jumper on the back seat of her car so we went home.'

'To deal with the stuck sheep.'

'That's it. To deal with the stuck sheep.'

Marco shifted his weight a little so he was properly facing her. 'Jude, I want you to know that I didn't call Clara the moment you left. She came round to return something she'd borrowed from me.'

Jude wasn't exactly sure what she was supposed

to make of that. 'It doesn't matter. I mean, I know I said that it had surprised me but you're a free man. I just didn't know how Clara would feel if I was always showing up and lurking in your house like we used to.'

'Clara knows that you're one of my closest friends.' Marco turned back to the steering wheel and slid the car into gear. 'And anyway, she's got nothing to worry about now that you're with Sami.'

Jude felt herself blush. She should put Marco right, tell him that there was absolutely nothing going on between her and Sami and that Marco had witnessed the totality of their brush with romance in that one fleeting half-kiss. But for some reason she held back. She longed for her friendship with Marco to return to how it had been and maybe that would be easier if he thought she was also in a new relationship.

Jude decided not to deny or confirm Marco's suspicion, instead she moved the conversation on to less problematic topics, keeping the tone light until before too long it was as though things really hadn't changed between them. They were chatting, teasing each other and laughing together as they always had. By the time Marco dropped her off at the farm, Jude felt completely at ease in his company again and so much happier for it.

* * *

As soon as she had word from the hospital that Binnie had been moved out of intensive care and was able to have visitors, Jude went to collect Sami to drive him over to Hereford. She'd offered so that they could carry on to Hope House after their visit to the hospital for Sami to collect Binnie's car which was still in the lay-by over there.

'Morning, Jude,' said Sami as he got into the Land Rover. The carefree ambience that usually radiated off him was missing and there was no smile on his face as he addressed her.

'She'll be fine,' said Jude. 'You know that, don't you?'

'Of course I do. Tough as old boots, is DI Binita Khatri.' He smiled at last but there was a nervous energy behind it. 'Look, Jude. About yesterday...'

It was then that Jude realised his jittery demeanour wasn't wholly to do with the fact that they were on their way to visit his boss and good friend in hospital. He'd clearly been thinking more about their kiss than Jude had and that threw her off balance, hoping that he wasn't about to declare something that would put her in an awkward situation.

'What about yesterday?' she asked.

Sami took a deep breath. 'Jude, you know I think you're brilliant, I really do, but I just don't think we'd be right for each other.'

Jude snorted reflexively before looking at the constant jester and realising that this time Sami wasn't joking.

'Oh, you're serious,' she said.

'Not as serious as I was a couple of minutes ago.' Sami cocked his head. 'I've been worrying about that kiss all night, thinking I'd taken advantage of you when we were both in an emotional state.'

'No advantage taken.' Jude leant over and took his hand. 'It was just one of those things. Like you say, we were both emotional and it had been a very long afternoon. That kiss was a reaction to the stress and relief we'd shared, nothing more.'

Sami sank back into the passenger seat and clipped his seatbelt in place. 'Good,' he said, returning to his usual self. 'Glad we got that cleared up.'

'Me too.' Jude set off towards the main road into Hereford. 'Now tell me everything new. Who's been arrested and what do we know?'

As they drove through the Herefordshire countryside, Sami updated Jude on everything that had happened since Penny had been arrested the day before. Although the drug raid and incident involving Binnie were being handled by a team from Hereford, it was so closely linked to the ongoing investigations into the two murders that Binnie had been leading that the Malvern team were also heavily involved.

Sami knew that Penny, Olivia, Zander and Tara had all been brought in for questioning, and their stories all tallied.

Penny had been alone in growing the cannabis in a container on the edge of the farm which she had told Tara was rented by someone else. She was adamant that Tara had no idea what she was doing and there was currently nothing to suggest otherwise so she had been released.

The whole thing had started when Tara brought Olivia back to the family farm during the summer break from agricultural college. One evening, Olivia had been telling them about her father and how he'd worked for a man who'd set up an inner-city cannabis farm and had earnt a fortune.

'According to Olivia, unbeknownst to her dad, his boss had registered the lockup where he grew the stuff to him,' said Sami. 'When the police raided it, her dad was the only one on site and he was too scared to turn grass.'

'So he took the rap for the whole thing.'

'Exactly. Although it sounds like he wasn't a nice man anyway so probably got what he deserved. He used to take Olivia down to the lockup and make her help him look after the plants when she was just a child. Not child-appropriate labour but it would come in very handy when she agreed to help Penny set up a similar enterprise.'

Jude thought about the woman she'd met at the Three Counties. Robust, unsinkable, full of gumption. Despite her short stature and advancing years, Penny had handled the sheep as though they were nothing more than cuddly toys. When she'd walked in on David in a threatening position with her daughter, she had been furious and mighty in her verbal attack. Jude had no doubt that Penny was capable of setting up a cannabis farm, although she was surprised at her morals.

'I'd have thought that producing drugs to make a quick buck would have gone against everything she believed.'

'It sounds as though her husband racked up a lot of debt behind her back,' said Sami. 'He overspent on new machinery, bought a brand-new combine harvester in the hope he could make his money back by contracting himself and the combine out to other farmers each harvest time. But his sums didn't add up and he didn't take into account that most of the farmers already had harvesting contracts in place so the money didn't come in.'

Jude knew that a machine like that was worth half a million new and not easy to sell on second-hand without a significant loss.

'That wasn't the only expense, either. It sounds like he was a farm machinery shopaholic and didn't know how to stop.'

'Bloody hell,' said Jude. 'The Imelda Marcos of tractors.'

'Something like that.' Sami drummed his fingers against the glovebox. 'The combine was the last straw though. It almost broke them and Penny gave him an ultimatum. Either he handed over full control of the farm's finances to her or she would leave him. He cut himself off completely from his credit cards and bank accounts but that didn't clear the debt.'

'So Penny needed to diversify quickly to save the farm?'

'Exactly. She contacted Olivia for advice on how to set up everything she needed to grow cannabis and Olivia used her contacts to help get the equipment.'

'That must have been an expensive and risky endeavour,' said Jude.

'Worth it though by the sounds of it as they started to bring in serious money within the first six months. By that time, Zander was establishing himself in the music scene and had introduced Olivia to a lot of people, plenty of whom were keen for clean weed with a good provenance.'

Jude flicked her indicator on as they came to traffic lights on the outskirts of the city. Her mind was a whir with the balls of the two women to risk everything in that way, and to be so successful in their enterprise. Up until they'd got caught.

'I wonder how long they'd have got away with it if David's murder hadn't led the investigation to Hope House.'

'Who knows,' said Sami. 'He obviously knew about what was going on though, so that puts everyone involved in the spotlight again although they're all obviously still denying all knowledge. Do you think Penny could have killed David?'

Jude remembered Penny's shocked reaction when she saw Binnie crumple and the blood pouring from her head. It wasn't a look that she could equate to a cold-blooded killer.

'I suppose she could have struck out at David if she felt cornered but I'm not convinced she'd have been able to set up Griff's murder and cut his wrist,' said Jude. 'What about Tara? I'm not sure I believe that she had no idea what her mother and close friend were up to.'

'Neither do I,' said Sami.

'Who have you still got in custody?' Jude asked as she pulled into a parking space at the hospital.

'Penny has been charged with grievous bodily harm and the production and supply of an illegal class B drug so she won't be coming out any time soon. Olivia is up on charges of supplying. We have nothing on Tara or Zander so they've been released.'

'But still nobody to pin the two murders on,' said Jude.

'Not yet.'

22

Binnie was asleep when Jude and Sami went into her room. White bandages were wrapped around her head and wires and tubes linked her to myriad machines.

'She's very drowsy,' said the nurse who showed them in, 'but she is aware of where she is and who she is. I'm sure she'll be pleased to see you when she wakes up.'

Jude and Sami sat down in chairs on either side of the bed. Seeing their strong, courageous friend reduced to a silent pile of sheets and a hospital gown was a real shocker. Of course, they'd known that it would take time for Binnie to recover from the injury and operation – having brain surgery was a pretty significant bump in the road – and yet it still took them by surprise to see her so broken.

'There's no part of her that isn't connected to some machine or other.' Sami pointed to the tube that was coming from her head. 'Is that one running straight into her brain?'

Jude nodded. 'I think it's measuring the pressure in her skull. I know it's a lot to take in but it's all here to help her get back on her feet as quickly as possible.'

Jude glanced down at the catheter bag attached to the side of the bed and was very glad that Sami had chosen to sit on the opposite side.

'She looks so fragile,' Sami said. 'Like if any one of those tubes comes loose, that'd be the end of her.'

'Sami!' Jude admonished.

'Sorry. It's just I'm so used to seeing her marching everywhere with a fierce look on her face just waiting to tell me off about something or other.' Jude could see tears in Sami's eyes. 'I won't be happy until she wakes up and tells me off.'

Binnie's eyes flickered open and she ran the tip of her tongue over her cracked lips but didn't move. Jude's heart soared and she took her friend's hand gently, delighted to feel how warm it was.

'Hey there,' Jude said. 'I'd ask how you're doing but I suspect that's a stupid question.'

Binnie gave the smallest of smiles.

'Okay, boss?' Sami took her other hand, his face virtually splitting in half, his grin was so wide. 'You had us all worried there for a while.'

Binnie turned to look at him. 'Sounded to me like you were working out which tube to pull out,' she croaked.

Sami's eyes crinkled in delight and he looked across at Jude. 'There it is,' he said. 'I take that as a telling off. I can relax now.'

Binnie was clearly exhausted and kept falling in and out of consciousness whilst Jude and Sami chatted, keeping the conversation light and away from cannabis suppliers and murder cases. There would be plenty of time for Binnie to catch up when she was well enough to do so.

After an hour or so, Jude thought it was best to leave Binnie to rest so she and Sami said their goodbyes and promised to visit soon.

'She didn't ask one thing about the case,' Sami said as they walked down the long corridor back to reception. 'I thought she'd want to hear how it was all going.'

'I'm glad she didn't,' said Jude. 'She needs a complete break from it all to recover properly.'

'I hope we crack this before she gets out.'

'So do I,' Jude agreed.

They pushed through the main doors and stepped back out into the sunshine.

'I'd be very surprised if Zander wasn't mixed up in all this somehow,' said Jude. 'He and Olivia are so close. He obviously bought Hope House for her and surely he can't just have thought that was so they could keep a few sheep out in the paddock.'

'Hope House was originally bought for Zander's mum,' said Sami. 'Lorna did move in for a short while, when Zander and Olivia first took Greener Days on, but she had a stroke soon after and they had to put her into a home.'

'That was handy,' said Jude, who couldn't help being suspicious when things like this worked out so perfectly for someone with criminal intentions.

'I thought that too, but it sounds like Olivia and Zander both genuinely love Lorna. She looked after them as best she could when they were growing up, gave Olivia the closest thing to stability when her father was locked up. I really do think that Hope House was bought with best intentions.'

'But it became useful when Lorna left as they now had the perfect place for breeding pedigree sheep and running a hash business.' Jude unlocked the car and they both climbed in.

'Yes,' said Sami. 'A business that Zander claims to have known nothing about.'

'Of course not.' Jude pulled the parking ticket from the windscreen and stuffed it into the central storage compartment with all the rest of the rubbish. 'Imagine the backlash if it came out that he was involved. It's going to be damaging enough to the reputation of Greener Days as it is.'

Jude thought about Zander and the other three that were either definitely or possibly involved in the drug supply. They all had something to lose once the truth came out. Penny would have faced a prison sentence even if she hadn't attacked Binnie. Olivia too and if Tara was involved then she would also be in deep trouble. The future of the Watsons' farm was hanging in the balance and yet it felt to Jude as though Zander was the one with most to lose.

If he was convicted of supplying drugs on the scale that it seemed had been going through the garage at Hope House, a prison sentence would be just one of many problems for him.

The more Jude thought about it, he was also the only one out of the four who she could imagine going round to Griff's house armed with an expensive bottle of whisky, similar to the one she'd seen in the photograph in his memoir, and use it to frame Griff's suicide.

Jude knew he had an electric motorbike which could have been the perfect means of escape whilst Jude and Binnie had been trying to save Griff's life. Zander was clever too. He knew how to lay a scene and create an illusion.

'Zander Pettiford doesn't have an alibi for the day Griff was killed, does he?' Jude asked.

'That's right,' said Sami. 'Why?'

'Because I think he might have been the one to kill Griff,' said Jude. 'I'm wondering if David confronted Olivia at the show and she reacted by stabbing him with the closest thing available. We know Griff wasn't above a little blackmailing, you only have to look at the Proctors and their prize ram to see that.'

'And you think he might also have been blackmailing Olivia because he knew that she'd killed David?'

'If he had then Zander would have two reasons to want him dead. He'd want to protect the two things he loved most in the world. His best friend and his reputation.'

* * *

Jude did not enjoy revisiting Hope House to drop Sami off by Binnie's car. The police car sitting at the end of the track only reminded her of the danger she had led Binnie into the day before.

She was glad to be on the road again and heading back to Malvern End.

But as she hit the junction where she should have turned east, she found herself drawn westwards to the Watsons' farm.

Jude didn't trust Tara when she said she'd had no idea that her mother had been growing cannabis for Olivia, the college friend she'd introduced to the family, to sell on. It just seemed inconceivable to Jude and, with Binnie incapacitated, she was ready to find out the whole truth.

She didn't know what to expect when she knocked on the door and was a little surprised Tara made it easy for her by not only opening the door but inviting Jude inside. They went into the kitchen and sat down but this time there was no cup of tea or slice of fresh bara brith on offer.

'I assume you're here about your friend.' Tara looked ashen, as though she hadn't slept since her mother had been arrested. 'How is she?'

Jude rested her hands on the table and glowered at Tara. 'I've just come from the hospital. She's had an operation on her brain and has a pipe drilled into her skull to relieve the pressure.'

'Oh Christ.' Tara exhaled and Jude could see that she was shaking. 'Will she be okay?'

Jude had to remind herself that it wasn't Tara's fault that her mother had flown at Binnie with a gardening hoe and that no purpose would be served by making her feel worse than she clearly already did.

'It's too early to say exactly what the repercussions will be but the doctors seem pleased with the way the operation went and, although she was sleepy, she was able to say a few things to us.'

'That's good,' said Tara. 'I hope she recovers well and quickly.'

'Thank you.'

'Look, Jude, I'm sure you're here because you're looking for answers but I already told the police. I don't know anything. I know it sounds ridiculous but when Mam told me that the lockup was being rented by someone else, I just believed her. Why wouldn't I?'

Jude searched her face for traces of a lie but had learnt not to trust the innocence that some people managed to paste on like face paints.

'Did you know about the debt your dad had got you into?' Jude asked.

Tara shook her head. 'Most of that was whilst I

was away at college. I did wonder about the new combine but just believed them when they told me it would pay for itself once the harvest contracts came in.'

She really did sound genuinely distraught and Jude softened. If she was telling the truth then all of this must have come as a whopper of a shock and with Penny out of the picture, it would be down to Tara to bear the burden of the consequences her parents' actions would have on the farm.

Tara buried her head in her hands and let out a strangled howl. 'What am I going to do, Jude? It's all such a bloody mess. Mam isn't evil.' She stopped and looked at Jude. 'You've met her. You know that. She only did what she did because she had to find money fast to save the farm. And I can't believe she meant to hurt DI Khatri, I really can't. She just lashed out in the heat of the moment. It happens all the time when someone is frightened or feels cornered.'

Tara scrubbed her knuckles against the pressure points at each side of her head. 'It's just like... gah! Oh, what did you do?'

'It's just like what?' Jude asked.

She had been certain that Tara couldn't have been so blind that she hadn't spotted anything that would alert her to what had been going on under her nose for so long. Now she wondered what else Tara knew about that she was hiding.

'Jude, I'm so worried.'

There was a knock on the door then and Tara visibly jumped, her nerves clearly in tatters.

Jude saw Tara glance at the window before scrunching her eyes shut as though to block everything out. 'It's the police again.'

She opened her eyes, her mouth set in a tight, straight line. 'I'd better go and see what they want.'

Jude watched her get up, a little unsteadily, and walk out of the kitchen. She heard voices and then footsteps told her that Tara was returning and she wasn't alone.

'They've come to search the house.' Tara sank back into her kitchen chair and wrapped her arms tightly around her body as though she was trying to protect and comfort herself.

Jude didn't want to stick around any longer. She felt bad leaving her but Tara wasn't the only one who felt wrung out. Jude had watched her best friend collapse in front of her after being cracked on the head by Tara's mother. She had spent the previous day in hospital worrying for Binnie's life and she'd spent the morning watching her struggle to do more than muster the odd sentence in the short spells she was able to stay awake. Jude had little capacity for any further feelings.

'I'm sorry.' She stood up. 'I have to get going.'

* * *

That evening, Jude called the hospital to find out how Binnie was doing and was told that she'd spent the day resting but that all signs were looking hopeful and they should be removing the ICP monitor from her brain the following day.

Jude called Sami to let him know and then tried to switch off for the night by watching television with Lucy and Noah. Of course, with Binnie in hospital and the murders still unsolved, relaxation of either the body or mind was impossible.

She sat on the sofa, fiddling with the corner of a scatter cushion and going through everything she knew, trying to uncover the one thing she'd missed that would point her to the truth. Earlier that day she'd been so certain of Zander's guilt when it came to at least Griff's murder. But as time passed she found other suspects creeping back in and her mind shifting. Tara definitely seemed to know more than she'd admitted to, for one thing.

What did she know for certain?

Penny had being producing hash for Olivia to distribute.

David had been getting a supply from somewhere, quite possibly either Penny or Olivia. It could have been either of them he was accusing of becoming greedy in the background of Zander's Instagram video.

Penny, Olivia, Tara and Zander all had a lot to lose if David blew the whistle on the whole set up at Hope House.

David was trying to blackmail Hugh Davies, which meant Ffion's family also had a lot to lose.

David was a womaniser. Jude had seen first-hand his inappropriate advances to Tara and had pinned him as a letch from the start. He was threatening and intimidating.

Griff had been blackmailing Carl and Ffion.

Griff had been planning on sharing a piece of important information with the police.

Someone had been at his farm when Jude and Binnie arrived and had managed to leave silently, getting far enough away from the scene before the police began their search.

Jim had arrived on the scene very quickly.

Jim had become attached to Olivia during her time working on his farm.

The list went on, tangling around itself and throwing up countless different possibilities.

Every person who featured had reason to want both men dead but who had been pushed far enough to make it happen?

As Jude picked at a thread on the cushion, Tara Watson was once more at the front of her mind. It felt as though perhaps she had been about to say more just before the police had arrived to carry out the house search. Something that explained her reaction and the things she said.

It's just like...

What did you do?

I'm so worried.

And when she'd been talking about her mother's attack on Binnie, Tara had reasoned that things like that happened all the time. People lashing out in the heat of the moment when they were frightened or caught by surprise.

She was right, Jude had already known that much, but the way Tara had been so emphatic in her proclamation, along with the other things she'd said, made Jude deeply suspicious.

As the credits rolled at the end of the David Attenborough documentary Jude hadn't been watching she was starting to feel certain that there was a very real chance that Tara was either the person who'd lashed out with the sheep clippers, or she knew who it was. She hadn't just been justifying her mother's attack on Binnie when she'd said those words, she'd been excusing David Martin's killer.

She had seemed near breaking point and Jude found herself wondering if she might be able to give her a little push, just enough for her to crack and off-load everything she knew. Perhaps another night on her own in a house with just her conscience and fears to keep her company would be enough.

Jude went to bed that night knowing that she had to be back in the Brecon Beacons first thing in the morning, ready to force that crack and uncover Tara's truths.

23

Once more, Jude left the farm and headed for the Welsh border. She went without telling anyone where she was going, knowing that if she mentioned her intentions to Sami, Lucy or Noah, they'd try to stop her. But Jude Gray was on a mission and she didn't want to be hindered by other people's misgivings. Besides, she had learnt a trick or two from her sister and picked up a small can of hairspray on her way out. She would keep it in her pocket at all times. The perfect weapon to stop any attacker long enough for her to make her escape.

The thought of Binnie lying in her hospital bed, head bandaged, oxygen prongs to help her breathe and an IV drip in lieu of food, lit a fire in Jude's core and revved her up to demand answers from Tara.

Tara's car was parked outside the house when she pulled up which meant she must be around, and yet when Jude banged on the door, nobody answered.

She waited but there was no sound from inside. Jude walked around the side of the house and peered through the kitchen window but there was no sign of Tara in there, nor any of the rooms that Jude could see. The sun was starting to warm the day and Jude took her jacket off and hung it over her arm.

Tara either wasn't there or she didn't want to be disturbed. There was a chance she was out in the fields of course, but if so then there was no telling how long she'd be.

Jude didn't want to hang around and wait for what could be hours so she decided to pay the Proctors a visit instead and see if Ffion could shed any light on the situation. At the very least, it would kill some time and then Jude could return to see if Tara was home and ready to talk.

She threw her jacket onto the back seat and climbed into the car, despondent but not ready to give up.

The sun was a long way off being at full height for the day and the house at Batters Farm was in the shadow of the three oppressive evergreens that stood guarding it.

Jude got out of the car and was instantly greeted by Tom who charged over to meet her.

'Hello, handsome,' she said as she ruffled his ears.

Carl was just coming around the side of the house and waved when he saw her.

'Hello there. What brings you to this neck of the woods again so soon?'

He smiled and Tom skipped between the two of them.

'I've been worried about Tara so I thought I'd come and check on her, but she's not in.' Jude decided that the closer she stuck to the truth, the better. 'So I decided to come and see you and Ffion and then try again a bit later.'

'No Ffion, I'm afraid, she was up and out first thing but you're welcome to come in and kill time with me and Tom for a bit if you like.'

Carl bent over the dog and nuzzled his face into the soft patch between the ears of his border collie and Jude was reminded again of the strong bond he had with his dog. It wasn't until she had followed Carl into the house that she realised why that suddenly seemed significant.

'Come and take a seat,' Carl said, ushering her into the little snug off the side of the kitchen.

Next to a hibernating log-burner lay an enormous dog bed and Tom went over to it, turned two and half circles on the plump cushion and only then lay down and curled up. Jude sat on the sofa pushed up against the opposite wall and found her mind trying to recall the details of the CCTV footage Binnie had shown her of Carl setting out on the long walk in the Wye Valley that had acted as his alibi for the time Griff had been killed. She was sure that there hadn't been any sign of Tom in the video and yet it seemed bizarrely out of character for him to go on a long hike without taking his dog with him. Hadn't Carl mentioned it in jest to Ffion as one of the reasons he loved Tom more than her? The long walks they shared together. So why had he left Tom behind that day?

'You said you were worried about Tara,' said Carl, sitting down next to Jude. 'You don't think she had anything to do with all this hash business that Penny was carrying on with, do you?'

'Not at all,' she said, erring on the side of safety. 'I feel so terrible for her and just wanted to let her know that I don't blame her at all for what happened to Binnie.'

As she spoke, Jude's eyes were drawn to the window next to her where she saw a shiny new-looking motorbike lurking in a shed. There was something about the bike that made her skin prickle and her internal warning radar gently beep.

'That looks like fun,' she said. 'Is it one of those new electric things?'

Carl followed her gaze and grinned. 'Yes. Sadly not mine though. It belongs to my brother but I'm looking after it whilst he's away on an extended work trip down under. He'll be back at the weekend so I'll have to give up my latest toy.'

Jude turned around to see that Carl had taken off his hoodie and was sitting in just a T-shirt. On the front was a cartoon picture of a sheep smoking a spliff. Jude looked at it in horror as all the clues started to fall into place. The Tom-less hike, the electric motorbike, the T-shirt that she had seen before on Tara. And then she saw a leather strap wrapped around Carl's wrist. On it someone had attached a little enamel Kerry Hill charm, same as the one Marco had bought her – the one Tara had bought for her secret lover.

Jude gathered her thoughts too late – Carl had already registered her shock. He looked down at the T-shirt and ran his hand over the picture.

'Oh God,' he said. 'More than a little insensitive I suppose, given the circumstances.'

Jude shook her head and plastered a smile back on her face. 'Maybe not the best choice but hardly the world's biggest crime.'

Inside her head, Jude's mind was whirling. Tara and Carl were having an affair, that much was obvious. He was the secret that Tara had been keeping from everyone.

But there was more to Carl's secret than simply cheating on his wife. There were far too many things that were screaming at Jude to pay attention. He'd gone for a walk without his dog and had parked his pickup directly underneath a CCTV camera, perhaps a deliberate move as it would give him the perfect alibi. But what if he'd stopped somewhere else first? Had he already dropped off the electric motorbike, then left the pickup on the pretence of going for a hike but only walking as far as the bike so he could tear off to Leigh Sinton with a bottle of drugged whisky and a suicide note?

Jude knew there were still things that didn't quite add up and yet she was certain she had stumbled on at least some of the truth.

'God, I'm a terrible host,' said Carl, jumping out of his seat. 'Coffee? Tea?'

Jude knew she should make an excuse, head for the door and tell Sami everything she knew – and yet she stayed put.

'I'd love a coffee,' she said. 'No sugar but plenty of milk please.'

Carl beamed at her and went out to make the coffee, Tom, as always, right at his side. Jude had the upper hand, at least. She had a grasp on what had happened and yet she was as sure as she could be that she hadn't given Carl any clues that she was on to him.

With a jolt of frustration, Jude remembered the can of hairspray she'd brought with her which was still in the pocket of her jacket, now lying uselessly on the back seat of the Land Rover.

She had been daft not to tell anyone where she was and she needed to rectify the situation before Carl came back in so she took out her phone to send Sami a text. But the one waiting for her made her stop in her tracks. It was a message from Sami containing five words and a picture.

Found in Tara Watson's bedroom.

The picture was of a handwritten note and Jude instantly recognised the odd, slanting stroke of Griff

Gould's handwriting. She used her fingers to enlarge it so that she could read what he had written.

Dear Mr Pettiford,

It seems we have a common problem in the shape of David Martin.

I know it was him who used the hair dye and he's not a bit sorry for what he did.

He's been a thorn in your side and now he's trying to ruin the place where I live and work with his killer development plans.

He needs to be stopped and brought to justise. I am sure you want this too.

I can't do much on my own but I think you can help me stop his development by using your internet videos to tell everyone what he's up to.

This is my plan and I hope you'll be willing to talk about it with me after the show.

With thanks
Griffin Gould.

Jude stared at the picture, homing in on the misspelling of the word *justise*. It was exactly the same as the error in the suicide note, which Jude had memorised in its simplicity. The handwriting was a match too which meant that the note found by his body must have been written by him.

Except – perhaps it hadn't. She stared at the words of the note on the screen of her phone and read them slowly out loud. Bits of it sounded familiar to her, and it dawned on her as she recited the suicide note again in her head why that was. Every single one of the words used in its construction could be found within the note that Griff had written to Zander Pettiford. Right down the misspelt final one.

I am David Martin's killer.
I can't live with what I did.
I am sorry. This is my justise.
Griffin Gould

That was why the note had been written on such cheap, flimsy paper. It was because someone had traced key words and phrases from the one that was still filling her phone screen.

But who? It had been written to Zander but found in Tara's bedroom.

'Everything okay?' Carl came in carrying two mugs of coffee. He passed one to Jude and put the other down on the table in front of the sofa.

Had he seen what was on her phone before she'd

managed to flick it off? Jude hadn't managed to get a message out to Sami but she didn't want to switch the phone back on again in case the picture was still there and Carl had another chance to see it.

He was already looking at her in a slightly odd way and she started to feel as though he knew exactly what her game was and how much she knew, or at least thought she knew.

Jude blew into her coffee and looked into the muddy liquid. Drinking it suddenly seemed like a very bad idea indeed knowing what she did about the way Griff had died.

She put it down on the table and carried on with the pretence that she was merely at Batters Farm on a social visit. 'How did the Cheshire Show go?' she asked.

'Really good, thank you,' said Carl. 'Caitlin gave us the presents. That was kind of you.'

'I was hoping to catch you before you went to say good luck and everything.'

'A long way to come and wish us luck.' Carl looked at Jude and she caught a glint of something dangerous in his eyes, just for a moment, and then it was gone.

Shit! Jude thought. What had Caitlin told Carl about Jude and Binnie's visit? Had he already had an inkling she was on to him before she stepped through his front door?

'Oh no, that's right,' said Carl. 'You were tying it in with another trip to that shop in Monmouth for your sister's wedding blankets, is that right?'

Carl took a sip of his coffee and Jude nodded at him. 'That's right.'

What should she do? Make an excuse and just leave? Would he let her go if he suspected she thought he was a murderer? She couldn't just rush out as he was sitting between her and the doorway.

Tom had had enough of lying in his bed and wandered over to sit next to Carl. When Carl didn't immediately give him the strokes and affection he had come for, Tom nudged Carl's hand and a little coffee spilled from the mug he was holding and splashed onto his T-shirt.

Carl cursed and put his mug down for a moment whilst he turned to reach the box of tissues on the shelf next to the sofa. Jude took her chance and quickly picked up her mug, pulling Carl's into its place.

'Here,' she said. 'Give me one of those.'

Jude took a tissue from the box and made a show of mopping the underside of the mug she was holding before passing it back to Carl. She picked up the other mug to hide the slight coffee mark on it and the fact that she'd made the swap and she put the tissue down to cover the wet ring it had left behind.

'Well, I guess Tom didn't think much of the T-shirt either,' Carl said with a little laugh.

He took another sip of his coffee. Jude blew into the one she'd stolen and sipped it carefully as though testing the temperature, aware of Carl's eyes on her.

'Tell me about Tara,' Jude said.

Carl's smile didn't drop but she saw him tense at her name and left it half a beat before continuing. 'She and Ffion knew each other from their Young Farmer days, didn't they?'

'That's right,' said Carl.

'I don't know her very well but she seems like such a lovely person,' Jude said. 'She was really kind to me when I was a newbie at the Three Counties, took me under her wing, you know?'

'Yeah, that's Tara all over. She's such a sweet girl, always looking out for the rest of us.' The look Carl gave her seemed full of such affection Jude realised that whatever was happening between them it was more than just a fling. There was love in his eyes and in his voice and Jude knew that love brought with it great power and made people do great things.

Jude sipped her coffee again and Carl instinctively mirrored the action.

'In a way, I think perhaps she was too nice sometimes,' said Jude.

'What do you mean?'

'I saw her with David Martin and heard the way he was treating her.' Jude was playing with fire and she knew she had to be careful but there was more she wanted to get to the bottom of. 'They were dating for a bit, I think Ffion said.'

Carl was bristling. 'That was years ago. Before she realised what an arsehole he was.'

Jude had obviously poured vinegar on a raw nerve. 'He really was an arsehole, wasn't he?' she said. 'Probably not all that surprising that he ended up the way he did.'

'Plenty at the show who would want him dead, that's for sure. My money's on Griff. We all saw how angry he was when David told him about the plans for development.'

Jude finished her coffee and put the mug down, noticing that there was still over an inch left in Carl's. She realised that he was watching her more intently now. If he had spiked the coffee with benzodiazepine as he potentially had Griff's whisky, how long before he expected them to start taking effect?

Jude decided to test the water and ran a hand across her forehead.

'Sorry. I missed what you just said.'

'Are you feeling okay?' Carl asked and his tone suggested he was asking more out of interest than concern.

'I'm just feeling a little light-headed,' said Jude. Hoping that she was choosing the right words and acting the right way.

'That's okay.' Carl's voice was silky smooth. 'Why don't you rest your head back for a bit. You do look a bit sleepy.'

Jude did as she was told, knowing for sure now that Carl had drugged one of the mugs of coffee. She watched as he took another deep swig before speaking to her again. 'How are you doing there, Jude? Eyes getting heavy? Feel free to shut them and have a little nap.'

Jude was not going to shut her eyes but she did try and make them look as though they'd lost focus as Carl continued to talk.

'I'm so sorry I had to do this to you, Jude. But sadly you left me with very little choice. You know too much, I fear. I saw your face when you noticed what I was wearing. I think you might have seen Tara in it before, am I right? Don't worry about trying to answer, I know how this goes. I saw Griff do the same thing, but then I think you know that too, don't you?'

Jude willed him to finish the coffee but Carl put the mug back on the table and Jude had no way of knowing if he'd had enough of the sedative to knock him out.

'You were too clever,' he said. 'I saw you looking at the note that I found the day after Tara killed David, that dirty letch. Forcing himself on my beautiful Tara, telling her that she was a dirty slut because he'd seen her with me. Saying that she could buy his silence if she showed him just how dirty she could be.' Carl let out a low growl of hate at the memory.

So Tara had been the one to kill David and Jude thought she now knew the rest of the story. Tara had gone to tell Carl what had happened and either he persuaded her to keep quiet or they came to that conclusion together. He was besotted with her and the thought of her going to prison for killing such an odious man was one he couldn't bear. But Griff must have found out somehow. Jude would have bet her farm on the fact that this was why he had to die as well. Carl was protecting Tara.

'Too clever, Jude.'

Was she imagining it or were Carl's words starting to slur just a bit?

'Too clever and now I have to decide what to do with you. Obviously you can't be allowed to go to the police and help them work out what Tara and I did. She'll come with me now, I know she will.' Yes, he was definitely slurring and she had seen his eyes close in an extended blink. 'The only reason she didn't before was because she said she could never leave her mother and the farm. Only, what's left of them now? Nothing, that's what.'

Carl's head slipped back to rest on the sofa and Jude saw his eyes close. This time they didn't reopen. Tom gave a little whimper and rested his chin on his master's lap, staring up into his unresponsive face, waiting for him to wake up.

Jude snatched up her phone and called for help, and it was at that moment the front door opened and she heard the sound of Ffion and Tara chatting in the hallway.

24

'Carl?' Ffion called out. 'Jude, are you here?' The Land Rover in the yard would have alerted them to the visitor.

Jude had no idea what she would say to the two women who were heading her way. She thought about cutting them off before they went into the snug and directing them to the kitchen where she might be able to manage the situation a little better until the ambulance arrived. But she knew she had to stay with Carl. He was breathing and there was a pulse, albeit a rapid one, but things could turn and Jude needed to keep him alive.

Ffion called her name again and then she and Tara were there, standing in the entrance of the snug, staring at the scene in front of them. Carl out cold on the sofa and Jude next to him, monitoring his pulse rate.

'Oh my God, Carl.' Ffion rushed forward and dropped to her knees on the floor next to her husband. 'Carl. Can you hear me?'

Jude stood up, feeling helpless and completely unsure of what to say other than, 'I've already called for an ambulance.'

She looked across at Tara, expecting to read deep signs of distress at the sight of her unconscious lover, but she was calmly watching with what looked like the tiniest hint of satisfaction, or was that amusement? Tara caught Jude's eye and her face suddenly filled with the expected compassion that certainly hadn't been there before.

'What's wrong with him?' she asked, moving to crouch next to Ffion and looking up at Jude.

'He...' Jude hesitated. The truth was too big for the moment and yet what other explanation was there?

'He what?' Ffion glowered at her. 'What exactly are you doing here, Jude?'

'I came to talk to you but obviously you weren't here, so Carl invited me in for a coffee.'

'Then he just collapsed?' Ffion was stroking her husband's arm.

Tara looked at the T-shirt he was wearing and then back at Jude. Was a little smirk playing with the corner of her mouth as she realised Jude must have put two and two together and knew the truth about them?

Carl's eyes opened for a moment and he stared at the two women crouching on the floor in front of him.

'I'm sorry.' His voice was sagging but the words were clear. 'I love you, Tara. I'm sorry.'

Ffion's face froze in shock and the colour drained from her cheeks. She let go of her husband's arm as though it had burnt her and turned slowly to face her old friend.

'He said your name,' she whispered.

Tara's smirk returned and this time it was bold and brassy, not hiding in the corner now but parading across the fullness of her features.

'Yes, he did,' Tara said, and Jude realised she was enjoying this. 'And the brilliant thing is that it's been going on for such a long time without you having a clue. Self-centred Ffion and her self-centred life. Too busy to look out for her friends, never there for people when they need help. Always looking after number one and immune to consequences. Well look who won in the end.' Tara sat back on her heels, her eyes shining with the power her words held as she watched the effect they were having. Cutting deep and leaving scars that would never properly heal. 'Poor old Tara, the sad-sack reject who was always in your shadow. Your husband loves me. He would do anything for me, anything I asked him to without batting an eyelid. He's only here with you still because I told him I wouldn't leave the farm.'

Ffion looked at Tara with such evident pain and Jude knew that the sudden change in character was a hundred times more shocking to Ffion that it was to Jude. Ffion had been friends with Tara for so many years and all that time there had been a deep resentment growing that had poisoned her to the point of such destruction. This realisation also made Jude rethink everything she thought she'd discovered about the two murders.

Tara was not the person she had portrayed herself to be, innocent, vulnerable, kind. She was a superb actor who had played her part immaculately and that made Jude wonder what else she was hiding. Who else had she manipulated to get what she wanted? Thoughts of ivy-edged notepaper swam into Jude's mind. Tara's notebook that she had seen at the farm, a page of which had been used to write a delivery note in the garage at Hope House. Had that note ever been picked up by the police? Had the handwriting been properly tested? Or had Penny managed to somehow get rid of the evidence her daughter had any involvement in the marijuana supply? She'd been in the garage alone for long enough, and had proven herself to be fiercely protective of her only child. And then there was Tara's *special delivery* to Olivia. She'd pretended that it was a forgotten batch of bara brith but Jude felt certain that fruit loaf was just a cover for the drug delivery that Tara had dropped in the garage whilst Jude had been hiding around the side of the house.

But why hadn't Olivia snitched on Tara when she'd been arrested for her part in the drugs scandal? Perhaps something had happened at college that gave Tara leverage and made Olivia keep her silence. After all, it wouldn't impact on her own sentence whether it was Tara or Penny who'd brought her a steady supply of weed.

And if Tara had lied about her involvement with the hash and her relationship with Carl, manipulating so many people to get her own way, what did that mean for David and Griff's murders?

'Why would you do that to me?' Ffion spoke quietly. 'Carl was my everything, nobody knew that better than you.'

'That's *exactly* why I did it to you, you stupid bitch.' All joviality had left Tara and she stood up, shaking with a dangerous white-hot rage as she pointed a sharp finger at Ffion. 'I had to take from you to make you pay for the damage you caused me.'

'Damage?' Ffion looked genuinely perplexed. 'What the hell are you talking about?'

'I'm talking about David.' Tara spat the words out. 'I'm talking about the fact that when we first met, I loved him and you knew that. He was the first person at any Young Farmers event who noticed me. Whilst you were off with your tongue down the throats of pretty much every boy there, I only had David.'

'But he was an arsehole.'

'Not at the beginning, he wasn't. He sat with me and talked to me whilst everyone else was off having fun around us. He was the only one and I loved him because of it. But then you had to come along and add him to your collection of trophies. One more conquest and bugger anyone else.'

'It was only one kiss and you know I was sorry.'

'It wasn't only one kiss though, was it? He told me what you two did at the summer party.'

Ffion shook her head. 'What? We didn't do anything.'

'Liar!' Tara bent down and slapped Ffion across the face leaving a red mark behind.

Jude tried to put herself between them to disperse the situation. Where were the police?

'Let's all calm down.' Jude felt the futility of her words at the same time as she felt a shove in her chest.

Tara pushed Jude hard and she stumbled back onto the sofa, landing next to a still sleeping Carl.

'David told me all about it,' Tara shouted. 'How you were willing to open your legs for him and give him what I wouldn't. He told me that if I wanted to stay with him then he expected more from me because you'd given him that first taste.'

'Tara, you know I would never have done that.' Ffion looked aghast. 'Surely you haven't been carrying that around all these years?'

Jude's disgust for David Martin deepened as Tara seemed not to have heard Ffion's plea.

'That was the start of the end for us. It didn't matter that I did what he asked me. You made him want more and once he'd started it was just one slapper after another. You ruined him for me, Ffion. So it's only right that I ruined Carl in return.'

The anger ebbed away again as Tara looked down at Carl who was starting to drift groggily back into consciousness.

'Well played, Jude,' she said, almost playfully. 'I assume he tried to give you some of that benzo he had left over? What did you do? Switch mugs?'

Jude nodded, unsure of exactly how dangerous the woman in front of her was and how best to play her next card.

'Right then, well I'd better be going before this ambulance arrives,' Tara said, suddenly brisk. 'If you'd worked out that he was trying to drug you then I assume you also worked out the rest of it which means you almost certainly asked for the police to join us too. It's a beggar of a place to find and you know what it's like trying to get a quick response to anything this far out in the wilds, but I don't want to risk it. Luckily I planned for a quick escape should I need it. Such is the way when tinkering with drugs and the likes.'

Tara backed towards the door. 'I knew it would all come out in the end somehow and that Mam and I would be discovered, so I've been filtering off our profits for years to give us something to fall back on when we lost the farm, as we inevitably would.' Tara looked sad for the first time then. 'It's just a shame Mam won't be coming with me.'

She turned as she got to the door. 'Bye then.'

Ffion launched forward to grab at Tara's legs but she sidestepped and Ffion ended up sprawled on the floor.

Tara snorted in laughter, picked up some keys from a hook by the door and disappeared through the kitchen door.

'Let her go,' Jude said as Ffion pulled herself up to follow. 'She's dangerous but she won't get far. The police will be here very soon.'

A noise outside made Jude look at the window and she saw Tara, now wearing a black crash helmet, mounting the electric motorbike.

'You're right,' said Ffion. 'She won't get very far at all. There's no charge on that thing. Carl ran it flat and never got round to finding the cable to plug it in.'

Jude could see Tara twisting the key backwards and forwards in the ignition and jabbing her finger at the starter button until she gave up and flung the bike angrily on the floor. She looked around for another means of escape but it was too late. The police were already screeching into the yard.

* * *

The extent of Tara's manipulation only became evident when Carl had recovered and been arrested.

Two weeks after Binnie's operation, whilst she was staying with Jude at the farm to rest and recover, they all discussed the case over a bowl of pasta. Sebbie had been invited to his first ever sleepover at Kai's house and the adults decided to make the most of it.

'Tara really was the mastermind behind everything, wasn't she?' said Jude. 'Did you ever find out what secret she was holding over Olivia to keep her quiet?'

'No,' said Sami. 'We had hoped Tara would tell us during the investigation.'

'But she didn't?' Lucy asked as she dished up five bowls of pasta for Noah to distribute to those assembled at the kitchen table.

'She treated the whole thing like a joke, playing the old *no comment* card with a grin on her face.'

'I think it's all a power thing with Tara,' Binnie said. 'She likes playing with people and it'll be enough for her to know that Olivia is worried she could talk at any point.'

'Olivia must have a whole load of secrets when it comes to Zander that she'd pay heavily to protect,' said Lucy.

'I always wondered about those two.' Sami rested his fork on his plate and picked up his glass of water. 'Surely they must have been schtooping.'

'Schtooping?' Binnie raised her eyebrows and elbowed him in the side. 'If you mean you think they might have been intimate with each other, then who knows for sure, but I suspect not. They seemed far too close for that.'

Jude smiled. It was lovely to see Binnie returning to her old self. She'd taken to wearing bright Indian headscarves to cover the patch of fuzzy hair that had only just started to grow back over the shaven site of her surgery. She was tired a lot of the time and her memory and concentration weren't back to full sharpness but every day she was a little bit better and the post-op checks were very encouraging.

'I didn't think you could get much closer than intimacy,' said Sami.

'That's because you're as shallow as a frying pan,' Binnie quipped back.

'Do you know exactly what happened then?' Noah asked. 'I mean, as far as the murders go?'

'We're as close as we're ever going to be, I think,' said Sami. 'We know Tara killed David and although her lawyer is claiming it was self-defence, personally

I think it was very much an act of revenge and anger. Although we'll never prove that.'

Whilst she watched Sami recall the details of the murders, Jude reflected on how much he'd changed since Binnie's attack. It had shaken him more than he'd admitted and had rubbed away at the old easy-going edges and constant jokes and banter. The new Sami seemed older and wiser as he'd been forced to confront the seriousness of his job and Binnie's.

'Whatever made her kill David that night, she went straight to see Carl knowing he would give her an alibi and help her get rid of the evidence. Between them they managed to trick Ffion into thinking they were with her when David was killed. It was a case of manipulating time and barefaced lies. Not only that but when Griff saw them getting rid of Tara's bloody clothes and tried to blackmail them both, it was Tara's idea to give him the ram to try and keep him quiet for a bit whilst she put together a plan to shut him up for good.'

'Ffion giving up her ram had nothing to do with her brother's role in the dodgy planning permission?' Lucy asked.

'I doubt Griff even knew about that,' said Sami. 'Carl convinced Ffion that this was why Griff was blackmailing them, knowing that Ffion would give him what he wanted.'

'So was it Carl or Tara who killed Griff?' Noah asked.

'That was Carl but according to him he was just Tara's puppet, doing whatever she told him to do in the hope she'd run off with him. She thought of everything. All the small details like how to use the note that Carl had picked up at the show.'

'The one Griff had written to Zander?' Binnie pushed her half full bowl away, her appetite still far off where it had been before the attack.

'That's the one. Zander must have dismissed it and Carl had been curious. But it was Tara who saw the potential to use it as the start of a clever plot to not only get Griff out of the way but also frame him for David's murder.'

'Perhaps if they'd had more time to finish the job properly before we turned up then they would have got away with it,' said Binnie.

Jude had been wondering the same thing. If both Griff's wrists had been cut and the blade just left to lie on the ground then she'd have been less suspicious of foul play. Carl had made sure he'd swapped the whisky bottle and glass, possibly tidying up before he put the final deadly part of the plan into action. But in the end he'd been rushing and left just enough questions to open the investigation wide. Would the contents of Griff's stomach have been tested if there had been less doubt in the words of the suicide note? It was that key piece of evidence highlighting the fact that both the whisky and the sedatives on the table didn't match what Griff had ingested that left no doubt it was not a case of suicide.

'Once Carl realised that Tara had never loved him and that he'd just been played as a pawn in her game of revenge he was very forthcoming with the facts,' said Sami. 'It was Tara who came up with the plan for him to go for a hike and found a car park with a camera that would capture him coming and going. She suggested putting the motorbike in the back of the pickup and she was the one to supply the expensive whisky and black-market liquid benzos to mix into it.'

'And then she stepped back so she wouldn't get her hands dirty,' said Jude. 'Making sure she was seen well away from Leigh Sinton by lots of people so she had the perfect alibi.'

'Poor Ffion,' said Lucy. 'Tara certainly got her revenge there, her life must be ruined.'

'Oh, I don't know,' said Jude. 'She's a strong

woman. She set up on that farm before Carl came along and she'll carry on without him. Ffion's young, she's got plenty of time to carve out a new start for herself.'

Jude thought about all the other people that Tara had caught up in her games. For many of them the consequences were far greater. Two men had died, her mother and college friend were facing prison sentences and the man she'd duped into loving her really had lost everything. Zander was the only one who seemed to have come out unscathed but Jude knew that he would still be suffering. Although some clever publicity had stopped Olivia's story making more than a minor dent on his public reputation, privately he would be lost without his wing-girl. Jude didn't know what sentence Olivia would be given for her part in the supply of large quantities of a class B drug but without her, Zander literally wouldn't know what to do. Not with the farm for certain, but not with himself either.

'Anyone know how Jim is doing?' Binnie asked.

With everything else that had happened, Jude had almost forgotten about the final player in this complex game of lies and secrets.

'Actually, my dad's been to see him a couple of times,' said Noah. 'Keep an eye on him and all that.

He was talking about selling up but Dad reckons he'll never do it. He's as much a part of that farm as the grass itself. He is parting ways with his Kerry Hills though. Says they're too much hard work for him now he's on his own and he doesn't have the stomach for showing any more.'

'Is he going to sell them off?' Jude asked.

Noah shook his head. 'No. I believe he's planning on giving them to Ffion. I suppose it's his way of passing something forward to the next generation of farmers now that he hasn't got any heirs of his own. No point in hoarding the money he'd make from them. He has enough to get by and he's reaching the end of his farming life.'

'That's a really amazing thing for him to do.' Jude remembered the accusation that Jim had once fired at her, suggesting that Ffion could have been involved in his son's death. In the end he had been wrong and perhaps he felt a little guilty about it.

'He knows it isn't Ffion's fault and he must feel sorry for her,' said Noah. 'Only a farmer truly knows how bloody hard it is to keep a farm going, let alone starting from the beginning like Ffion's trying to do. Don't forget that Jim's known her since she was a baby. That's the power of the farming community, I suppose.'

Jude knew he was right. She'd seen farmers stand by each other many times before and had felt the power of that community herself when the chips had been down for her personally. Even Griff, at the end, had left his Kerry Hills to Jim. Sheep, including the prize ram, that would now form part of a flock on the emerging farm of a diligent, hardworking woman who deserved a bit of good luck going forward.

'I'm really sorry but I'm going to have to be a party pooper again,' said Binnie. 'I just can't keep my eyes open, I'm afraid.'

Binnie took herself off to bed and Sami went home, leaving Jude, Lucy and Noah to settle down for the evening. Once more a little peace and stability descended on Malvern Farm. Jude wasn't sure how long it would last this time but it was nice to be able to take a moment to pause in between the dramas.

With a wedding on the horizon and a summer of harvest to complete before then, life was not going to stand still.

She had made mistakes with huge costs attached. It had been Jude who'd persuaded Binnie to go to Hope House where she'd been attacked and almost lost her life and it would be a while before she'd be able to start forgiving herself, despite the fact that Binnie already had.

And then there was Marco. She'd really messed up there and now it was too late. But at least they'd found a way to get back the friendship that had been lost for a short while.

Things were not perfect, but when had they ever been?

Something on the television made Lucy and Noah laugh and the sound made Jude smile despite the fact she had missed the joke.

She had her team around her, imperfect as they all were, and that made her strong enough to tackle anything.

* * *

MORE FROM KATE WELLS

Another book from Kate Wells, *Murder on the Farm*, is available to order now here:

https://mybook.to/MurderOnTheFarmBackAd

ACKNOWLEDGEMENTS

I couldn't have written this book without the help and expertise of a generous farmer and Kerry Hill breeder who I had the absolute pleasure of meeting at the Three Counties Show.

Helen, thank you! You have been so generous with your time and wisdom and it's been such a joy to talk with you, learn from you and of course meet the Kerries!

Any mistakes or bending of truths in this book are all my doing and not Helen's and any similarities between any of my characters and any real members of the Kerry Hill community are purely coincidental.

Thank you to Emily Yau, my editor, for all you do to improve every book in the series, and thank you to Amanda Preston, my agent, for your constant support.

To the entire Boldwood team of superstars and Gary Jukes, proofreader extraordinaire – a huge thanks for being part of the much bigger picture.

Always enormous thanks to the wonderful indie bookshops who have put the series on your shelves and into readers' hands. And to the readers who have bought, gifted, read, passed on and recommended it.

To my writing buddies, critique group and all the wonderful authors I've met on this journey.

Cara, Annaliese and Nicola – we've got this!

And thank you and much love to my family.

ABOUT THE AUTHOR

Kate Wells is the author of a number of well-reviewed books for children, and is now writing cosy crime set in the Malvern hills, inspired by the farm where she grew up.

Sign up to Kate Wells' mailing list for news, competitions and updates on future books.

Visit Kate's website: www.katepoels.co.uk

Follow Kate on social media:

facebook.com/KatePoelsWest

instagram.com/KatePoelsWrites

ALSO BY KATE WELLS

Murder on the Farm

Stranger in the Village

A Body by the Henhouse

Death in the Hills

Killer at the County Show

Poison
& Pens

POISON & PENS IS THE HOME OF
COZY MYSTERIES SO POUR YOURSELF
A CUP OF TEA & GET SLEUTHING!

DISCOVER PAGE-TURNING NOVELS FROM
YOUR FAVOURITE AUTHORS &
MEET NEW FRIENDS

JOIN OUR
FACEBOOK GROUP

BIT.LYPOISONANDPENSFB

SIGN UP TO OUR
NEWSLETTER

BIT.LY/POISONANDPENSNEWS

Boldwood

Boldwood Books is an award-winning fiction publishing company seeking out the best stories from around the world.

Find out more at www.boldwoodbooks.com

Join our reader community for brilliant books, competitions and offers!

Follow us

@BoldwoodBooks

@TheBoldBookClub

Sign up to our weekly deals newsletter

https://bit.ly/BoldwoodBNewsletter

www.ingramcontent.com/pod-product-compliance
Lightning Source LLC
Chambersburg PA
CBHW010658100726
47900CB00010B/2705